OPERATION BEAST SLAYER

JOHN RUST

SEVERED PRESS
HOBART TASMANIA

OPERATION BEAST SLAYER

ISBN: 978-1-922323-98-9

Acknowledgements: A thanks to the people who helped with this novel. Lt. Grant Temple, USAF; friends of mine at Embry-Riddle Aeronautical University; and my critique group, Heidi, Sally, Leta, & Melody.

ONE

"What the hell happened here?"

Captain Makato McShane stared out the canopy of his AH-1Z Viper attack helicopter, focusing on the two structures below. Both had large holes in their roofs. Nearby lay an overturned truck.

"Looks like some rundown old farm," a voice came through his helmet's internal communications system. First Lieutenant Scott Johnson, the gunner/co-pilot sitting in the front seat of the chopper's tandem cockpit. "What's the big deal?"

McShane didn't answer. His brow furrowed beneath his helmet. The damage would make one think the structures had been sitting in disrepair for years, maybe decades. But something didn't feel right.

He zoomed in with the Viper's Target Sight System. The overturned pickup filled the colorized display screen. Even upside-down he could still make out the Toyota logo on the rear. It didn't look rusted or dirty, like it had been sitting in the middle of the forest for years. Aside from the dents, the vehicle appeared in pretty decent shape.

McShane slewed the camera toward the structures, a house and a barn, he guessed. Damage aside, neither showed the kind of rot he'd expect from years of exposure to the harsh Norwegian weather.

"You seeing this on your screen?"

"Yeah." Johnson shrugged. "Again, I don't see the big deal. Place looks like it's been abandoned for years."

"No way. That truck looks like a newer model, and the house looks lived in, in spite of the damage." McShane chewed on his lip as he passed over the farm. Something bugged him about this scene.

"Hammer Flight, Hammer Four," he radioed the three other helicopters in his group. "Loiter over the farm. I'm going to take a closer look."

"What for, Mack?" This from Lieutenant Wes Cain in Hammer Six. "The place looks like shit. No one's probably lived there for years."

"Actually, the damage doesn't look that old. Hang tight."

"Roger, Four," Cain replied, doubt coating his voice.

McShane banked the Viper right and descended toward the farm.

"I hope we're not going to be late for the exercise," said Johnson. "I don't feel like getting reamed out."

"We have plenty of time to get to the exercise. And if we do run late, I'll take the full brunt of any yelling."

"Seriously?" Johnson glanced over his shoulder.

"My call, my responsibility."

"Um, thanks."

McShane nodded, though he had no desire to get chewed out himself.

He circled the area, carved out among a thick pine forest. His brows knitted together when he spotted a couple of fallen trees, still lush and green. They must have come down recently. Some indentations stood out in the ground. Rectangular in shape, maybe two, two-and-a-half car lengths in size. The way some of them were staggered out, they almost resembled . . .

He shook off the thought. Just way too crazy.

A large animal pen sat east of the damaged barn. Maybe for sheep or pigs or cows. But not a single animal roamed within its wooden fences. He used the TSS camera for a closer look.

"Look at this."

"What?" asked Johnson.

"There's still food and water in the troughs. No way that feed would still be here if this all happened a long time ago. The birds would have picked it clean."

Johnson swung his head around, looking up at McShane. "So what caused all this? It couldn't be a storm. We've had good weather for the past three days."

"Yeah, I don't know." He got on the radio. "*Tripoli,* Hammer Four."

"*Tripoli,*" replied an air controller back on the amphibious assault ship in the Skagerrak Strait. "Go, Four."

"We may have an emergency situation involving civilians near Drangedal." McShane described the scene below. "Request permission to land and search for any survivors."

"Standby, Four."

"Seriously, Mack?" Johnson looked over his shoulder. "This is something for the local fire department or EMTs."

"Look around, Johnson. We're not exactly surrounded by urban sprawl. It might be a long time before any help arrives."

"And what are we supposed to do? We're not medics."

"We've got basic first aid training. It's better than nothing."

Johnson faced forward, a brief sigh coming over the ICS.

McShane rolled his eyes. Johnson had been his co-pilot for three months, but it didn't take long for him to realize the man's biggest drawback. He was a self-centered prick. If someone or something couldn't help advance his career, he wanted nothing to do with it.

Apparently, aiding anyone who might be hurt in the middle of the Norwegian wilderness wouldn't help him get those captain bars pinned to his lapels.

McShane circled the farm again. If a storm hadn't caused all this damage, what did? An attack would seem the most logical assumption, if this were the Middle East or Africa. He didn't think Sweden suddenly got a wild hair up its ass and bombed Norway.

Even if they had, they sure as hell wouldn't blow up a farm in the boondocks.

Could something have fallen off an airplane? The air traffic in Norway had picked up over the past few days with the commencement of NATO's Winter Huskie Exercise.

"Hammer Four, this is Rambler Six."

McShane straightened in response to the voice of Colonel Dave Esposito, the Marine ACE - Air Combat Element – commander for the *USS Tripoli.* "This is Four."

"Describe the farm for me."

He ran down all the damage, capping it off with, "If I had to guess, this must have happened in the last twenty-four to forty-eight hours. Someone down there might need help."

A pause. Did Esposito think he was overreacting?

"Hammer Four, you are cleared to land and investigate. We'll contact the local authorities. The rest of Hammer Flight is to proceed to the exercise area."

"Roger, Rambler. We're setting down to investigate."

McShane radioed the rest of the flight and told them to continue north. "Cain, you're in charge till we get back."

"Copy, Mack."

The three other Vipers headed off. McShane landed on a large expanse of grass about a hundred-fifty yards from the house. He stared at it, then the barn, wondering, hoping, someone would stick their head outside. No way the folks who lived here could miss the loud thumping of helicopter rotors. At least one of them would appear to check out the noise, especially if they needed help.

No one did.

The rotors started spinning down as McShane removed his black TopOwl helmet, catching the reflection of his round face, buzzcut hair, and half-Japanese, half-Irish features in the bug-eyed visor. He reached into his survival pack, pulling out a first aid kit, a water bottle, a couple of energy bars, and his Ka-Bar knife. No Marine worthy of the name went anywhere without their trusty Ka-Bar, even in a friendly nation.

He then took out his 9mm Beretta pistol and checked the magazine.

"You're really bringing that?" asked Johnson.

"Look around." McShane swung his free hand left to right. "We've got forest all around us. What if a wolf or a bear wanders in here?"

Johnson's cheek twitched. "You think that might happen?"

"I'd say there's a ninety-nine percent chance it doesn't." McShane held up the pistol. "This is for that one percent chance."

Johnson stared at McShane's weapon, then looked out the canopy at the surrounding woods. "I guess that would be a good idea."

He got his pistol, along with a few other items from his survival pack.

McShane opened the canopy and hopped out of the Viper, followed by Johnson. He readjusted the flight jacket over his lean yet solid 5'9 frame and zipped it up. The September air was chilly, but not bitterly cold like it would be three months from now.

"Hello!" McShane shouted. "United States Marine Corps. Is anyone here?"

No answer.

He called out a second time. Again, no one responded.

"Let's check out the truck." McShane started toward the overturned pickup, his co-pilot in tow. He focused on the indentation on the vehicle's side. It didn't look like something had hit it. It looked more like something had . . . crushed it.

He bent down by the driver's side door and peered inside. Empty. He checked the ground for any sign someone may have crawled away from the pickup. Nothing.

They made their way to the other side of the truck. It had the same sort of indentation.

"What the hell could have made this?" Johnson stared down at one of the rectangular depressions nearby.

McShane also eyed it. "I don't know."

His gaze drifted to the animal pen. An entire section of fence had collapsed. All the animals probably escaped. He wondered if by now some of them would have returned. This was the place where they got fed, after all.

They headed for the house. Looking at the front of it, everything seemed fine. Simple brown wooden siding, a door, two windows, all well cared for. Just your typical farmhouse.

Except for the big-ass hole in the roof.

McShane tried the doorknob. Unlocked. He pushed it open.

"Holy shit," he muttered.

The ceiling above them was gone, along with a big chunk of the living room floor. Debris lay in the cellar and along the sides of what remained of the floor.

"Hello," McShane called. "United States Marines. Anyone here?"

No answer.

"Look at this." Johnson reached down, picking up a cracked, framed photo that had fallen from the wall. It showed a stocky blond man, a squat dark-haired woman, a tall teen boy, and a young girl with her black hair in pigtails.

"I guess this is the family who lives here," he said.

McShane nodded and took out his flashlight. He shined the beam through the hole into the basement. No sign of survivors, or bodies.

"Hello. United States Marines. Is anyone down there? We're here to help."

Again, no response. His shoulders sagged.

"Let's try around --"

"Hjelpe. Hjelpe."

The small, female voice filtered up from the basement. McShane crouched and played the beam toward the back of the cellar. "Hello. Are you okay?"

Someone poked their head up from behind a cabinet that had fallen on its side, shattered jars in front of it. The little girl from the photo, still in pigtails, eyes wide in terror.

"Hang on, kid. We're coming."

The girl just looked at McShane. Had she understood him? The majority of Europeans could speak English. Maybe she hadn't learned the language yet.

He shone the beam around the cellar until it settled over the stairs, which led up to the kitchen in the back of the house.

"Don't worry." He held up a calming hand. "We'll be down to get you in a minute."

The girl continued looking at him, unblinking.

McShane and Johnson hurried to the rear entrance. Luckily, this part of the house had suffered little damage. McShane opened the cellar door, tried the first step to make sure it was stable, then descended the stairs, Johnson behind him. The girl pressed her back against the wall, shaking, as they approached.

"Hey, hey, hey," McShane spoke softly, holding up a hand. "It's okay. We're not gonna hurt you. Are you okay?"

The girl drew her knees to her chest and hugged her legs. She took a shaky breath and sputtered out a few words McShane couldn't understand.

He squatted in front of her. "Don't be scared. I just want to check and see if you're okay." McShane spoke even softer and slower. *Oh yeah. Because* that *will make her understand you.*

She gave a terrified squeak and scooted a foot away from him.

McShane lowered his head. Sympathy swelled in him for the girl. All alone in a destroyed house, no idea where the rest of her family was, and two strangers showing up out of the blue speaking a language she couldn't understand.

He tried another approach. "Mack. Mack." He poked himself in the chest, then pointed to Johnson. "Scott. Scott."

McShane pointed at the girl. She took a breath before answering. "Liv."

"Hello, Liv." He reached out his hand. She stared at it for a couple of seconds, then gave it a brief shake.

"Okay, I guess we're all friends now." McShane smiled down at her. "What happened?" He swung his hand around the debris-filled cellar, hoping she'd get the idea.

Jaw trembling, Liv said something in Norwegian, followed by, "Mama. Papa."

Finally, two words I can understand.

She continued on. McShane had no idea what she was saying.

He sighed, resting a hand on his knee. "Well, we're not gonna get the story until the local authorities get here." He took out his water bottle and held it out for Liv. She didn't make a move for it.

"It's just water. Um . . . *wasser."* McShane did know German, having lived in the country twice when his parents were stationed there. Hopefully it was close enough to the Norwegian word for her to understand.

Whether she did or didn't, Liv took the bottle from him. She took one sip, then another. McShane unwrapped one of his energy bars and gave it to the girl. She took a hesitant bite, then dug into it.

McShane turned to Johnson. "I'm heading back to the chopper to tell *Tripoli* we have one survivor. Stay with her."

"And do what?"

"Keep an eye on her."

Johnson looked down at the girl, wincing.

McShane rolled his eyes. "All you need to do is watch her for a few minutes, not adopt her. Okay, Go Around?"

Johnson bristled, as he usually did when someone used the call sign he'd been stuck with since flight school. McShane liked to throw that out whenever his co-pilot got on his nerves.

"Okay," Johnson grumbled.

McShane started up the stairs when Liv shouted, *"Nei. Nei. Nei."*

Brow furrowed, McShane looked at her. "What is it?"

Words flew from her mouth. One in particular she repeated with urgency. *"Oo-hay-ray,"* or something to that effect.

Johnson's face scrunched. "I don't know what the hell she's talking about."

McShane continued up the steps. Liv's voice grew louder. He picked up the word again. *"Oo-hay-ray. Oo-hay-ray."*

The word echoed in his mind the entire walk back to the Viper. Whatever it meant, it had to be important to Liv. Actually, from the tone in her voice, she sounded terrified saying it.

He stopped next to the cockpit, gazing around at the farm. He felt the barest hint of a breeze. Something else stood out to him. No birds were chirping. The quiet settled over the farm like a heavy blanket. The whole atmosphere felt . . . eerie.

Get a grip. This isn't the fucking "Twilight Zone." They'd sort it all out when the Norwegian cops and paramedics got here.

He got into the cockpit and switched on the radio. The air controller back on *Tripoli* handed him off Colonel Esposito.

"Give me your SITREP, Captain."

"We found one survivor. A girl, eight or nine years old. Judging by a photo we found in the house, it looks like a family of four lived here. No idea where the other three are."

"What's her condition?"

"I think she's all right. I didn't notice any serious injuries. She is pretty scared, though."

"Stay on site until the local authorities arrive," said Esposito. "It might be a while, given how far from civilization you are."

"Roger . . . And sir, can someone back on *Tripoli* translate a word for me?"

"What word?"

"Oo-hay-ray. The girl said it over and over again. She sounded pretty freaked out when she did."

"How do you spell it?"

"No idea."

"Then how the hell are we supposed to translate it?" snapped Esposito. "Just let the Norwegian police figure it out when they get there."

His discipline urged him to respond, "Yes, sir." But that word by Liv clung to his mind. Not even so much the word, but the urgency in which she said it. He couldn't let it go.

"If we learn what that word means, sir, it could give us a clue what happened here. Something's just . . . I don't know, it doesn't feel right."

"I'm not interested in your feelings, Captain. I . . ." Esposito fell silent. Several seconds passed before he said, "Hammer Four, Standby."

A longer pause followed. When Esposito returned, his tone was stiff. "Captain, we'll have someone look into that word."

"Thank you, sir." McShane wondered why the sudden turnaround. The only thing he could think of was the *Tripoli's* skipper, Captain Mazzilli, must have been nearby. Apparently, the guy was more reasonable that the ACE commander, and not as big a dick.

McShane settled back in his seat, watching the sun as it neared the mountain range in the distance. They should still reach the exercise area well before night. This time of year in Norway, the country only experienced a few hours of actual darkness.

A voice burst from the radio a couple of minutes later. Not Esposito. Probably one of the Combat Information Center personnel. "Hammer Four, we have your translation. According to Google, the word is spelled u-h-y-r-e. It translates to 'monster.'"

"Monster?" McShane scrunched his face in puzzlement. "What the hell did she mean by that?"

"Um . . . I don't know, sir."

"Sorry, *Tripoli*. Just thinking out loud. We'll keep an eye on the girl until the local authorities get here."

"Copy, Hammer Four."

McShane stared down at his lap, turning the word over and over in his head. *Uhyre.* Monster. What would make Liv keep saying that? Well, an actual monster. But he doubted something out of a Japanese *kaiju* movie from the 1960s was roaming around Norway.

Could it be a human monster? Maybe some big bearded ax-murderer-type wrecked Liv's home and did God knew what to her family. That would make him a monster in her eyes.

But the damage to the home looked much more extensive than what a crazed ax-murderer could do unless he had a wrecking ball.

McShane snorted. *Time to knock off the mental gymnastics.* He wasn't going to come up with any answers. Best leave it to the Norwegian cops.

He looked over at the barn. They still had not searched it. Could the rest of Liv's family be there? *And are they alive or dead?*

Hopping out of the cockpit, McShane strode off to the barn. The ax-murderer theory hovered in the back of his mind, making him glance down at the Beretta in his holster.

A tremor rippled beneath him.

He froze, the breath caught in his chest. His mind flashbacked to when he was eleven. His mother had been stationed in Anchorage when an earthquake hit the city. It had been one of the most terrifying moments of his life.

Another tremor rolled beneath him. He swore he heard a rumble nearby. Did Norway even have earthquakes?

A third tremor rattled the ground. McShane's brow furrowed. This was nothing like the earthquake he went through in Anchorage. That had been a constant rumble and shaking. Here, the shaking was intermittent.

He heard another rumble and felt another tremor. The ground calmed for a couple of seconds. Then came another rumble and tremor. The pattern continued. If he didn't know better, he would swear this felt and sounded like . . .

Footsteps?

No. What could make . . .?

Movement caught his eye. He swung around, staring at the distant woods between the barn and the house. The tops of several trees shook. A couple fell over.

The rumbles grew louder, the tremors stronger. McShane took a few steps forward, trying to peer between the breaks in the trees.

He halted, mouth agape. What appeared before him scared him far more than the Anchorage earthquake.

TWO

"My God." McShane could not take his eyes off the . . . thing. The monster, the *uhyre* as Liv called it.

The creature stood at least thirty feet tall, dark brown in color, its skin resembling rock. No, not resembling. This thing was actually *made* out of rock.

Its tree trunk-shaped legs supported a thick, barrel-chested torso. The rectangular head reminded him of the famous and mysterious statues on Easter Island. The eyes resembled dark, sunken holes. And the feet. Also rectangular, just like the indentations throughout the farm. Those feet sent one tremor after another through the ground as the monster crashed through the trees and toward the farmhouse.

McShane gritted his teeth, pushing down his shock and terror. Time to be a Marine. Time to act.

He dashed toward the shattered farmhouse.

"Johnson! Johnson, get out of there!" He kept shouting until he reached the front door. Across the hole in the floor, he saw Johnson emerge into the kitchen, holding Liv's hand. The little girl screamed.

"What the hell's going on?" the co-pilot blurted. "Is this an earthquake?"

"No. It's a fucking monster."

"What?" He drew his head back in disbelief.

"Move your ass, Lieutenant, unless you wanna get squashed."

Johnson's face wrinkled in a befuddled look, but he hurried out the back door with Liv. The girl screamed louder. The tremors grew more violent.

McShane jumped off the porch and ran to the side of the house. Johnson and Liv sprinted toward him, the co-pilot's eyes and mouth wide open. "I don't believe it. I don't believe it," he muttered.

"Go, go, go!" He smacked Johnson on the back and took off with him.

The stone monster let out a deep bellow, like a foghorn and stomped forward. The tremor made the trio stumble. They quickly righted themselves. Johnson angled toward the Viper.

"Forget the chopper," McShane barked out.

"What are you talking about?" The response shot out of Johnson's mouth.

"No way we can start the engine and get airborne before that thing gets us. Make for the woods."

Johnson's face stiffened, but he obeyed.

McShane checked over his shoulder. The monster passed the farmhouse, bellowing again. *This can't be real.* He shook off the thought. Hard as it was, he had to accept the fact a thirty-foot rock monster was chasing them.

The mini-quakes from the creature's footfalls nearly knocked them off their feet more than once. But they kept going.

The three made it to the woods when a loud, metallic crash sounded behind them. They all swung around. The monster's left foot hung in the air. The mangled fuselage of the Viper flew across the field.

"Down!" McShane grabbed Liv's shoulder and shoved her to the ground with him. Johnson hit the deck a second before the helicopter smashed into the trees. Debris leapt off the airframe. Thankfully, it hadn't exploded.

He hauled Liv to her feet. "Move. Move," he urged Johnson.

The co-pilot jumped up. They ran deeper into the forest.

The monster bellowed. The ground buckled as it pursued them.

McShane's lungs burned. His breaths became deeper. Still he kept going. So did Johnson and even little Liv. What choice did they have? If they stopped, they died.

A wooden crash went up behind them. McShane glanced over his shoulder as a tree toppled over. The rock monster swatted away another pine, snapping it in half.

What the hell do I do? Anger flashed through him. He was a Marine, an officer. He had to come up with some idea to get them out of this alive.

Nothing came to mind. Except running.

The ground sloped. McShane, Johnson, and Liv slowed a bit to keep their balance. The rock monster bellowed.

Think, damn you. Do something!

"*Der borte!*" Liv pointed to her right. "*Der borte!*"

"What's she saying?" Johnson asked, nearly breathless.

McShane stared in the direction of Liv's outstretched index finger. Toward the bottom of the incline, a large hump grew out of the earth, one with a round opening.

A cave!

McShane sucked down a breath, hope surging through him. "Let's go."

The three dashed toward the cave. God bless Liv for spotting it. Or maybe she knew it was there all the time. Maybe she and her brother played in it.

Whatever the case, they had a place to hide from the giant.

He waved Johnson and Liv into the opening, then followed. They ran deeper into the cave until they came across a rock outcropping bulging from the side. The trio hid behind it, all breathing heavily.

"I don't believe this," Johnson spoke as he gulped down air. "Where did that thing come from? How can it be real?"

McShane shook his head as he, too, breathed deep. "You really think I have an answer?"

Johnson turned back to the opening. "This is just . . . I can't . . ."

"Hey." He grasped his co-pilot's shoulder. "Get it together, Marine. We're gonna get out of this."

Johnson stared at him in silence for a couple of seconds. "Yeah. Yeah. It's just . . ."

"I know." McShane looked over to Liv. "You doing okay, kid?" He made an OK sign with his right hand.

The girl nodded as she drew deep breaths.

A tremor shook the cave. Liv yelped.

"Ssh!" McShane held up a finger to his lips. They all pressed against the outcropping, trying to stay out of sight.

More tremors followed, stronger, closer. Then they stopped. The cave grew darker.

McShane peered around the outcropping. One of the giant's legs blocked the cave opening, letting in only slivers of sunlight. Had it seen them go in here? McShane prayed it hadn't. What else could they do against this monster except hide?

He became conscious of the Beretta in his holster and stifled a laugh. He'd wanted to bring it along in case of a chance encounter with a wolf or a bear. Always best to be prepared for any eventuality, that's what his parents told him growing up. Same with his instructors throughout his Marine Corps career.

Well who could have imagined this eventuality? His little 9mm pistol may have stopped a bear or a wolf, but it wouldn't do jack against a giant made out of fucking stone.

McShane thought about the *USS Tripoli* sailing off the Norwegian coast. It had F-35 fighters that could be here in minutes to blast that thing with JDAMs or small diameter bombs. Too bad he had no way of contacting his ship.

The monster grunted. Its leg still blotted out much of the cave entrance. In spite of the cool air, sweat broke out on McShane's face.

Just go away. Please go away.

Another grunt from the monster. It backed off. McShane tensed. Was it leaving?

The enormous leg angled down. McShane's eyes widened. The damn thing wasn't leaving. It was kneeling.

A thunderous blow rocked the cave. Liv screamed. Dirt and pebbles rained down from the ceiling.

Another blow shook the cave. Larger chunks of debris fell around them.

"I think it's trying to dig us out." Johnson stared above him, swallowing.

McShane turned to the opening. The giant's leg blocked it. Their only choice was to go deeper into the cave . . . and risk being buried alive.

His eyes settled on Liv. She trembled, tears streaming down her face. A black cloud of failure threatened to consume him. His anger, his will, tried to force it back. This little girl was his responsibility. No way would she die on his watch. No *fucking* way!

But how could he . . .?

A sustained, trumpeting wail echoed from outside. McShane whipped his head back to the cave entrance. That sounded nothing like the rock monster.

He heard it again.

"What the hell's that?" Johnson blurted.

McShane didn't answer. He kept watching the entrance. The monster's leg twisted around. It was turning, away from them, facing . . . something.

Another trumpeting roar blared, much closer. The monster let out a deep bellow in response.

A crash rattled the air, like a thousand bass drums pounding all at once. Two tremors followed, then a massive quake. Liv cried out as she tumbled to the ground along with McShane and Johnson. A fist-sized rock fell inches from McShane's face. His chest tightened as he looked to the cave ceiling, praying the whole thing didn't fall on top of them.

Liv curled up in a ball, crying. McShane checked her over. She didn't seem injured, just scared out of her mind.

She's not the only one. But he couldn't let it overwhelm him.

The earth rocked again, and again. More debris shook loose and rattled on the cave floor.

"We need to get out of here." Johnson looked above him, face tense.

McShane agreed. Problem was, how? The giant's legs moved back and forth in front of the cave mouth. Whatever made that trumpeting noise also remained outside.

More crashes shattered the air. More tremors rocked the cave. McShane's body rattled with each blow. A chunk of rock the size of a car hood crashed down just a couple of feet from Johnson. He gawked at it.

"All right, we've got no choice," McShane said, his heart hammering. "We gotta make a break for it before this whole thing comes down on us."

Johnson swung his head around, mouth agape.

"Yeah, I know. I wish I had a better idea, too."

McShane clutched Liv's shoulder. "C'mon, sweetie. We gotta go."

"No! No! No! Mama! Mama!" The girl thrashed about.

McShane gritted his teeth. He didn't have time for this. "Liv, move!" He tried to scoop her up in his arms. She cried louder.

Another sound ripped through the air, a shrill whooshing noise. Silence followed, to the point McShane wondered if the others could hear his heart slamming against his chest.

A large shape fell in front of the opening. The crash pounded McShane's ears and shook the cave, knocking him on his side. All his muscles clenched, expecting the ceiling to collapse and crush him, Johnson, and little Liv.

It didn't happen.

The air became still. The shape outside didn't move. The trumpeting roar lashed the air. Another sound followed. A half-whoosh, half-snap. Like . . . flapping?

The sound grew fainter, then faded to nothingness. McShane pushed himself to a sitting position, staring outside. The shape lay motionless. His gaze remained locked on it, waiting for any movement, any sound. Neither happened.

"Stay here with Liv," he told Johnson. "I'm gonna check outside."

McShane crept along the cave wall, staring at the opening, half-expecting the shape to jerk back to life. It remained motionless.

His jaw clenched as he stuck his head outside.

The rock monster lay nearby, unmoving. Wisps of smoke rose from its torso.

McShane scrambled to the top of the cave, staring down at the giant. "What the hell?"

A blackened, smoldering circle marred the rocky chest. The hole looked big enough to drive a pair of pickup trucks through side-by-side. Fissures ran down the thing's right shoulder and arm, which reminded him of . . .

Claw marks?

He climbed down and shouted into the cave, "All clear. This thing's dead . . . somehow."

Johnson emerged, Liv hiding behind him, peeking around his leg. She let out a frightened squeak and pulled her head back

"Don't worry," McShane told her, "it's dead."

They climbed atop the cave and stared down at the charred hole in the creature's chest.

"This is just . . . how is something like this possible?" Johnson shook his head.

"Beats me."

"Well hopefully someone can figure out what this thing is and where it comes from."

"Actually," said McShane, "there's something I'm even more curious about."

"What?"

McShane slowly turned to his co-pilot. "I wanna know what killed it."

THREE

"You two are confined to quarters until further notice."

The statement froze McShane in shock. They'd just gotten off the V-22 Osprey that had flown them back to the *Tripoli* when Colonel Esposito met them near the entrance to the amphibious warship's island.

"Wh-What?" Johnson sputtered. "I don't understand, sir."

"That goes double for me," added McShane.

Esposito's brows knitted together in annoyance. McShane figured he spoke a little sharper than intended. How could he not? He'd just survived being chased by some sci-fi monster and now his CO wanted to lock him up? What the fuck for?

"There are some people that need to talk to you two about your . . . incident," the bald, stocky colonel explained. "They do not want to risk you revealing what you saw to the crew or anyone outside this ship. What happened in Drangedal is top secret. They also don't want you two talking about the incident in case you want to change any details to compromise their investigation."

"That's bullshit . . . sir," blurted McShane. "What the hell are we going to lie about? Johnson and I both saw the same thing, and almost got killed."

The colonel bristled, his lips tightening. Concern flared within McShane for pissing off the ACE commander. Well, that last bit Esposito said had pissed *him* off.

McShane caught movement to his left. A compact man with dark skin held his right hand at his side, patting the air a couple of times. *Settle down,* was the silent message from Lieutenant Colonel Eric Whitaker, the ACE's executive officer.

"Those are your orders, Captain McShane," snapped Esposito. "And they don't come from me. They come straight from the Pentagon. You and Lieutenant Johnson are to remain in your quarters until your debriefings are finished. You are to turn over your cell phones and any other electronic devices you have. You are not to speak to any of the crew about the Drangedal incident. Is that understood?"

Johnson straightened. "Yes, sir," he belted out the reply.

McShane felt the retort on his tongue, but bit it back. "Yes, sir. Understood." His tone was much more subdued than that of his co-pilot.

Esposito glared at McShane as he and Johnson followed Whitaker through the *Tripoli's* passageways.

"You need to dial it back, Mack," the XO told him. "Colonel Esposito isn't someone who puts up with a lot of shit. Actually, he doesn't put up with any shit."

"Noted, sir. But this is still bullshit. Do they really think Johnson and I are going to sit down and concoct some crazy-ass story before we're debriefed? What do we have to make up? That damn . . . whatever it is, is sitting in the middle of a Norwegian forest. The cops who got there saw it, photographed it, and told their superiors about it."

"You've been in the Corps for what, now, five years? You really expect the military to do stuff that makes sense?"

"No, sir," McShane responded. "Definitely not."

Whitaker turned around, his face softening in sympathy. "Believe me, I wish this was handled differently. But when Fort Fumble -" He used the derisive nickname for the Pentagon – "tells you to do something, you smile, salute, and do it."

"I'll salute and do it, but I can't promise a smile."

Whitaker chuckled. "This, too, shall pass, Captain."

McShane nodded, grateful for the XO's understanding. It was nice to have Whitaker as the good cop to Esposito's bad cop. He'd served in one squadron where both the commanding officer and executive officer had been huge pricks. To say the experience had not been fun would be an understatement.

They neared the section of the ship that contained the berths for the USMC aviators. "Both of your bunkmates have been moved to temporary quarters until the debriefs are over. Your meals will be delivered to you, and I'll arrange to have some reading material from the ship's library brought to you."

"Thank you, sir," said McShane. "Though I feel like I should change into an orange jumpsuit."

Whitaker sighed. "No need to overreact, Mack. This is just a security precaution. You're not a prisoner."

They turned the corridor leading to McShane's quarters. Two Marines stood on either side of the door.

"Not a prisoner," McShane grunted. "Right."

He wished Johnson good luck and approached his quarters. The Marine sentries snapped to attention. McShane went inside, handed over his cell phone and laptop to one of his "guards," then closed the door.

The day dragged on. When he had to go to the head, one of the Marines escorted him.

"The last time someone walked me to the bathroom I think I was six," McShane grumbled.

"Sorry, sir," said the guard, a private first class who couldn't be older than twenty. "I'm just following orders."

McShane nodded to him. "I know, Marine. I'm not blaming you."

He ate the dinner they sent to him, then tried to pass the time reading one of the paperbacks from the library, Weston Ochse's *Grunt Life*. He zoned in and out of the battles between PTSD soldiers and alien invaders, his mind's eye calling up images of the rock monster towering over him.

Who needs this when I'm living a fucking sci-fi novel? McShane stared at the book, recalling the creature stomping through the woods. The fear of the cave collapsing around him. The smoking hole in the monster's chest. So many questions and absolutely zero answers. Was there anyone in the world who knew what that thing was and where it came from?

He looked at the alarm clock on the desk. 2130. He wasn't that tired, but he didn't feel like spending any more time staring at the four walls of his cramped quarters or barely registering the words in his paperback. He stretched out on his bunk and closed his eyes. It took a while, but sleep eventually came.

McShane sat in the cockpit of his Viper, body stiff. A lone pickup sped along the road below. Fear swelled as his eyes shifted to the sandbagged positions farther down the road.

No. No. No. His finger hovered over the trigger of his cyclic stick. His brain screamed at him to fire the gatling gun. His finger remained paralyzed.

Sharp bangs engulfed the world. The pickup, the road, the sandbagged positions all vanished.

A series of knocks reverberated through his quarters.

McShane groaned and blinked, cursing the dream. He checked the clock. 2243. He'd only been in bed a little over an hour.

Whoever stood on the other side of the metal door banged on it again.

"Coming," grumbled McShane. He slid off his bunk and opened the door.

Two men in dark suits stood before him.

"Captain Makato McShane?" asked the fatter of the two.

"Yeah."

He held up his ID. "I'm Agent Castillo, and this is Agent Powell. CIA. We're here to debrief you on the Drangedal Incident."

"You couldn't wait until tomorrow?" McShane tried to blink away the remnants of sleep from his eyes.

Castillo drew his head back, as though stunned by the comment. "After what you and your co-pilot experienced, we need to do this as soon as possible, while the details are fresh in your mind."

"Yeah, right." McShane stepped aside to let the two Agency men in. He tried to be more upbeat. The sooner he was done with this, the sooner he'd be sprung from his quarters-turned-cell.

Agent Powell set up a small video camera on the desk to record the debriefing. It went a lot smoother than McShane expected. They had him run down everything from the time he saw the wrecked farm to when he boarded the V-22 and headed back to the *Tripoli*. There was no hostile questioning, no doubting his mental stability. He didn't think there would be. All the proof he needed lay in a Norwegian forest.

"What about the kid? Liv?" asked McShane. "How's she doing?"

"She's okay," Castillo answered. "She's in the care of Child Welfare Services until one of her relatives gets her."

"Any idea what happened to her parents and brother?"

Castillo frowned. "No. Sorry. No one's found any sign of them."

McShane's shoulders sagged. He had a bad feeling no one would ever find them, alive at any rate. Sympathy swelled within him. Poor girl. At least she had some other relatives. Still, to lose your immediate family like that . . .

The debrief took around ninety minutes. It ended with him signing a non-disclosure form that threatened him with massive fines and a long stay in prison if he publicly revealed any of what happened at Drangadel. It didn't faze him. His mother had been in Army Intelligence since the first Gulf War. She took matters of secrecy and national security *very* seriously and made sure it rubbed off on him.

When the agents left, McShane figured he'd be back on duty later that morning.

He was wrong. The CIA had just been the start of a parade of alphabet soup agencies and organizations. Representatives from the DIA, NASA, NATO, MCIA (Marine Corps Intelligence Activity) ODNI (Office of the Director of National Intelligence), and ONI (Office of Naval Intelligence) interrogated him. The Norwegians also sent their own people from the National Security Authority, the Ministry of Defense's Intelligence Service, and the Defense Security Department.

Most of his interrogators acted in civil and respectful manners. One dickhead from the NATO contingent actually accused him and Johnson of staging the whole incident.

"Yeah," McShane had responded. "Me and my co-pilot hauled thirty or forty tons of rock into the middle of the forest, chiseled it into the shape of a giant monster, and burned a big-ass hole in his chest. Then for good measure, we flew our Viper into a tree and somehow got out without a single scratch."

The NATO rep had glared at him. "I do not appreciate your sarcasm."

"Well, I don't appreciate your stupid question."

When they asked what had killed the stone giant, McShane could not provide them with an answer. That did not sit well with one of his interrogators from MCIA.

"You mean you didn't even poke your head out of that cave to get a look?"

"No."

"Why?" the interrogator demanded in a sharp tone.

Eyes narrowed, McShane leaned forward. "Because I'm not a fucking moron."

The interrogator matched his glare. "So you hid in a cave instead of gathering intel on a situation like this? What kind of Marine are you?"

McShane clenched a fist, wanting to put it through this asshole's scowling, compact face. Who the hell did he think he was to doubt his courage?

He drew a breath, barely calming himself before speaking. "I'm the kind of Marine who wanted to stay alive, and who didn't get crushed so I could bring back some intel on this thing instead of none. You're welcome."

The interrogator's face reddened. McShane's eyes stayed locked on him until the other man grunted and continued his questioning.

On the opposite end of the spectrum, the pair from the DIA went out of their way to be polite. He figured it had a lot to do with his mother's position in the agency. That bugged him. McShane prided himself in making it this far in his career without any special favors from his mother. Then again, Mom wasn't the sort of person who'd grease the skids for him.

"I got where I am by hard work, not by asking for handouts or kissing anyone's ass," she had told him. "I expect you and your sister to do the same."

The NASA reps asked him about seeing any strange lights or other phenomena since *Tripoli* entered the North Sea. McShane answered no. Did they think the monster was an alien?

Two days. That's how long it took all the alphabet soup agencies to get their pound of flesh from him. Half-an-hour after the last de-briefing, Lt. Colonel Whitaker came by his quarters.

"Congratulations, Captain, you're a free man."

"Well Halle-freakin-lujah." McShane strode into the passageway.

"Don't celebrate yet." Whitaker held up a hand. "Colonel Esposito wants to see you and Johnson."

"What the hell did we do now?" McShane flung his arms out to his sides.

"You have a guilty conscience, Mack?"

"Do you know anyone who gets psyched when their boss says they want to see them?"

"Fair point," Whitaker conceded. "C'mon."

McShane followed the XO, retrieving Johnson along the way, and headed for officer's country.

"Any of our visitors give you a hard time?" asked Whitaker.

"A couple were dicks," replied McShane. "But for the most part, they were all right."

"Same here," said Johnson as they started up a ladder. "It wasn't as bad as I thought it was going to be. But repeating the same story nine or ten times got to be a pain in the ass. Why can't they have one guy record it and send it out to everyone else?"

Whitaker barked out a laugh. "You want efficiency from government agencies? Why don't you ask for whiskey to fall from the sky instead of rain?"

McShane chuckled as they reached the door to Esposito's quarters. The ACE commander sat at his desk when they entered.

"Captain McShane. You've been given a new assignment."

He held back a snort. No "How are you doing?" or "How did the debriefings go?" Just all business with Colonel Esposito.

"What will we be doing, sir?"

"You're heading back to Drangedal. The Norwegians have cordoned off the area around the Jotunn."

McShane cocked his head. "The what?"

"It's what they're calling the rock monster. They got the name from some stupid Norse myth. Anyway, we're assisting them in studying it. The Pentagon and the scientists on site want you and Lieutenant Johnson there since you two have first-hand experience with that thing, and survived. That's one part of your mission."

"What's the other part?"

"You're to provide security in case more of those Jotunn things show up."

FOUR

McShane glanced at the Viper's wing stubs as he flew over the forest, his confidence surging. If another one of these Jotunns – actually, he'd learned the proper plural was Jotnar -- showed its ugly rock face, he wouldn't be taking it on with a useless pistol. He and Johnson were packing serious heat. Two rocket launchers, eight Hellfire missiles – the same kind his dad used in the First Gulf War to blast Saddam's tanks to scrap – and 750 rounds of armor-piercing ammo in the chin-mounted gatling gun.

Part of him wanted to run into another Jotunn, especially when he thought of Liv and her family. Just going through a normal day of doing farm things, not bothering anyone, and that big son-of-a-bitch comes by and kills them all, except Liv, leaving the poor kid traumatized.

Well, next time it wouldn't be crushing or eating a bunch of farmers. It would go up against two Marines and a fully loaded out attack chopper.

Better reach around and kiss your rocky ass goodbye.

McShane flew parallel to the road leading to Drangedal. He spotted two green boxy vehicles parked nose-to-nose blocking the roadway. Colonel Esposito told him the Norwegians had cordoned off a twenty-mile radius around the dead Jotunn. They had even established a no-fly zone over this stretch of the countryside.

A glance to the west showed McShane how serious they were to enforce it. The sleek forms of two F-16 fighters circled the area. But so long as his IFF – Identification Friend or Foe – kept squawking the right frequency, they wouldn't blow his ass out of the sky.

"Damn." Johnson leaned forward in the front seat. "They've been busy since we left here."

McShane shifted his gaze to the front. His eyes widened at the sight ahead of him.

Several dome-shaped tents sprouted from one end of the farm to the other. What had been the animal pen now served as a motor pool. Two Leopard II main battle tanks and two shoebox-shaped M113s guarded the perimeter. In an open space near the southern end of the farm, two Norwegian Hueys and three USMC Vipers sat side-by-side.

The sight brought a smile to McShane's face. The Marines and their Scandinavian friends were ready to dish out one major ass-kicking to any Jotunn that showed up.

He set down his chopper. The blades had barely stopped spinning when a group of Marines in green flight suits headed toward him.

"And our fearless leader has finally arrived," said one of them as McShane and Johnson climbed out of the cockpit. "Now we're invincible."

"Yeah, let's hope." McShane gave a half-smile to Lieutenant Ken Eastwick. The stout, angular-faced man stood there with his trademark toothy grin.

McShane exchanged handshakes, fist bumps, and shoulder slaps with the rest of Hammer Flight. Johnson stuck to nodding to everyone. The other pilots appeared fine with that.

"The spooks and the suits treat you all right?" asked Lieutenant "Stripes" Cain.

Johnson cocked his head. "You heard about that?"

"C'mon," the strapping Cain scoffed. "*Tripoli* ain't that big a ship. A bunch of people in suits show up, people notice, and talk."

"Sorry, we're sworn to secrecy." McShane held up a hand and shook his head. "But I can tell you there was no waterboarding, thumb screws, or electrodes to the junk. Actually, most of them were pretty polite."

"I still can't get over it," said Eastwick. "Just . . . damn, man. A real-life fucking monster."

"So has anyone learned anything about our big friend?" McShane nodded in the direction of the dead Jotunn.

"Beats me." Eastwick shrugged. "All the scientists here are being tight-lipped. Only authorized personnel are allowed to see the thing. They even covered it up with tarps so you can't see it from the air . . . before we got here, of course."

A black woman of medium height with short hair let out a small grunt. "It's need to know, Captain," said Lieutenant Colbi "Clubber" Hunter. "Our superiors don't think we need to know."

"'Course they don't." The lanky Lieutenant Dave Nunez scowled. "Gonna be like those alien crashes at Roswell and Kecksburg. Keep everything close to the vest."

"Oh please." Hunter gave him a dismissive wave. "That's all bullshit."

"You know that for sure? You can still be a skeptic with some big-ass monster just over that way?" Nunez pointed to the forest.

"Just because there's a creature no one's ever seen before doesn't mean flying saucers actually crashed decades ago and we recovered them."

"It's not just Roswell and Kecksburg. Lots of other places where UFOs crashed, or other weird shit happened, and the government came in and hushed it up." Nunez slapped his hands against his legs. "And now I'm part of a government coverup. Fuck me."

"Aw, don't worry, Tin Foil." Eastwick, using Nunez's call sign, put an arm around him. "Just wait till you're out of the Corps, then post an anonymous video on YouTube about all this."

"You think anyone's going to believe it?"

"Probably not. But it'll be just as funny as the videos from the Flat Earth morons." Eastwick belted out a laugh.

"Man, fuck you, Flameout." Nunez pushed the pilot away.

"Knock it off, you two," Hunter said in an annoyed tone.

McShane gazed around the farm. The combined U.S./Norwegian force had deployed more firepower than he'd seen from the air. The M113s carried anti-tank missiles. Several fighting positions had been dug out for crew-served weapons like Javelin missiles and heavy machine guns. Sentries not only carried rifles – M4s for the Marines, HK416s for the Norwegians – many also had rocket launchers slung over their shoulders.

"At least they're not messing around."

Cain's brow furrowed. "What'd you mean, Mack?"

"We brought enough firepower to level a small town. Probably two."

"That's nothing." Eastwick gave a dismissive wave. "There's plenty more tanks and APCs in this area."

"There's no way they can keep all that equipment hidden," said Johnson. "There have to be some civilians asking what it's all about."

"Oh, they gave us a cover story." Nunez glanced toward the sky. "A Chinese satellite crashed here and there might be radiation contamination."

McShane shrugged. "Well, it sounds more convincing than a downed weather balloon."

He caught movement out the corner of his eye. A young woman in camouflage strode toward him. Not the pixelated green-olive-black MARPAT of the Marines, but the wavy green-olive-beige pattern of the Norwegian Army.

"Excuse me. Are you Captain McShane and Lieutenant Johnson?" She pronounced the "J" like a "Y."

"Yes we are."

She saluted. "Corporal Knutsen, sirs. Please follow me. You need to be processed. After that, the scientists want to interview you."

"Fucking seriously?" Johnson threw his arms up. "Didn't we get interviewed enough back on *Tripoli?*"

Knutsen winced. "Um, I am sorry, sir. I do not know about that. I am just following orders."

"That's okay, Corporal," McShane spoke in an even tone. "We can put up with a few more questions."

A lie, he knew. He'd had enough of debriefs and answering the same questions over and over and fucking over again. But he wasn't going to take it out on some poor corporal acting as a messenger.

Unlike Johnson. He shot a glare at his co-pilot. The man didn't seem to notice. His face scrunched, eyes boring in on Knutsen like it was her fault.

McShane looked around at his fellow pilots. "Time to become official." He turned back to Knutsen. "Lead the way, Corporal."

She escorted him and Johnson to an elongated green tent – or DRASH, Deployable Rapid Assembly Shelter. Desks and work areas took up most of the inside, which was heated. A far cry from the simple cloth tents his great-grandfather slept in when he fought in World War II.

They went from one work area to another, having their names put into "the system," getting the orders for their new assignment approved, and being photographed for ID badges.

"These badges are to be worn at all times within the area of operations," Knutsen explained. "If your badge is not visible, for any reason, you will be disciplined by your respective country and service branch."

She gave them a map of the area of operations, explaining they were not allowed to leave it without permission from the command staff unless they were on aerial patrol. Use of personal computers or phones was prohibited, along with contact with anyone beyond the scope of the operation. She also showed them a diagram of the camp layout; HQ tent, personnel quarters, defensive positions, mess tent, armory, supply tents, bathroom and shower facilities. Next, McShane received the aerial patrol schedule. His first one was set for 2100 to midnight.

"If you spot any Jotnar, you are to contact headquarters immediately," Knutsen told them.

"You don't have to worry about that," said McShane. "What about rules of engagement?"

"Per order of General Tellefsen, the operational commander, you are cleared to fire if attacked or if other lives are in danger. Otherwise, you must receive permission from headquarters before you engage the target."

McShane nodded, glad that the higher-ups running this show actually displayed some common sense in the ROE. That hadn't always been the case during his one tour in Afghanistan.

He grimaced, thinking about that pickup from his dream.

Last but not least, they had to sign another non-disclosure form.

Knutsen then led them to the DRASH for the helicopter crews. Whoever set it up did not splurge on the decor. The interior had two rows of cots, each with a footlocker and a small nightstand with a travel alarm clock. Like the administration tent, warm air pumped in from the environmental unit.

Great-Grandpa would definitely be jealous of this.

Once they stowed their gear, Knutsen led them to the DRASH used by the scientific contingent. McShane was brought to a partitioned area to the rear, which had a folding table and a few chairs. Knutsen took Johnson to another part of the tent, probably with the same sort of set up.

The scientists came two or three at a time. Their disciplines varied. Biology, geology, earth sciences, space physics – again, making him wonder if that Jotunn was actually an alien.

"I would have thought you got the notes from all the debriefs I did on *Tripoli,*" McShane said to the first two scientists to question him.

"We did," one of them, an American, replied. "But there are some questions that never occurred to your interrogators."

One such question concerned the Jotunn's movement. Had it been quick? Sluggish? McShane wondered if it had something to do with operating in Earth's gravity. The alien theory took a firmer hold on his mind.

They asked if he had seen its chest rise. No, McShane answered. Would a rock monster need to breathe? he wondered.

Had he seen it eat? No. Had it tried any attempt at communication? Definitely not. Did he think the creature had followed them by sight or scent? McShane had no idea.

Then came the dumb question.

"When the Jotunn was attacked, why didn't you check and see what was attacking it?" This from a lean, gray-haired Norwegian biologist.

McShane sighed, leaning his head back. *Seriously? This again.*

He returned his gaze to the biologist. "Because it looked like there was one hellacious fight going on out there, and I didn't feel like getting turned into a big red stain on the ground."

"But you are a soldier --"

"No," McShane cut him off. "I'm a Marine. There's a difference."

The biologist's forehead wrinkled in confusion. Then again, most civilians didn't understand how different the Corps was from the U.S. Army.

"Um, okay." The biologist gave a slight shake of the head. "As I said, you are a sol . . . er, Marine. You are used to dangerous situations."

"It doesn't mean you do stupid things. If I'm in a trench and hear a machine gun open up across from me, I'm not gonna poke my head up and say, 'Ooh, what's that?'"

The corner of the Norwegian's mouth curled, obviously not liking the answer. "Captain McShane. An unbelievable event occurred a few meters from you. Yet you did not risk even a brief glimpse of what went on. Were it me, I would have looked outside."

"Oh really?" McShane plopped his folded arms on the table. "A thirty-foot giant made out of stone is trying to dig you out of a cave. You've got rocks falling all around you. Then who the hell knows what shows up and offs the thing. You're responsible for a little girl who just lost her entire family, and all you have is a dinky pistol. Please tell me how you would stick your head out of that cave to see what's going on."

The biologist opened his mouth, but no words emerged. He cast his gaze to the floor.

Yeah. Thought so.

The Norwegian had no more questions after that. Once he left, McShane exhaled loudly and stared up at the DRASH's ceiling. When the hell was this going to end? He'd had it with the never-ending questions. Plus, he was friggin' starving. McShane hadn't eaten since breakfast. All he wanted was some chow, get back in his Viper to search for any other Jotunn, and launch a Hellfire up its ass.

Then again, those things were big and made of stone. He'd probably need more than one missile.

A woman entered the makeshift interrogation room. McShane straightened. She couldn't have been more different from the other scientists who'd questioned him. Whereas they mainly wore casual dress shirts, slacks, and name brand light jackets or windbreakers, this one had on a jeans jacket with some white threads showing on the cuffs and pockets. She wore it unbuttoned, showing off a black t-shirt with the characters Ichigo and Rukia from the anime *Bleach*. Her dark hair hung just above her shoulders and a pair of glasses stood out from her heart-shaped face.

McShane's annoyance faded. This was certainly the most pleasant-looking scientist who'd seen him. He hoped she had the personality to match.

"Captain McShane?" she asked with a distinct Norwegian accent.

"Present." He gave her a brief smile.

The woman smiled back. "I've been looking forward to meeting you. Professor Ylva Tande, University of Tromsø." She extended her hand, which McShane shook.

"A pleasure to meet you."

Ylva smiled again and sat across from him, pulling out a notepad and a small tape recorder. She looked at the device and frowned. "I'm used to recording things on my phone. But the army won't let us have our own devices. They're trying to keep this whole matter secret." She shrugged. "I guess it's a small price to pay to see an actual giant."

"Yeah, I've been through the whole security spiel myself." McShane tilted his head, processing the woman's appearance again. "So what kind of professor are you?"

"History." Her jaw tensed for a moment. "But I specialize in mythology."

"Mythology?" McShane spoke a little louder than he intended. But after all the biologists, geologists, and physicists that had paraded in and out of here, that answer had surprised him.

Ylva's gaze fell to the table. Her shoulders drooped. Was she embarrassed?

"Well, I guess it makes sense," McShane continued. "That Jotunn looks like it stepped out of a Thor movie. You might be the closest thing to an expert we have on it."

Ylva stared back up at him, a warm flush tinting her cheeks. "Thank you. It would be nice if the others thought so."

McShane tilted his head. "Problems?"

"Most of the other researchers do not believe someone who wastes their time talking about fairy tales can make a serious contribution here. Their words, not mine."

"Apparently your government thinks differently."

"I guess. But if that isn't bad enough, a couple of them were trying to get in my pants. One of them had to be older than my father." Ylva cringed.

"Well, you've got an officer and a gentleman here," said McShane.

Ylva grinned. "So, um, sorry about going on about all that. We need to talk about the Jotunn." She turned on the recorder. "I never imagined such a creature could truly exist. I've examined the corpse, but you've seen it alive. That must have been incredible."

"Honestly, incredible is not the word I would've used."

"Oh." Ylva shrank back in her seat. "I apologize. The Jotunn was chasing you, trying to kill you. It must have been scary."

"Now that is the word I'd use." McShane tacked on a grin, just to show her no offense was taken.

She responded with an apologetic smile.

"So, before you start with your questions," McShane leaned closer to the table, "do you mind if I ask a few of my own?"

"No, of course not."

"Thanks. So, you're the expert in mythology. You have any idea what that thing could be?"

"I cannot say for sure. There are very few creatures made of living stone in any mythology. The closest one is the Golem from Hebrew folklore, which can be a statue of stone or clay. But most stories have Golems two or three feet taller than the average person."

"So I guess we can rule them out."

Ylva nodded. "I've concentrated mostly on Norse mythology. There are not many creatures that fit the Jotunn's description. Rock trolls were a common creature, but they lived among the rocks, they were not actually made of rock. The closest I've found is Mokkurkalfi."

McShane drew back his head. Damn, that was a mouthful.

"According to legend," Ylva continued, "it was created by giants using clay from a river bed and sent off to fight Thor. Mokkurkalfi was said to have been so large its head reached the clouds."

"Our monster was big, but not that big."

"This is what happens when dealing with myths. The people who write them, perhaps even witnessed them, tend to exaggerate. Fear can sometimes affect a person's perception of reality."

McShane nodded. Ylva had a point. To someone like Liv, the Jotunn could look tall enough to stretch toward the clouds. But . . .

"You said this Mokor . . . kalfee or whatever was made of clay, not rock."

"Clay can be hardened."

"True."

Ylva picked up a pen. "So, my turn to ask a question, if you don't mind."

"Shoot."

"In your report, you said something else appeared while you were hiding in the cave. Do you have any idea what it might have been?"

"Nope." McShane shook his head. "Honestly, we couldn't make out a lot from our vantage point. Plus, I had other things on my mind, like if the cave was going to collapse and crush us. All I know is I heard a few roars and some other weird sounds."

"Can you describe the sounds?"

"Like . . . whooshing. Best word I can think of."

"It sounds as though you encountered another creature," said Ylva.

"That's what I figure. What it was, I have no idea."

Ylva clutched her pen in both hands. "Every mythology has many monsters, and Norse mythology is no exception. You encountered at least two of them, and if there are two . . ." She bit down on her lip.

Concern flooded through McShane. "There could be a lot more weird-ass monsters roaming around Norway."

FIVE

Arms folded, McShane stared at the man sitting in the pilot's seat of his Viper. He moved his head left, right, up, down, then looked at McShane, nodding.

"I like this." Lieutenant Ole Hattestad tapped the side of the TopOwl helmet. "Good graphics, good field of vision. The symbols do not block your forward vision. Much better than the helmets we have."

"That's because we fly helicopters older than we are," replied Hattestad's lean, blond co-pilot, Lieutenant Tore Stenerud, who stood next to the Viper's starboard wing stub. "The guys in the NH90s and 101s get helmets like this."

"Well, I did hear you'll be phasing out the Hueys over the next couple of years," said McShane. "You'll probably get bumped up to one of the newer helos."

"Not me." Hattestad shook his head. "I love my Huey. It's a classic, easy to fly, not some complicated monstrosity."

Stenerud snorted. "You suffer from too much nostalgia, Ole. Besides, what we need is a real attack chopper." He looked over his shoulder at McShane. "An Apache, to be specific."

And here we go. Not the first time McShane had been in the Apache vs. Viper debate. As always, he relished it. "You don't want to sit in the best attack helicopter in the world?"

Stenerud's face wrinkled, as though offended. "Of course I do. The Apache."

Snickers rose from behind McShane. He glanced back at Eastwick, Cain, and Hunter.

"Please set our Norwegian friend straight, Mack," urged Hunter.

"Gladly, Clubber." McShane puffed out his chest. "For one, the Viper is faster than the Apache, has a better rate of climb, and carries more weapons. Avionics and sensors are on par with the Apache, and in some cases, better. We have improved countermeasures and increased crash survivability."

"Plus, if you want to deploy an Apache somewhere, you have to bring 'em in from the States," Cain chimed in. "Us, we're already on amphibious ships and can drop ordnance on any asshole anywhere in the world."

Stenerud grunted. "Maybe, but Apaches look much cooler."

McShane shrugged. "They just get better PR than Vipers. There's also one other advantage Vipers have over Apaches."

"What is that?"

"They're flown by United States Marines."

"Oo-rah!" Cain, Eastwick, and Hunter hollered in unison.

Hattestad laughed. Stenerud wore a sour expression.

McShane and the others continued to show the Norwegian pilots the Viper. Hattestad enjoyed himself. Stenerud, though unsmiling, seemed to pay attention whenever any of the Hammer Flight pilots spoke. He surely had some interest, given the Royal Norwegian Air Force had no dedicated attack helicopters. The best they could do was slap some machine guns and rocket launchers on their Hueys, which were used primarily for transport.

Most importantly, it gave McShane and his Marines the chance to get to know their Norwegian counterparts better. Knowing what made the other guy tick made a fighting unit more effective.

It also gave them something to do besides sitting around doing fuck all.

The gathering broke up when Hunter and her co-pilot, Keith "Tooti" Tudoran, left to prepare for their patrol. McShane made his way toward his DRASH when he spotted Ylva walking across the expansive front yard. She made eye contact and waved.

A smile grew across McShane's face. "Good afternoon, Professor."

Ylva chuckled as she angled toward him. "Please, we are not in a classroom. Even then, I get uncomfortable when students call me professor. It makes me sound old."

"I'd go with it makes you sound wise."

"'Wise' also makes me sound old."

McShane shrugged. "Oh well, I tried."

Again, Ylva softly chuckled. She looked at him, smiling, a very pretty smile at that.

"Taking a study break?" he asked, walking side-by-side with her.

"You could say that." She sighed. "Not that there is much to study. I cannot tell you how many books I've pored over, and yet have not found any stories that tell us anything about what that Jotunn might be. There have been many examples of stone creatures in movies, television, and comic books. But in mythology, not so much. Plus, all that reading was making my eyes glaze over. I thought I'd take a walk."

"Well, at least you've got something to do. Unless I'm flying, I'm sitting around my tent twiddling my thumbs. After nearly three days, that becomes old really fast. How my dad dealt with it for three months in the Gulf I don't know."

"Your father was a soldier, too?"

"Army helicopter pilot. He fought in the First Gulf War back in '91. He told me about what it was like the months leading up to the fighting. Yeah, they'd do some flight ops, PT, go over intelligence briefs. But they still had hours and hours of sitting around their base being bored out of their minds." He gave a brief laugh. "He said in some ways, that was worse than combat. At least you're doing something when you're fighting, your thoughts are focused. When nothing's going on, you start to run out of things to talk about with your buddies, you get tired of reading the same books or magazines lying around the barracks. You think about home, family . . . whether or not you'll make it out alive."

Ylva winced. "Are you . . . thinking those same thoughts?"

"Yeah, I guess. But at least if another Jotunn shows up, we've got enough firepower to turn it into a rock pile. Till then, I guess I'll try to find ways to keep from being bored."

McShane took a couple of steps, then tilted his head. "You know, if you ever need help reading all those books on mythology, give me a holler."

Ylva's mouth hung open wordlessly. A brightness lit up her eyes. "That's . . . I . . . um, sure. Though several of my books are written in Norwegian."

"Then God bless Google Translate. Then again, since we're not allowed personal computers or phones, I can't use it. So there goes that brilliant idea."

Ylva laughed. "Then I guess you'll have to read the English language books."

"Fine by me. Maybe we can eventually find something useful about the Jotunn. Heh! This is probably why Mom had it easier during Desert Shield than Dad."

"How so?"

"Mom was Army Intelligence. While Dad was wallowing in boredom waiting for the balloon to go up, Mom was analyzing all sorts of reports on Iraq and its armed forces. She didn't have the chance to be bored."

"So both your parents were in the military? Is that a tradition with your family?"

"Yeah." McShane nodded. "On my dad's side, we've had relatives serve as far back as World War One. For my mom's side, World War Two."

"So you could have had one relative fight another relative."

"I suppose. Though with my mom's side, I was talking more about my great-grandfather."

Ylva's brow furrowed. "What about him?"

"He was with the U.S. Army in World War Two."

Ylva stopped, mouth agape. "What? But if he was Japanese, how could he be with the American Army?"

"Great-Grandpop Fujio was *Nisei,* second-generation Japanese-American. He got thrown into an internment camp after Pearl Harbor, but ended up joining the Four Forty-Second Regimental Combat Team with other Japanese-Americans. He fought all over Europe, won two Bronze Stars and got two Purple Hearts."

"I don't understand. Why would he fight for a country that imprisoned him?"

"Great-Grandpop and the other *Nisei* considered themselves Americans, not Japanese. They wanted to prove their loyalty to their country. They did it in spades. Became one of the most decorated American units in World War Two."

"I had no idea," said Ylva. "So that's why the rest of your family joined the military?"

"Pretty much. What about you? Do you come from a long line of mythology enthusiasts?"

She grinned, but more of a forced one. "Both of my parents are civil servants in Drammen. They do not have much imagination. They think I am wasting my life teaching students about things that do not exist."

Ylva stuffed her hands in her jacket pockets. "What can I say? I find these stories interesting. Powerful heroes. Evil villains. Horrific monsters. Quests. Battles. Magical forces. I loved all that. But my parents did not. They tried to discourage me from learning about it. My classmates would make fun of me. It made for a difficult time growing up." She hung her head.

"I'm sorry." He lifted his hand a few inches, wanting to put it on Ylva's shoulder, but stopped. He did not know if it was appropriate, having known her for just a couple of days.

His sympathy for her grew. He'd known his share of outcasts while in school. Sometimes, he'd felt like an outcast. The risk of being an Army brat. Rarely had he spent more than two years in the same school. Some places it had been easy to make friends fast. Other places, the cliquishness and the peer pressure permeated the atmosphere to the point he'd rather be by himself than hang out with a group of ass-hats.

"At least you didn't give in," he said.

"Huh?"

"You didn't let other people kill your love of mythology. I'm sure it was tough, but you held on to it. You're even making a living out of it. Hell, you're so knowledgeable, you're working on a top secret project.

That's something you can rub in the faces of all the people you went to school with." McShane glanced up at the overcast sky. "Well, I guess not, since this project is top secret."

Ylva laughed, then gave him a warm smile, one that sent an electric jolt through his chest.

"Thank you, Makato."

"You're welcome, and like I said, I'm sure you'll find out something about this Jotunn, and whatever the hell else is out there."

"That may be easier than digging up something on the Jotunn."

"Sounds like you have some theories," said McShane as they resumed walking. "Care to share?"

"The wounds to the Jotunn's shoulder look like claw marks. It makes me think of a wolf, which in Norse mythology could mean Fenrir."

"The problem with that is I didn't see any footprints that looked like they could have been left by a giant wolf," McShane pointed out.

"That is probably a good thing," said Ylva. "According to legend, Fenrir was supposed to have eaten Odin during Ragnarök."

"Yeah, I guess we don't want a wolf that can gobble up the king of the Norse gods running around Norway."

"Definitely. But the chest wound, the scientists agree that it was made with some sort of intense heat. That makes me think of fire-breathing dragons. There are quite a few of them in Norse mythology. Actually, dragons are part of the mythologies of most countries throughout Europe."

"But can fire burn a hole through solid rock like that?" asked McShane.

"Perhaps not regular fire."

McShane stared at the grass around him, thinking. Did Ylva mean magic? Was that truly possible?

Well, rock giants are possible. But there should be some natural explanation for its existence. Shouldn't there?

"Maybe we should hit those books of yours and try to find out --"

Klaxons wailed throughout the compound. Ylva jumped and gasped, putting a hand on her chest. McShane stiffened.

"Alert! Alert!" the loudspeakers blared. "Jotnar approaching the compound. Repeat, Jotnar approaching the compound."

SIX

McShane's chest tightened. His fear spiked, memories of being chased by the rock creature played in his mind.

That fear vanished, replaced by resolve to face these damn monsters. He wanted to show them what a Marine can do with one of the world's most advanced attack helicopters instead of a wimp-ass nine-millimeter. He wanted payback for Liv, whose world had been suddenly and violently changed by a Jotunn.

Ylva stared at him, her wide eyes lit up with what appeared to be a mix of terror and curiosity.

McShane started to run for his chopper, then halted. He took in Ylva's pretty face and clutched her shoulder. "Be careful."

That seemed to snap the mythology professor out of her daze. "Y-You too."

With a nod, McShane sprinted away.

U.S. Marines and Norwegian soldiers rushed about the compound. Some jumped into trenches, readying their heavy machine guns or anti-tank missiles. Others scrambled into their tanks or APCs. McShane pounded across the grass toward the helicopters. He glanced around him. The other pilots of Hammer Flight, along with the Norwegian pilots, Hattestad and Stenerud, charged for their aircraft.

McShane vaulted into the pilot's seat in the rear of the cockpit and shoved on his TopOwl helmet. A few seconds later, Johnson climbed aboard. McShane shut the canopy and started the engine. The rotors of the other helicopters around him started to spin.

The comm unit in his helmet crackled to life, with the voice of a Norwegian air controller in his ears. He relayed the position of the Jotnar from Lieutenants Berdal and Oftebro, the crew of the other Huey. Three of them, twelve miles north of the Drangedal compound. The GPS coordinates showed up in McShane's navigation system.

The Vipers lifted off, along with Hattestad and Stenerud's Huey. McShane took a last look at the compound below, his eyes lingering on the shattered farmhouse. He thought of Ylva, sending up a quick, silent prayer that she'd be all right.

She will be. Everyone down there will be. I'll make damn sure of that.

Staring straight ahead, the Viper buzzed over the treetops, followed by the rest of his flight.

It didn't take long to spot the dark shape of Berdal and Oftebro's Huey in the distance, marking the position of the Jotnar. McShane pulled back the stick a bit, gaining altitude, looking for any sign of –

There! Several trees snapped up and down or side to side. A couple toppled over.

"I've got movement in the forest, dead ahead," McShane announced.

"I see it, too," said Hunter.

"Man, they're knocking around those trees like . . . whoa!" Nunez blurted. "Holy shit, look at 'em."

A Jotunn stomped out of the trees and into a clearing. Another followed. Another.

McShane's jaw stiffened, thinking how enormous the one that chased him had been. Even from this height, they still looked big, but sure as hell not as intimidating as last time.

"My God," Hunter stammered.

"Unbelievable," Hattestad practically whispered.

"Look at those things." The awe in Cain's voice was evident. "They're . . . How . . . I don't --"

"All right, can the chatter," snapped McShane. "Flameout," he contacted Eastwick. "You and me target the one on the right."

"Copy, Mack."

"Stripes, Clubber," he radioed Cain and Hunter. "You guys have the middle one. Hattestad, Berdal, take out the one on the left. Lock up Hellfires. Fire on my mark."

Everyone gave two clicks of their mikes to acknowledge the order.

McShane held the Viper steady, watching the Jotnar march through the forest. One swung its arm, snapping off the tops of two trees like toothpicks.

"Hellfire One locked," reported Johnson. "Hellfire Six locked."

The other gunner/co-pilots of Hammer Flight radioed they had lock with their missiles. Berdal slid his Huey near Hattestad's, lining up the left Jotunn for a rocket barrage.

The monsters knocked down more trees. One looked to the sky. The other two did the same.

McShane aimed a harsh gaze at them. "Fire."

Two Hellfires whooshed off the Viper's rails. More contrails raced through the air. Yellow streaks flew from the Hueys' rocket launchers. McShane held his breath, watching the eight missiles draw closer to their targets. He leaned forward in his seat, waiting . . .

Clouds of black and orange sprouted across the large torsos of the Jotnar. Other explosions churned up the ground around the monsters. Unguided rockets from the Norwegian Hueys.

Suck on that, mother fu—

"What!?" Eastwick blurted. "Are you kiddin' me?"

All three Jotnar tromped through the smoke, unfazed by the explosions.

"No." McShane blinked, not wanting to accept the sight. The Hellfire could turn the best main battle tanks in the world into burning scrap and fortified bunkers into rubble. Against the Jotnar, they did nothing.

He shook his head, ridding himself of his shock. "Fire at will. Keep hitting the bastards until they go down." And they would go down if they kept pumping missiles and rockets into them.

Wouldn't they?

Another volley of Hellfires streaked away from the Vipers. The Hueys spat out more rockets. Explosions blossomed across the Jotnar's massive bodies. McShane zoomed in with the Target Sight System. Each stone beast showed scorch marks, pockmarks, and cracks. Superficial wounds. Nothing close to fatal.

Fear clenched the pit of his stomach. Fear for everyone back at the Drangedal compound. For Ylva. Would they all die if they couldn't stop these things?

"Keep firing," he ordered, hoping he kept the rising panic out of his voice.

Hellfires and rockets rained down on the Jotnar. Flames licked several trees. The giants continued their march. One stared up at the helicopters, its mouth wide open. Was it roaring?

"We're down to our last Hellfire, Mack," Johnson told him.

McShane stared at the Jotunn's angry face. That's when it hit him. "Head. Aim for the head." He radioed the same instructions to the rest of the flight.

Let's see how good these things are with their brains blown across the forest.

Their last Hellfire shot off its rail.

"All missiles expended," Johnson announced.

McShane watched the Hellfire barrel over the forest and straight at the Jotunn on the right. Its large, hollow eyes locked on the approaching one-hundred-pound missile.

A fiery cloud blotted out its rectangular head.

"Direct hit!" blared Johnson. "Blew its damn head o--"

The Jotunn remained on its feet, a scar marring the left side of its face. It kept stomping through the forest.

"No!" Johnson surged forward in his seat. "How is it still alive?"

"It's no good," radioed Hattestad. "Nothing we do hurts them."

"How the hell do we kill these things?" Hunter wondered aloud, not bothering to hide her frustration.

McShane slowly shook his head, trying to think of some new strategy. Nothing came to mind.

"Go for broke. Keep firing and try to wear 'em down." He had his doubts they could actually do that. But what else could he do? Hover and jerkoff while these things made a beeline to the base?

Yellow streaks zipped through the air. Rockets crashed into the Jotnar, the trees, and the ground, sending up a storm of flames, sparks, and dust.

The monsters didn't stop.

McShane backed up the Viper, rockets still shooting out its pods. Worry clutched his chest. What the hell would they do when they ran out of rockets? He doubted the gatling gun would work where high explosives failed.

"What the hell's that?" He heard Nunez's query over his headphones.

One Jotunn raised its arm through the debris cloud, holding . . .

"Is that a tree?" asked Eastwick.

McShane's eyebrows knitted together. It was a large pine. He took a short breath and held it. Was that thing about –

The Jotunn hurled the tree like a spear.

"Stripes!" McShane hollered. "Evasive action!"

Cain banked his Viper right. The tree missed by a good fifty yards and dropped into the forest.

Another tree rocketed into the sky. Another.

"Reverse. Reverse." McShane backed up his Viper, putting more distance between him and the Jotnar. The other helicopters did the same.

The monsters ripped more pine trees out of the ground, as easily as a person would tear out a weed. They hurled them through the air. Some fell short. Others did not. The Vipers and Hueys jerked left, right, or up to dodge them.

"Echo Three, Hammer Four," McShane radioed the base. "We are taking ground fire."

"Say again, Hammer Four," came back the puzzled voice of the air controller. "Ground fire? How?"

"The bastards are throwing trees at us."

"Trees? Are you sure?"

"Mack!" shouted Johnson, pressing his back into his seat.

A large pine knifed through the air straight at them. McShane jammed the stick left. The tree missed by fifteen feet.

"I just had one go right past my cockpit," he growled at the controller. "So yeah, I'm fucking sure!"

"Skywolf One!" Cain yelled. "Break left!"

McShane's head snapped toward Hattestad and Stenerud's Huey. His throat tightened as the large pine closed with the chopper. The Huey twisted left.

The tree shuddered as it struck the spinning rotors. Blades snapped off.

"We're hit!" Hattestad shouted. His Huey spun like a top and tumbled toward the forest.

"Can't pull up!" The Norwegian's voice cracked with fear. "Going down. Can't control-"

The Huey slammed into the treetops. A cloud of needles and bark burst around it. McShane's stomach collapsed as the Huey vanished from sight.

A gusher of flame and smoke brewed up from the forest floor.

"No," McShane said in a sharp whisper. He almost closed his eyes, but didn't. The Jotnar were still throwing trees.

He dodged another pine. So did Eastwick. McShane opened up with the three-barrel gatling gun in the chin turret. He swept the line of 20mm rounds left and right. He doubted it would hurt the rock monsters, but maybe it would throw off their aim.

Another tree missed his Viper by twenty feet.

Not throwing it off by much.

"Hammer Flight, Echo Three," radioed the air controller. "Pull back to base. Repeat, pull back to base. Air strike is coming in."

"Copy, Three. Hammer Flight pulling back to base."

McShane swung the Viper around and sped south. The others followed. He checked his rearview mirror. The Jotnar continued chucking trees, but all fell far short of the helicopters.

He lowered his chin. Hattestad. Stenerud. Barely twenty minutes ago he and his Marines had been joking with them, showing off their Vipers to them. Now . . .

Mourn later. This fight was far from over.

The farm appeared in the distance when something caught McShane's attention. He looked right. Two sleek shapes dove toward the forest. F-16s. The air strike.

Several dark green vehicles sped down the road away from the farm. Probably evacuating civilians. He prayed Ylva was in one of those vehicles.

McShane slowed as he neared the tree line and spun the Viper around. Just in time to see a massive cloud of gray rise from the forest, almost like a mini-volcano. Paveway laser-guided bombs, he guessed. More than 900 pounds of high explosives.

"Oh yeah," Eastwick cheered. "Ain't nothing coming out of that alive."

"I was starting to wonder if anything could kill those things," added Hunter.

Johnson switched from the flight net to the internal communications system. "Yeah, great. The Air Force gets the credit for this, and the Norwegian Air Force at that."

McShane shot his co-pilot a glare. Johnson probably worried not taking down the Jotnar would look bad on his record and hurt any future promotions.

"Be glad you're still alive. Hattestad and Stenerud aren't."

Johnson glanced over his shoulder, his lips curled. "Um, yeah. Yeah, right."

The large cloud still hung above the forest. McShane scanned the treetops for any movement. Nothing. Had they really done it? Were the Jotnar a smoking rock pile? Unlike Johnson, he didn't care that he wasn't the one to deliver the killing blow. It could have been the Norwegian Air Force, the U.S. Air Force, or the fucking Boy Scouts. He just wanted the things dead.

"I got . . ." Cain stammered. "I got movement."

McShane gripped the cyclic stick tighter. Trees swayed in the distance. A couple fell over.

"How?" Hunter spoke in breathless shock.

McShane couldn't take his eyes off the shaking trees. His brain fought to process the reality. They had survived a hit from a bomb.

"Echo Three, Hammer Four," he contacted the air controller. "They're still coming. Repeat, they're still coming."

A few seconds of silence passed before the Norwegian on the other end replied in a stunned tone, "Copy, Four. Jotnar still approaching base."

The trees rocked to all sides as the monsters neared. McShane inhaled deeply, pushing aside his disbelief. "Hammer Flight, weapons status."

Everyone reported they had a few rockets left and most of their cannon rounds.

"Big deal," grumbled Johnson. "Nothing we have can hurt them."

"We have to try," said McShane.

"What for?"

"Because we're Marines," McShane snapped. "That's what we do. We fight. We don't quit, no matter what." *For all the good it'll do.* If a Paveway couldn't take out those fuckers, what chance did they have?

"Hammer Flight, ready all rockets. Standby cannons. We don't stop shooting until we're empty."

"Copy," his fellow Marine aviators replied. They all sounded determined. At least, McShane thought so. But he wondered if in the back of their minds they thought it would be futile. Lord knew he thought that way.

The Jotnar were a half-mile away, their heads sticking above the treetops.

"Fire!" ordered McShane.

Orange snaps erupted from the rocket launchers. Explosions raked the forest. The Jotnar didn't break stride.

Trees collapsed as the three giants stomped into view. All of them bore deep black burn marks and cracks. In some places, chunks of rock had been blown off their bodies. They were hurt, but not close to dead.

But they could die. McShane saw it himself. Whatever it was that fought the other Jotunn used something to burn a hole right through its chest. Too bad they didn't have that something.

Contrails from anti-tank missiles rose from foxholes and armored vehicles. Flame and smoke sprouted from the 120mm guns of the Leopard II tanks. Tracers from machine guns zipped through the air.

None of it affected the Jotnar. They charged forward.

McShane fired a long burst from the Viper's gatling gun in a vain hope it would distract the monsters.

It didn't. He shuddered as one of them kicked an M113 across the farm. Two others were crushed under their enormous feet. One of the Leopards fired into a Jotunn's thigh. It paused for a split second, then snatched the 55-ton metal beast off the ground. It reared its arms back and slammed the tank into the grass.

Soldiers and Marines dashed away from the monsters. One Jotunn grabbed a pair of men.

"Holy shit," yelped Nunez.

Hunter gasped. McShane almost gasped as the Jotunn dropped both men into its large mouth. Horror and rage collided inside him. Had that happened to Liv's parents? Had she actually witnessed it?

Sneering, he crushed the trigger on his cyclic stick. Twenty-millimeter rounds hammered the Jotunn. It ignored the barrage.

The three tromped back into the forest, leaving wrecked and crushed tents, vehicles, and people in their wake.

No one spoke. McShane just watched the Jotnar lumber through the trees. He forced his mouth open and switched the comm unit to his ship's frequency.

It took a second to find his voice. "*Tripoli,* Hammer Four. Base is destroyed. Repeat, base is destroyed."

SEVEN

Failure clung to McShane the entire flight to the *Tripoli*. They could have laid waste to an entire armored division with the firepower they expended. Against the Jotnar, it did nothing. They had knocked Hattestad and Stenerud's Huey out of the sky with a tree. A fucking tree! They trashed their base. How many had been killed or wounded? Had Ylva gotten out all right? Now the Jotnar were roaming around Norway. How many more people would they kill?

The *Tripoli* appeared in the distance, resembling a small aircraft carrier. The four Vipers set down on the flight deck. Colonel Esposito was waiting for them near the entrance to the island.

"Hit the head and make it quick," he told Hammer Flight. "Briefing in ten."

Looking forward to it. McShane sighed as he made his way to the bathroom.

Minutes later, he entered the briefing room, his gaze going to the small stage in the front. The veins in his neck stuck out. Along with Colonel Esposito and Lt. Colonel Whitaker, three others were seated. A lean man with a narrow face and piercing dark eyes, a balding, portly man with glasses, and a solidly-built black man with large forearms. Captain Frank Mazzilli, the *Tripoli's* skipper, Captain Daniel Owen, commander of the Amphibious Ready Group, and Colonel Ed Gordon, CO of the Marine Expeditionary Unit.

A nice, big brass ensemble for him to explain how the most advanced attack helicopters in the world failed to take out a trio of rock monsters.

He took a seat in the front row as the rest of his flight filed in. All unsmiling, all stiff.

"All right, let's get started," said Esposito. "Captain McShane."

Squaring his shoulders, he ran down the battle, their tactics, how the Jotnar counter-attacked, and the minimal damage inflicted on the monsters.

"At least we know they can be hurt," said Captain Owen. "If we can hurt them, we can kill them. Hell, that first one we found was killed, somehow."

"If we are going to kill them, sir, we're going to need something bigger," said McShane. "Bunker busters or maybe even MOABs. These things are essentially hardened bunkers with legs."

The brass ensemble went down the row, having each pilot recount the battle. It was a repeat of what McShane had said, for the most part. Johnson did put a CYA spin on his account.

"I lazed the target properly. All Hellfires I fired flew true. All rockets were aimed properly and on target. It's just . . . none of our ordnance could penetrate them."

"I'm sure you did everything according to procedure," noted Mazzilli. "That goes for all of you. But let's face it. This is an enemy we've never faced before, never even dreamed could exist. We have one hell of a learning curve in front of us."

Next, they played footage from the Vipers' gun cameras to further break down the attack and hopefully learn of some weaknesses they could exploit on the Jotnar. McShane was damned if he could find any. No one in the briefing room could.

In the end, the best strategy anyone could come up with was from Colonel Esposito. "Keep hitting them. Sooner or later you'll have to blast through all that rock and hit something vital."

"We may run out of things that go boom before that happens," Hunter chimed in.

"Do you have a better idea, Lieutenant?" Esposito glared at her.

"No, sir." Hunter lowered her gaze.

McShane's eyes narrowed at the colonel. He didn't like one of his pilots being berated for making a legit comment.

Not that he could scold his CO for it, unfortunately.

"The Norwegian Air Force has almost every aircraft in their inventory up searching for the Jotnar," Captain Owen told them. "We've committed our F-35s and helicopters to the search. U.S. Air Force Europe is sending some F-16s from the 480th Fighter Squadron in Germany to help."

Eastwick raised a hand. "If I may, sir, how the heck did anyone lose sight of something that big?"

"The forest is pretty thick in that part of Norway. Maybe they decided they had enough of being shot at and have gone to ground. But you're right, Lieutenant. They're big, and we have a lot of eyes in the sky. We'll find them eventually."

"You're also going back out to assist in the search," said Whitaker. "Your Vipers should be refueled and rearmed within the hour. As soon as they are, get in the air."

"Yes, sir," replied McShane. Lips tight, he looked over to Colonel Gordon. "Any word on casualties for our side?"

Gordon's face tightened in a grim mask. "Last I heard, around thirty dead, several more wounded. We're still trying to get a final tally and ID the dead, but some . . . ." He grimaced. "Some we'll need a DNA test for that. Others . . . well, there won't be any bodies."

McShane nearly shuddered. He knew what the colonel meant by that. Those men the Jotnar had eaten.

"What about the scientists?" he asked. "Did they make it out okay?"

"I'm sure they did, Captain," Esposito answered in an abrupt tone. "Just concentrate on finding those damn monsters."

McShane clenched his teeth. *Fucking excuse me for caring about someone.* "Yes, sir," he nearly hissed.

A short time later, their flight plans and search grids had been generated. Esposito and Whitaker briefed them on the topography of their assigned area, where other air units were searching, their frequencies, and rules of engagement, especially in populated areas. The briefing done, everyone headed out.

McShane hung back in the passageway, waiting for Esposito to leave. When Whitaker emerged from the briefing room, he went up to him. "Colonel?"

"Yes, Captain?"

"If you can do me a favor, sir. Could you find out the condition of one of the scientists at Drangedal? Her name is Professor Ylva Tande. I . . . I just want to make sure she's all right."

Whitaker cocked his head, brow crinkled, not speaking. McShane took half-a-breath and held it. Would the XO not honor his request?

"I'll look into it."

"Thank you, sir." McShane turned to leave.

"Mack?" Whitaker called out.

"Yes, sir?"

"Keep your head on straight. You're going into a dangerous situation and you have seven other people you're responsible for. Focus on that."

"Yes, sir." McShane nodded.

He stepped into the passageway, thinking of the search for the Jotnar, trying to bury his worry for Ylva.

That proved impossible.

***

McShane had been assigned a patch of forest to the west of the small town of Akland, some twenty miles south of Drangedal. He and his wingman, Lieutenant Eastwick, buzzed over trees, hills, and lakes. He scanned for any shaking treetops, downed pines, or rectangular footprints. Anything to show a group of thirty-foot-tall giants had stomped through the area.

Neither McShane nor Johnson found any sign of the Jotnar. The same for Eastwick and his co-pilot/gunner, Lieutenant Paul Koosman. Several times McShane concentrated on his headphones, hoping for some U.S. or Norwegian pilot to sing out they had spotted the monsters.

Someone did. The crew of a Norwegian Sea King helicopter found large, rectangular footprints in the hills outside Nome, about twenty miles north of Drangedal. The *Tripoli* ordered them to the area.

McShane and Eastwick discovered the huge footprints heading into a river. They checked the forests and fields on the other side of the water. They saw no more footprints.

"Maybe they fell into the river and drowned," Eastwick pondered aloud.

"We should be so lucky," McShane replied over the radio. "I don't think the river's that deep. Even if it is, do the Jotnar even breathe?"

No one could answer that. Plus they were near bingo fuel. Time to head home.

A darkish hue settled across the sky when McShane and Eastwick swung their Vipers to the southeast, making their way back to the ship. Their post-mission brief was mercifully short. How many different ways could one say, "We didn't find shit,"?

Next came the after-action report. The deeper he got into it, the harder his fingers banged on the keyboard. He snorted again and again, trying to expel his sense of failure. McShane repeated Captain Mazzilli's words in his mind, how no one had ever faced anything like the Jotnar, how they had no idea their strengths or weaknesses or what it would take to kill them. The skipper was right, though it did little to ease McShane's anger.

It was after 2330 that he finally finished his report and sent it off to Esposito, Whitaker, and Mazzilli. His stomach had turned into a void. Aside from an energy bar before his second sortie of the day, he had not eaten since breakfast.

McShane made a beeline for the O3 wardroom, or "the dirty shirt mess," where air crews could eat in their flight suits. The mess crew had laid out heated trays of sliders and fries for midrats, or midnight rations. At the end of the serving line sat small plates of chocolate sheet cake with white frosting. He stared at it for a few seconds, then looked up at the nearest cook, a husky African-American.

"Heard you guys had a rough day," the man said. "Just our way of trying to make things a little better."

"Much appreciated. Thank you."

"You're welcome, sir."

McShane loaded his plate with three sliders and two handfuls of fries and grabbed a slice of cake. He ate that first, and damn it was good. Sweet, moist. Most people could probably never comprehend how something as simple as a piece of cake could be so important to him after a horrific day like this. But for at least a minute or two, the treat made him forget about giant rock monsters that wouldn't die.

The sliders and fries did not have that same effect. He chewed, barely noticing the taste, thinking about waves of missiles and rockets exploding harmlessly against the Jotnar, of the beasts stomping through the base.

Of Ylva.

He looked toward the entrance of the wardroom, hoping someone would come in. No one did. Just him in here, him and his thoughts.

She's all right. She has to be.

McShane held a fry between his thumb and index finger, staring at it. He'd only known Ylva for a few days, had only a handful of conversations with her. Yet he worried so much for her safety.

And why not? He liked her. Ylva was just . . . different. Interesting. Smart. Beautiful. He liked being around her. Wanted to be around her more. Wanted to protect her.

Tried to, anyway.

He laid down the French fry, suddenly not hungry.

"Captain."

McShane spun in his seat. Lt. Colonel Whitaker entered the wardroom.

"Good news. That professor you've apparently taken a liking to is safe and sound."

He closed his eyes and leaned back in his chair, all his muscles unwinding. "Thank you, sir."

Whitaker nodded as he took a seat across from him. "All the scientists got out before the Jotnar hit the base. They're temporarily quartered at an army base in Heistadmoen until the Norwegians figure out where to stage for future anti-Jotunn operations."

"Speaking of which, has anyone found the ugly bastards?"

"Nope. Damn things vanished off the face of the Earth."

McShane said nothing, just eyed what remained of his midrats. He had a bad feeling the Jotnar wouldn't stay vanished for long.

EIGHT

The United States Marine Corps was invading Norway.

At least, that's how it seemed to McShane.

Circling the beach over the Krokstrand campground, he watched half-a-dozen bulky AAV-P7 amphibious assault vehicles chugging through the water and rolling onto land. Each one contained twenty grunts. Behind them, three oval-shaped vessels skimmed over the waves. LCACs, or in civilian terms, hovercraft. A fourth one slipped out the rear of the landing dock ship *USS Gunston Hall* sitting offshore. Two of the LCACs carried Humvees or LAV-25 armored recon vehicles. The remaining two held M1A1 main battle tanks.

McShane and the rest of Hammer Flight provided air cover. So did a pair of F-35s high above. About a mile south of them, the littoral combat ship *USS Omaha* gave them added firepower with its 57mm gun. All in all, it was an impressive force.

At least it would be against a human enemy. Against the Jotnar . . .

He tried to shake off such defeatist thoughts. Hard to do when he thought about their futile attacks on the three Jotnar in Drangedal two days ago. The pilots of the ACE had gone over the footage of the battle multiple times, bandied about theories and ideas. The best tactic they could come up with was, "Hit them in the same spot over and over again."

They decided to make that spot the head. It couldn't be as thick as the torso. Pound it with enough Hellfires and bombs and whatever passed for its brains would eventually be blown all over the Norwegian countryside.

At least, that's what they all hoped.

McShane continued circling the landing force. The official story from NATO stated this was a rapid deployment exercise in conjunction with Winter Huskie. In reality, the Marines would be headed to Gardermoen Air Station outside Oslo, the new center of anti-Jotunn operations.

Once all the vehicles assembled on the beach, Hammer Flight took turns topping off their fuel tanks on either the *Gunston Hall* or the *Omaha* before starting their seventy-plus mile trek north. Because of the narrowness of the Oslofjord, this was the closest the landing ship could get to the Norwegian capital.

The Marine ground force wound its way along a forest road. McShane scanned the countryside for any sign of Jotnar. No rock giants popped up. All he saw were miles of trees and farmland broken up by small clusters of buildings. That changed once the convoy got on the E18 motorway. Actual cities stretched around them. More civilian vehicles flowed up and down the roadway. He could picture the wide, surprised eyes of drivers and passengers as they watched the massive M1 tanks and their armored escorts roll by.

Buildings outnumbered trees as they entered Oslo, the USMC convoy guided by a car from the Norwegian Home Guard military police, lights flashing. McShane gazed around the big city with its mixture of modern and classic architecture. He thought of the Jotnar, of the people below. How many lived in Oslo? Over a million if he recalled.

"If they only knew," he muttered.

"What was that?" asked Johnson.

"Just thinking of the folks down there. Going about their lives, no clue there are monsters roaming around their country and killing people."

Johnson shrugged. "That's the way the higher-ups want it. Don't want to panic the general population."

McShane scoffed. "Well there's gonna be a shitload of panic if some Jotunn stomps into this town, or any other town."

"Someone will find a way to stop them before that happens."

"What if they don't?"

Johnson grimaced. His mouth opened, closed, and opened again. "They will. I mean, they have to."

McShane groaned. Even in the privacy of their cockpit, Johnson wouldn't voice any doubts. Did he worry McShane would tell Colonel Esposito he had no confidence in the superior minds of the senior officers to defeat the Jotnar? It wouldn't surprise him. Johnson's father made it to light colonel before retiring from the Corps. His older brother was a flight leader for a Marine tilt-rotor squadron. Johnson was determined to outshine them both and would go to great, even semi-paranoid lengths, to keep his nose clean for the sake of his career.

Outside of flight-related matters, the pair flew in silence the rest of the way to Gardermoen Air Station. All manner of aircraft were parked along the two runways, so many McShane wondered if the air controllers had a place for him and Hammer Flight to land.

They did. McShane and the others had to wait for a transport plane to take off before they touched down. Once out of the chopper, he gazed around the airfield, taking in the vast array of aircraft. C-130, C-17, and V-22 transports, F-35, F-16, and F-15 fighters, Huey and NH-90 helicopters. Not all the aircraft bore the star for America or the triangle inside the circle for Norway on their fuselages. Black iron crosses adorned the sides of four German Tornado multi-role fighters. Two Apaches had a roundel divided into three equal sectors of the Royal Netherlands Air Force. A Seahawk helicopter had a red circle with a white interior emblazoned on its side for the Royal Danish Navy.

No longer was this simply a joint U.S./Norwegian operation. The NATO Alliance had gotten fully involved.

The flight reported to the administration building for processing, where McShane again ran into the female corporal from Drangedal, Knutsen.

"Good to see you again, Corporal. Glad you got out all right."

"Thank you, sir, though some people . . . didn't." Her face sagged.

"Yeah. Damn shame about that."

The corporal nodded and gave Hammer Flight their billet assignment. No DRASH this time. They'd be staying in an actual dormitory.

"What'd ya know," said Eastwick. "We're moving up in the world."

"Yeah," Cain chimed in. "Maybe the mess has steak and shrimp cocktail."

Tudoran barked out a laugh. "If only."

Knutsen pointed out the location of various buildings, including the mess, then told them to report to air operations for their patrol assignments.

"Thank you, Corporal," said McShane. "By the way, do you know where I can find Professor Tande?"

"The research group is housed in Building Twelve, north of the mess hall."

McShane thanked Knutsen before heading out with the rest of his flight. Anticipation at seeing Ylva built up by the second. He walked a little faster, head high, drawing deep breaths of the cool air.

"Damn, Mack," said Nunez. "You in some kind of hurry to get to ops?"

"No, Tin Foil." Hunter glanced at him, then at McShane. "He's in a hurry to meet up with that mythology professor he's smitten with."

McShane swung around to face "Clubber" Hunter, raising an eyebrow.

She shot him a wry grin. "Come on. Deny it."

He shrugged. "Nothing to deny. You're absolutely right."

Nunez and Koosman hooted. Eastwick slapped his shoulder. "Go get her, Mack. Just keep talking to her about dragons and weird shit and she'll be all over you."

"Shut up, ass-hat." McShane knocked away the other pilot's hand. Eastwick laughed.

"Grow the fuck up, Flameout," Hunter scolded him.

Koosman waved a dismissive hand. "Aw, he's just jealous 'cause he knows he wouldn't have a chance with her."

"Sorry. Myth girl ain't my type."

"Of course she isn't," said Hunter. "Because she actually has a brain . . . and good taste."

The other pilots howled.

"Burn by Clubber, yeah." Nunez gave her a fist bump.

Eastwick flipped them the middle finger. The group laughed even harder.

Except Johnson. That didn't surprise McShane. His co-pilot wasn't much for good-natured ribbing. Probably afraid of saying something that could be deemed politically incorrect and earn him a reprimand. Also, Johnson didn't have much of a sense of humor.

"What I mean, you jackasses," said Eastwick, "is she looks like one of those girls you see at those ComicCons. The ones who dress up like cartoon characters. Sorry, I'm not into women who are still into kid stuff."

"I don't know." McShane shrugged. "When I was in college I dated a girl who was bigtime into cosplay."

"And that didn't embarrass you, Mack? Being with a girl who never outgrew Halloween?"

"You wouldn't say that if you'd seen her dress up like Chun-Li from *Street Fighter.*" McShane waggled his eyebrows.

They got to air ops and received their schedules. McShane and Eastwick drew the patrol from 1800 to 2000 hours for a grid twenty-five miles west of Gardermoen. Plenty of time to get his gear stowed, see Ylva, and grab some chow.

He'd packed simply. Change of clothes, a couple of jackets, toiletries, and a couple of paperbacks to fight the boredom of downtime. When he got to his four-bed dorm, McShane stored everything quickly, to the snickers of some of his fellow pilots.

"You think the hot prof is gonna find a new guy if you don't see her in the next five minutes?" Nunez joked.

"No, but why take a chance?" McShane grinned.

"Go forth and conquer, Mack." Cain pumped a fist in the air.

McShane waved him off as he left the dorm.

He powerwalked to Building 12, the engines of a big, chubby C-17 rumbling as it touched down on the nearby runway. A Norwegian soldier directed him to the third floor, where the research team had set up shop.

The large space was laid out like a typical office bullpen, with several pairs of desks pushed together.

It didn't take him long to spot Ylva. She sat at a desk in the far corner, by herself, wearing a black *Rick and Morty* sweatshirt. Smiling, he strode over.

He was halfway across the bullpen when Ylva looked up. "Makato," she beamed.

"Hey, Ylva."

"I'm so glad to see you. I was . . ." She bit her lip for a moment. "I was worried when those Jotnar attacked."

"Well, I was worried about you."

Ylva's face flushed as McShane continued. "I'm glad you got out okay."

"It was a close call." She clutched her hands, staring down at them. Probably reliving the evacuation from Drangedal, he guessed.

She looked back up at him. "I could see them above the trees as we were pulling away. And I . . ." She shook her head. "You will think me strange if I say it."

McShane raised his right hand. "You have my word as an officer and a gentleman, I will not think you're strange."

Ylva managed a weak smile. "Part of me did not want to leave. I actually wanted to stay and watch those Jotnar. Actual monsters, like the ones I've studied all my life, right before my eyes."

She took a slow breath before going on. "I know how dangerous they are, how many people they killed, but I still cannot help being fascinated by them. Wanting to see them, find out all I can about them. Perhaps find other creatures we have only believed existed in fiction. I think this, and it makes me feel guilty about those who died. Like I am being insensitive."

"I think you're being human," said McShane. "And it's not like you're giving zero thought to everyone who died back at Drangedal. Besides, even I have to admit a sort of morbid curiosity when it comes to the Jotnar. Won't stop me from blowing them into a smoking pile of pebbles, if that's even possible."

"Yes, they showed us the footage from the battle."

McShane folded his arms. "There's gotta be some way to take them out."

"I truly wish I could tell you." Ylva swiveled in her chair, staring at the piles of books that covered her desk. "But I cannot find anything in any of these books that will give me a hint as to what the Jotnar truly are, never mind how to kill them. I do have contacts at a few museums and universities both here and in Sweden that have journals and documents on Norse mythology dating back centuries. They might have some clues about the Jotnar. I put in a request to General Tellefsen for them. He said asking for so much material could raise suspicions as to what is really happening here."

"Seriously?"

Ylva snorted. "It makes no sense."

"Welcome to the military world. I guess the U.S. doesn't have the monopoly on senior officers doing things that make no sense." For a second, McShane's mind flashed back to the speeding pickup truck, to that damn order.

Ylva's soft chuckle reeled him back to the present. "Well, he is letting me use the internet, in a limited manner," she told him. "But there has to be a soldier with me to make sure I do not look at unauthorized websites. It is rather . . . uncomfortable."

McShane wondered if those soldiers watched Ylva more than the computer screen. That set off a flicker of anger in him.

"So what sites are you allowed to look at?"

"Some deal with the statues on Easter Island. A connection between them and the Jotnar is possible, given the similar looks of their heads. There is one theory that suggests those statues had been living creatures. There is still debate on whether or not the people of that time had the necessary tools to move the statues, given how large they were."

Eyebrows knitted, McShane said, "So say those statues were alive. They dug a hole, jumped in, covered themselves up to their necks, and just sat there?"

"I know. It sounds implausible. But it leads to another theory." Ylva directed her stare to the ceiling.

McShane followed her gaze, then gave her a knowing nod. "You're thinking aliens, right?"

"That is another theory for the Easter Island statues, just as with Stonehenge and the pyramids. I have looked at several UFO sites and found three accounts of mysterious lights over the Telemark region over the past month."

"Which could be anything."

"That is true." Ylva nodded. "Also, these Jotnar do not seem intelligent enough to build a ship capable of traveling from one star system to another."

McShane leaned against Ylva's desk. "You said the Jotnar might be based on Norse legends of giants or trolls. How intelligent were they?"

"Giants could be very intelligent. Some were kings, some devised cunning plans to defeat their enemies, some even played musical instruments. Trolls, however, had below average intelligence, and that might be giving them too much credit."

McShane grinned at the sarcastic comment. "And if they were aliens, they'd probably have laser rifles or something. They wouldn't be ripping trees out of the ground and throwing them."

"Trolls did use trees and boulders as weapons, according to legend."

"So it looks like we're ruling out the alien theory," said McShane. "If they're not from space, where the heck could they have come from?"

Ylva shrugged. "They could have been hiding in the mountains until now. They could have been frozen in a glacier a long time ago and released when it started to melt. I can give you a dozen other theories and all of them could be wrong."

"There is one thing we know for sure. These Jotnar don't like us very much."

"Unfortunately."

"Well, I better let you get back to work." McShane patted a stack of books on Ylva's desk. "I need you to find something in these books that'll let us kill those butt ugly bastards."

"Ha. If only everyone else here had that kind of faith in me." She smiled. "Thanks for stopping by."

"My pleasure." McShane took a step, then paused. "By the way, if we get some free time, I'd like to take you to dinner."

Ylva's face brightened.

"And I don't mean the mess hall here with a hundred of our closest friends and acquaintances. I mean an actual restaurant in town."

"I'd love to. Thank you."

McShane left the bullpen, chin held high. *Unbelievable.* He actually asked someone out on a date while giant stone monsters threatened the country.

Perfect time to do it, when you think about it. If they couldn't come up with an effective way to destroy the Jotnar, he and everyone else here might not have a long-term future. Might as well have a little bit of happiness in case the worst happens.

NINE

McShane found jack shit on his first patrol. The same with his second patrol, and his third, and his fourth. More than a week since the attack on Drangedal, not a single NATO aircraft had come across any trace of the Jotnar.

Despite the days of inaction, McShane and Ylva found it impossible to sync up their schedules for a dinner date. Given all the briefings, flight planning, patrols, research, writing reports, and maintenance checks, neither had much free time.

On his fifth day at Gardermoen, McShane and Johnson drew the 1200 to 1400 patrol with Eastwick and Koosman. They were assigned a grid in Skrim-Sauheradfjella, a heavily forested area along the Telemark/Buskerud border. They flew around and around, seeing nothing but trees, mountains, and lakes.

Another day of burning up fuel. But at least he was flying. Contrary to popular belief, military pilots did not spend all day, every day in the air. They spent lots of time in classrooms being lectured on everything from enemy weapons systems to tactics to being told that sexually assaulting people was bad, something he had known for, well, *ever.* They took part in flight planning and mission briefs. They were evaluated, or in McShane's case as Hammer Flight leader, performing evaluations.

Times like this, he entertained the idea of one day sitting down and calculating how many hours he had spent in a cockpit compared to how much time he'd spent on the ground since he graduated from flight training. He had yet to work up the courage, fearing the result would be depressing.

"One hour of boredom down, one more hour to go," Eastwick said over the radio.

"Would you prefer to have some Jotunn chucking trees at you?" McShane answered. "Boredom isn't always a bad thing."

"I dodged those trees before. I'll do it again."

McShane opened his mouth, about to say that Hattestad and Stenerud had tried avoiding flying trees and wound up deep-fried for their troubles. He held his tongue. Sometimes, a little jovial banter was needed to –

"All fights! All flights!" the voice of an air controller back at Gardermoen blasted through his headphones. "Jotnar spotted five kilometers west of Skien. Three Jotnar, repeat three Jotnar. West of Skien. Approaching the city."

McShane's hand tightened around the cyclic stick. He glanced down at Johnson. The co-pilot let out a long, tense breath over the chopper's ICS.

The air controller rattled off the names of various flights, ordering them to converge on Skien. That included Hammer Flight.

"Looks like you got your wish, Flameout," McShane radioed Eastwick. "No more boredom."

"Fine by me. I'm looking forward to getting me some payback on those ugly bastards."

"You and me both."

McShane shoved the throttle. His Viper sped over the thick forest, Eastwick following. Worry surged through him. Would they be able to stop the Jotnar? Would their attacks be as futile as last time? Would he and Johnson wind up smeared across the Norwegian countryside like Hattestad and Stenerud?

"Hammer Flight, Echo Base."

"Go Echo."

"Handing you off to NATO AWACS, call sign Monarch Three."

"NATO AWACS, call sign Monarch Three. Copy."

Seconds later, a new voice came through his headphones. Heavily accented. Czech, McShane guessed.

"Hammer Flight, Monarch Three," said the weapons controller on the E-3 Airborne Warning and Control Systems aircraft high above Norway.

"Go Three."

"We have you on radar. Come to heading zero one niner for intercept."

"Copy on heading zero one niner." McShane gently moved the cyclic stick right.

"Be advised, there is increased military air traffic in the area of operation," reported the Czech. "All civilian air traffic is being diverted."

"Roger, Monarch Three."

The green and brown checkerboard of farmland appeared in the distance. Beyond that, the mass of buildings and roads that made up Skien. Certainly nowhere near as big as Oslo, but still a fair-sized city.

McShane leaned forward, noting four dark dots in the sky southwest of the city. Helicopters. Orange flashes streaked down from them. Rockets or missiles. Several columns of greasy black smoke rose from the outskirts of Skien.

"I don't think we're going to be able to keep these things a secret anymore," said McShane.

"No, I guess not." Johnson flicked a couple of switches on his console. "Hellfires ready."

"Copy. Flameout?"

"Locked, cocked, and ready to rock, Mack," replied Eastwick.

"All right, we're not screwing around with these bastards. Four-missile volley from each of us. All headshots. Hopefully that'll put 'em down for good."

"Oo-rah!" blurted Eastwick.

"Oo-rah." McShane contacted the AWACS. "Monarch Three, Hammer Flight. Moving to engage Jotnar."

"Roger, Hammer Flight. You are cleared to engage."

McShane tried to tune out the thumping of his heart as he soared over Skien. Numerous vehicles packed the roads, the vast majority heading north. Dots crowded the sidewalks, looking like ants from this height. People. All fleeing the Jotnar.

Yup. The secret is definitely out.

A large brown form lumbered ahead of him.

"Monarch Three, Hammer Flight. I have eyes on a Jotunn. Moving east from what looks like a soccer field."

"Copy, Hammer Flight. Fire at will."

McShane put the Viper into a hover. Eastwick did the same off his starboard side.

"You're on, Johnson. Let's decapitate this sucker."

"Roger that." Enthusiasm filled Johnson's voice. "Four Hellfires, locked on."

"Hammer Eight," radioed Eastwick's gunner, Koosman. "Four Hellfires, locked on. Just say the word."

McShane's eyes bore in on the Jotunn as it smashed a house beneath its enormous foot.

"Fire."

"Missiles away," both Johnson and Koosman called out.

Eight contrails raced across the sky. McShane held his breath as he watched the missiles draw closer to their target.

Fireballs blossomed along the Jotunn's head and shoulders. The beast stumbled and fell.

"Yeah!" Johnson threw a fist in the air.

"We did it!" Koosman hollered. "Oo-rah!"

A cheer erupted from Eastwick. "That's what you get when you mess with the United States Marine . . . Corps." His voice trailed off.

The Jotunn rose to its knees.

"Dammit," hissed McShane. "Go for broke. Fire all Hellfires. Go for the head."

Both Vipers launched their remaining Hellfires. Six hit the Jotunn. When the smoke and flames cleared, its rectangular head was scorched, a few chunks blown off. But the monster remained very much alive.

"Mother . . ." Eastwick stammered. "What the hell does it take to kill these things?"

"Zip it. Keep shooting."

Rockets flashed from the pods of both Vipers. Sparks, smoke, and dust jumped off the Jotunn's body. It threw its arms out to the side, mouth wide open. Roaring?

"Monarch Three, Hammer Flight," McShane called the AWACS. "Jotunn took multiple hits to head with Hellfires and rockets." He pressed his lips together, frustration taking over. "All ineffective."

A second or two of silence passed before the Czech weapons controller responded, "Acknowledged, Hammer Flight." Another pause. "Recommend you clear the area. I have a flight of two A-10s rolling in."

"Roger, Monarch. Hammer Flight vacating the area."

McShane swung the Viper around, taking up position three miles from the Jotunn. It hurled some rubble, which fell far from both helicopters.

"Warthogs to the left," Johnson alerted.

McShane turned his head. Two ungainly aircraft dove at the Jotunn. Long wings, fat engines on either side of the fuselage near the twin tails. A-10 Warthogs. The attack jets had gained just as fearsome a reputation during Gulf War One as the Apaches his father had flown. And they still kicked ass in the present day.

He hoped they'd continue doing it today.

Smoke sprouted from the chin of the first A-10. The GAU-8 rotary cannon. A storm of 30mm uranium-depleted rounds battered the Jotunn.

The first A-10 peeled away. The second also hit the monster with a sustained burst.

McShane scowled. The legendary cannon that had ripped apart Saddam Hussein's tanks had done nothing to the rock monster.

The Jotunn grabbed more debris and flung it into the air. It didn't come close to hitting the A-10s. Both jets swung around. An elongated object fell from each one. JDAMs.

The first bomb exploded close to the Jotunn. It fell backward as the second JDAM scored a direct hit on its massive chest.

There was no victorious yelling this time by the Marine pilots. McShane focused on the massive black cloud that blotted out the Jotunn and the neighborhood it stomped through.

"Standby rockets," he ordered. "Just in case."

He eyed the smoke cloud for any movement. Maybe the bomb had done its job. He so wanted to believe that. But after all the other unsuccessful attacks . . .

The Jotunn charged out of the dark cloud. A blackened gouge had been torn out of its chest. McShane shook his head, stunned. The thing had to be better armored than a World War II battleship.

Houses collapsed under its footfalls. It ripped out a thin pine tree and flung it skyward, not hitting any aircraft.

The A-10s made another run. The giant tore out a light pole and threw it. A miss. It grabbed a car and hurled it. The lead A-10 banked right.

The car clipped its wing. The jet corkscrewed into the ground near one of the main roads. A snaking trail of fire cut through several homes. The second A-10 broke off the attack.

"Monarch, Hammer Flight. Permission to re-engage."

"Hammer Flight, permission granted. Re-engage target. Be advised, two Apaches have entered your area of operations to assist."

"Copy, Monarch," replied McShane. "We'll take all the help we can get." *If it'll do any good.*

McShane surged the Viper forward. To his left, a pair of Apache attack helicopters entered the fray. The Jotunn stomped on another house, moving toward a main thoroughfare crowded with vehicles. McShane tensed as he gazed at the line of cars, trucks, and vans. One word blared in his mind as the monster neared the road.

Ammunition.

Hellfires flashed off the rails of the Apaches. The missiles exploded against the Jotunn's torso. One struck its head. The beast didn't slow.

Johnson launched a volley of rockets. Eastwick's Viper did the same. Several missed as the Jotunn bent down and came up with a minivan. It hurtled toward the Apaches. Both dodged the spinning vehicle.

Another vehicle flew through the air. Another. The fourth one came McShane's way. He easily avoided it.

The Apaches raked the Jotunn with their 30mm chain guns. No effect. Two more Hellfires slammed into the giant. It flung a pickup truck at one of the Apaches. The chopper banked right, just avoiding the collision. Johnson loosed another barrage of rockets. That earned them a streetlight soaring toward them. McShane jammed the stick left, glancing at the big, improvised spear as it whizzed past.

"We're running out of rockets," Johnson told him.

"Same here," Eastwick chimed in.

McShane snorted. Soon all they'd have left to fight with would be their 20mm gatling guns. *Like they'll do any good.*

The Jotunn bent down, a Hellfire exploding against its shoulder. It rose with another vehicle, this one requiring both hands.

"Holy shit," Eastwick stammered.

McShane's eyes bulged as the Jotunn lifted a fuel tanker over its head.

"I have weps!" he shouted.

"You have weapons," replied Johnson.

McShane lifted the Viper's nose. His thumb mashed the fire button. Six rockets flashed away from the launchers. The Jotunn leaned back, ready to heave the fuel tanker.

Four rockets missed. The fifth burst against the monster's forearm.

The sixth barreled into the oblong storage tank. An enormous fireball consumed the Jotunn's upper body.

"Oo-rah!" hollered Eastwick. "That SOB is deep fried."

Jaw stiff, McShane stared at the conflagration. He desperately wanted to believe that.

The Jotunn emerged from the black cloud, burning fuel snaking down its body.

"Shit!" yelled Johnson. "We didn't do anything to it."

The monster stood still, its gaze aimed at their Viper. A chill shot up and down McShane's spine.

"We did something. We pissed it off."

Rockets fired from Eastwick's chopper. The Jotunn ignored the explosions and charged ahead.

McShane swung his Viper around. "Monarch Three, Hammer Four. That Jotunn is chasing us."

A car flew by, missing them by twenty feet.

"And throwing stuff at us."

"Go higher, Four."

"I was about to . . ." An idea sprang into his head. "Scratch that, Monarch. That bastard wants to chase us, we'll let him."

"What?" Johnson practically yelped, looking over his shoulder.

McShane zigzagged the Viper, hoping to throw off the Jotunn's aim. An egg-shaped electric car tumbled by, missing them by a good thirty feet.

"We can lead it out of Skien. Get it somewhere not so built up."

"Mack! Break right!" warned Eastwick.

He shoved the stick right. A van flew past.

"We'll get it somewhere deserted," McShane told the AWACS weapons controller. "Then send in every bird you've got and bomb the hell out of it."

No response for several seconds, then, "Standby, Hammer Four."

"Standby my ass," McShane grumbled. He checked the chopper's mirrors. The Jotunn kept after them. He returned his gaze forward, still jinking.

"Bank right!" yelled Eastwick.

McShane threw the Viper into a sharp turn. The car didn't come close to hitting them.

"Thanks, Flameout. Keep singing out if it throws anything."

"I got your back, Mack."

Eastwick shouted another warning seconds later. A van soared well past the Viper.

"This is nuts," blurted Johnson. "That thing's gonna kill us. We need to go faster."

"Negative." McShane jerked the Viper right. "We pull away from him, he'll stop chasing us. There are thousands of civilians down there. We need to get that monster out of the city."

Another car went flying by. Johnson pressed his back into his seat. "My God, my God."

"Pull it together," snapped McShane. "Check those mirrors. Keep an eye on it."

Johnson drew a sharp breath. "Yes, sir."

A moving truck whizzed past. McShane gritted his teeth. Was anyone inside it? Or any of the other vehicles the Jotunn had thrown?

"Hammer Four," the Czech weapons controller finally returned to the airwaves. "Try to lure it to the west. There is a forested area, water on three sides. We are preparing a strike package."

McShane glanced left. A few miles past the local airport, a large finger of land poked out into the water. He saw all green, no buildings.

"I see it, Monarch. Making my way there."

"Cop . . . Wait one, Four."

McShane furrowed his brow. What the hell was that about?

"Break right!" hollered Eastwick.

McShane jerked the Viper right. A sports car whizzed by.

He swung the chopper around and ordered another rocket barrage.

"Why?" asked Johnson. "It's not gonna hurt it."

"No, but I want to keep it good and pissed off at us."

Rockets flashed out of the pods. Most hit the Jotunn's face and neck. It ran faster.

"Yup. Still pissed." McShane turned and headed toward the archipelago.

"All units. All units, Monarch Three," radioed the Czech. "Bogey approaching Skien from the west." He read off the coordinates. "Appears to be flying at treetop level. Speed, ninety knots. Estimated size, fifteen meters. Sixteen klicks and closing."

McShane scanned the west. He saw no sign of the bogey, or unidentified object.

"What the hell now?" Johnson threw up a hand in exasperation.

"No idea. Just focus on our job."

He tuned out the AWACS directing aircraft to intercept the bogey. To the south, more smoke rose from the city. Jets and helicopters zipped about the sky, spitting out yellow streaks. Missiles and rockets, aimed at the other two Jotnar, no doubt.

McShane spotted a flying tree in his side mirror. It fell far short of his Viper. The Jotunn now tromped across a forested area near the airport. A few roads lay beyond it, and another town. Worry bubbled up. How many people still tried to flee this battle? How many would be trapped when the Jotunn came through? How many would die?

He grimaced. Collateral damage, unfortunately, came with the territory. All he could do was keep this Jotunn focused on him, get it out to the archipelago, and have NATO strike planes drop enough bombs to put it down for good, with as few civilian casualties as possible.

Won't be much comfort to the families of the ones who die.

McShane banked away from another tree-turned-spear.

"Mack," Johnson called out. "Something dead ahead."

A large object soared over the forests in the distance. A plane? That's what McShane originally thought. But something about it looked . . . strange.

No, definitely not a plane. He zoomed in with the Target Sight System.

His mouth slowly fell open.

"No fucking way," Johnson spoke in a stunned whisper.

McShane blinked a couple of times, then got on the radio. "Monarch Three, Hammer Four. I have a visual on the bogey."

"What is it?"

"It's . . . a dragon."

TEN

"Hammer Four," the Czech replied in a dumbfounded tone, "say again. What is it?"

"A dragon, Monarch," snapped McShane. "I am looking at an honest-to-God dragon."

Silence hung in his headphones.

"Dragon, Monarch! Delta, Romeo, Alpha, Golf, Oscar, November." He used the NATO phonetic alphabet to spell it out. "Dragon."

"Um, Roger, Four. Dragon."

And that dragon drew closer to McShane's Viper.

"Evasive action!" He swung the chopper to the left. His finger kissed the trigger of the cyclic stick, ready to let loose with the gatling gun.

"My God." Johnson gaped.

McShane couldn't blink as the dragon soared by. Its skin was a shade of dark red that almost looked black. Scales covered its body, resembling plate armor. The snout was sharp and angular, with curved, ivory horns growing from its skull. Ridges ran down its back and tail, which ended in a round club with four spikes. It flapped its enormous bat-like wings and flew past the Viper.

Right at the Jotunn.

The dragon barreled into the other monster like a gigantic, living missile. The Jotunn collapsed to the ground. The dragon landed and whirled around, jaws open. Roaring perhaps?

The Jotunn picked itself up on all fours. The dragon leapt at it and swung its tail. The spiked club tore into the stone giant's left arm. Shards of rock flew in all directions.

"Holy shit!" blurted Eastwick.

McShane said nothing. His eyes remained locked on the scene below, enthralled. A dragon, an actual fucking dragon, was fighting a giant stone monster in the middle of Norway.

The dragon leapt on the Jotunn's back. It slammed its large talons into the rocky skin. McShane's eyes widened when he saw fissures going down the Jotunn's back.

The giant shook back and forth, throwing off the dragon. On one knee, the Jotunn took a swing with its left hand. The dragon ducked, then snapped up its head. The horns impaled the Jotunn's forearm.

"Mack," Eastwick called. "Do we keep hovering around like spectators or do something?"

The dragon jerked its head left, right, then up. The Jotunn's arm snapped off, hanging from the two horns.

"That thing's doing a lot more damage to the Jotunn than we did," replied McShane. "I'm not gonna do anything to stop it." But once the fight was over . . .

The dragon launched itself at the Jotunn again, knocking it on its back. Mouth wide open – roaring again? – it raised its front right leg, then brought it down. Talons cut through the Jotunn's neck. Another slash . . . another.

The Jotunn's head rolled away from its body.

"Did you . . ." Johnson stammered, leaning forward. "That thing . . . damn."

McShane didn't speak. He just gaped at the severed, rectangular head lying in the field.

The dragon turned away from the dead monster. Its wings snapped up and down, throwing up massive dust clouds. It rose into the air, heading toward Skien proper.

Eastwick fired a burst from his gatling gun. McShane squeezed the trigger on his stick a second later. Tracers stitched the dragon's body. The beast whipped its head toward Eastwick's helicopter.

McShane swallowed, expecting the dragon to make a beeline for his wingman's Viper. He let loose another long burst from the cannon. The 20mm rounds had no effect. Cold gripped his body. Would the dragon smash Eastwick's chopper, then his?

The dragon looked away from the Viper and continued on.

Head cocked to the side, a puzzled McShane watched it go. The damn thing could have turned their helicopters into metallic confetti. So why didn't it?

"Flameout. Stay with it."

"Copy, Mack."

The two choppers pursued the dragon.

Two F-35s dove on the dragon. Yellow lines zipped out of the 25mm cannons mounted above their left wing roots. The beast shrugged them off. Same with the 30mm armor-piercing rounds from an A-10. A damn shame none of the planes carried air-to-air missiles. No reason to have them dealing with ground targets like the Jotnar.

The dragon glided over farmland, suburbs, and commercial areas. McShane tensed, expecting the beast to start smashing buildings.

It didn't.

Just beyond the dragon, the remaining two Jotnar stood in the rubble of what McShane guessed had been a shopping center. Both giants eyed the flying monster as it approached, then bent down.

Wrecked vehicles, pieces of wall, and lampposts hurtled through the air. The dragon avoided larger objects. Smaller ones harmlessly bounced off its hide.

The dragon went into a dive just as one Jotunn hefted a tractor-trailer. It didn't throw it. Instead, the giant swung it like a baseball bat.

The trailer smashed against the dragon's head. The creature rolled on its side and crashed to the ground. The Jotunn threw the crumpled trailer down on the other monster's body. Both stone giants stomped toward their fallen foe.

The dragon's head sprang forward. Its jaws bit down on the leg of the nearest Jotunn, then pulled to the side. The giant's arms flung out as it tumbled on its back. The other Jotunn sidestepped its partner and reached out for the dragon.

The tail whipped around. The spiked club crashed against the side of the Jotunn's head in an explosion of stone shrapnel. The giant stumbled.

The other Jotunn got to one knee. The dragon roared and raked it across the chest with its talons. Deep, jagged lines stretched across the Jotunn's torso.

McShane's gaze locked on the wounds. How the hell could those claws tear through thick stone when bombs and missiles only made the barest of dents?

The Jotunn shoved the dragon away. Its friend charged forward and kicked the winged monster. It soared into a rectangular building across the street, steel and glass collapsing like building blocks. The dragon rolled to a stop near the lake. The two Jotnar advanced.

The dragon swung its tail. The Jotnar jumped back. The closest one lunged forward and launched its fist. The blow sent the dragon's head snapping to the side. It staggered into the lake. One Jotunn ripped out a nearby pine tree and raised it like a club.

Spinning faster than McShane expected of such a large creature, the dragon jumped up. Its jaws clamped down on the Jotunn's wrist. The tail lashed out again, keeping the other Jotunn at bay. The dragon's mouth remained locked around the giant's wrist.

Until it severed it. The hand, and the tree it held, fell to the ground.

The dragon propelled itself off the wounded Jotunn and slashed the second one across the throat. Its wings flapped, making it hover in place. It slashed a second time, a third.

The Jotunn's head toppled off its body.

The remaining stone giant punched the dragon in the back. The humungous reptile slammed into the ground. The Jotunn stomped on it once, twice.

The dragon sprang forward. It flattened several trees when it landed, then spun toward the Jotunn. The stone creature charged. The dragon's mouth opened. Another roar? A very long roar considering –

A blast of sunset-red flame erupted from the dragon's maw.

McShane slammed his back into his seat, eyes bulging in shock.

"Shit!" yelled Johnson.

"What the hell?" clamored Eastwick.

The tongue of flame burrowed through the Jotunn's chest and exploded out the other side. The giant stood still for a few seconds, then toppled over.

"Did . . ." Johnson stuttered. "D-Did you see that? I . . . my God, how . . ."

McShane took a few breaths to compose himself. "I think we know what killed that one Jotunn in Drangedal."

The dragon eyed the fallen Jotunn, then raised its head, taking in the aircraft above Skien.

"Trigger fingers ready," warned McShane. "Looks like it's our turn."

He slewed the gatling gun toward the dragon's head. Maybe he could nail its eyes. Surely they had to be vulnerable.

The dragon leaped off the ground, flapping its wings. Both McShane and Eastwick fired. Several tracers hammered the monster.

It paid them no attention and flew west.

"All units, Monarch Three," the air controller on the AWACS called. "Pursue the dragon. Bring it down."

McShane grunted. "Yeah. Easier said than done."

ELEVEN

McShane's Viper roared over the Norwegian countryside, the air speed indicator hitting 175 mph.

He still couldn't catch up to the dragon. Just how in the hell could any animal fly that fast, especially one so big?

The beast's large wings snapped up and down at a furious rate. It blasted through a low-hanging cloud, banked left, and shot through another cloud.

McShane gritted his teeth, scanning the horizon. More low clouds floated above the forests and fjords of the Telemark region. Lots of opportunities to throw off its pursuers.

Yellow flashes zipped past the dragon. McShane glanced up as a Norwegian F-16 pulled out of its dive, its strafing run unsuccessful.

He goosed the throttle, pushing the chopper to 180 mph. With a turn of the head, the helmet's tracking system slewed the gatling gun right. McShane squeezed the trigger on the cyclic stick. All his rounds fell short.

"Dammit," he hissed under his breath. He upped the chopper's speed to 185 mph. The dragon ducked behind a hill. McShane waited until it came out the other side and fired.

Another miss.

"Mack, we're running low on fuel," Eastwick radioed.

McShane checked his own fuel gauge in the helmet-mounted display. He had just enough gas to make it back to Gardermoen . . . barely.

With one last, harsh stare at the dragon, he contacted the AWACS. "Monarch Three, Hammer Four and Hammer Eight disengaging. Low on fuel."

"Copy, Four. RTB." The Czech used the acronym for return to base.

"Lucky," McShane snorted as the dragon barreled through another low cloud. He swung the Viper to the northeast and backed off his speed, Eastwick following. A glance at the map on the kneeboard on his right leg showed all the air fields between here and Gardermoen, just in case he needed to make a pit stop.

"Everyone keep sharp," he told the others. "Just in case that dragon shows up again. Or some other weird monster."

"Don't say that, Mack," said Eastwick. "Like rock giants and dragons aren't bad enough." The pilot paused. "Jeez, did you see that thing take out those Jotnar? Damn thing even breathed fire. Just . . . how?"

"I wish I knew, Flameout."

Both attack choppers made it back to Gardermoen without the need for a refueling stop. McShane couldn't find Cain or Hunter's Vipers. Probably up searching for the dragon.

He and Johnson jumped out of the helicopter when the rotors stopped spinning. Groundcrew hurried over, ready to refuel and rearm the aircraft.

"Colonel Esposito wants you back in the air ASAP, sir," said the stocky crew chief, Sergeant Tamargo. "It's all hands on deck looking for the dragon." He shook his head. "Shit, I can't believe I said that."

"Yeah, well I'm still trying to believe I saw it."

McShane headed for air ops for a quick piss and maybe to shove a protein bar down his throat before hitting the sky again. He was halfway to the building when Ylva raced toward him.

"A dragon!" Her eyes blazed with excitement. "You really saw a dragon?"

"That we did," McShane replied.

"My God, my God." Ylva bounced on the balls of her feet. "They exist. This is unbelievable. You have pictures, right?"

"We do . . . and we're also okay."

Ylva's face fell. "Oh. Oh, I'm sorry. I didn't mean to . . . sorry."

"It's okay." McShane grinned and gently clasped her shoulder, letting her know it was a joke. Ylva stiffened, glanced at his hand on her shoulder, and formed a weak smile.

"Captain McShane."

He swung around to see Lt. Colonel Whitaker striding toward him.

"Debriefing. Now. We need to break down the footage from Skien." He shook his head. "A dragon. How much crazier can this all get?"

"I don't know if I want to find out, sir."

McShane took a couple of steps toward Whitaker when Ylva called out, "Excuse me, Lieutenant Colonel?"

"Yes?"

"May I be part of this briefing?"

"Sorry, ma'am. Marines only."

"If I may, sir." McShane held up a hand. "This kind of stuff is right up Professor Tande's alley. She might have some valuable insight on the dragon."

Whitaker's eyes shifted between him and Ylva. "All right, Professor. You're in. Johnson, fetch Eastwick and Koosman and bring them to the second floor conference room."

"Yes, sir." He hurried off.

Ylva beamed at McShane. "Thank you, Makato."

"C'mon. Who am I to deny you the chance to see footage of a real-life dragon?"

McShane didn't think it possible, but Ylva smiled even wider.

They headed to the air ops center, Ylva powerwalking the whole way. When Johnson, Eastwick, and Koosman joined them in the conference room, each pilot gave a quick rundown of the battle, up to the point where they broke off pursuit. Whitaker then hit a few keys on the laptop at the head of the polished table. A screen on the front wall played the footage from McShane's gun camera, showing the dragon flying straight at them.

Ylva gasped. "My God. Incredible." Her mouth hung open in awe.

Whitaker turned to her. "Sorry, Professor. You're here to give us your expert opinion on this thing, not marvel at it."

The comment set McShane's emotions on fire. He took a breath to settle himself. Whitaker's tone came off as more matter-of-fact than scolding. Unlike if it had been Colonel Esposito. Then again, his CO likely would never have allowed Ylva in here in the first place.

She reeled in her jaw and stared at the carpet for a moment. "I apologize, Lieutenant Colonel. You are right."

The footage continued. Whitaker stood off to the side, arms folded, watching the dragon sheer off the heads of two Jotnar. Ylva's jaw dropped again when the winged monster unleashed its fire breath at the last Jotunn. So did Whitaker's.

"You've gotta be shittin' me." The ACE executive officer gaped at the screen for a couple of seconds before turning to McShane. "So Hellfires and JDAMs can't do crap to these things, but . . . dragonfire goes through it like a bullet through cardboard?"

"Apparently so, sir."

Whitaker's face tightened. His attention shifted to Ylva. "Professor Tande. Any thoughts?"

She blew out a breath and set her clasped hands on the table. "This dragon has similar features to one called Fafnir. According to legend, he was originally a dwarf, but killed his father in order to possess all his gold. Fafnir became so greedy that he turned into a dragon to guard his fortune. Tolkien even used Fafnir as the basis for Smaug in *The Hobbit.*"

Eastwick drew back his head. "You think that actually happened?"

"Perhaps not, though with everything that has happened recently, can we really dismiss anything?"

Eastwick's face scrunched in a doubtful expression.

"So here's the next big question," said Whitaker. "Did anyone kill this dragon?"

"Yes," Ylva answered. "The hero Sigurd."

"How?"

"He dug a trench between the cave where Fafnir lived and the stream it drank from. Sigurd waited for Fafnir to crawl over him, then stabbed him in the heart."

"So maybe the underbelly is where it's vulnerable," said McShane. "I raked its side with the gatling gun and it didn't do a damn bit of good."

"That is, if there is any sort of truth to this story." Ylva turned up her palms as she spoke.

"Let's hope there is," said Whitaker. "Because if a sword can kill this thing, then a missile should have no problem."

"Um, yes. But the sword Sigurd used, Gram, was brought to this world by Odin. He plunged it into a tree and said anyone who pulled it free would have the best sword of any warrior. Several tried and failed before Sigurd's father, Sigmund, pulled it out."

"So basically, the Norse version of Excalibur," said McShane.

"Yes." Ylva nodded. "So that means there could have been a magical element to the sword Sigurd used to kill Fafnir."

Whitaker rolled his eyes. "Magic? That's all we need."

McShane glanced at Ylva. Giant monsters were one thing, but magic? Could that really exist? It seemed far-fetched, but up till an hour ago, so did fire-breathing dragons.

"But that is one possibility. Dragons such as this one," Ylva pointed to the screen, "are common in British folklore."

"Kinda far from home then," Koosman chimed in.

"It is only a few hundred miles across the North Sea from the United Kingdom to Norway. I doubt a flying dragon would have much of a problem crossing it."

"Do you need a magic sword to kill those dragons, too?" asked Whitaker.

Ylva winced, then stiffened her shoulders. "No. Not necessarily. There are many stories about English dragons. Some were killed by regular swords, some by more magical means. A few were poisoned. One, the White Dragon, was captured by two brothers who got it drunk."

"Great." Eastwick clapped his hands. "All we need to do is fill up a lake with Heineken and we're in business."

McShane and Koosman chuckled softly. Johnson groaned.

"Or more realistically," said Whitaker, "we go for that thing's underbelly. From everything Professor Tande's said, that's going to be our best bet to take it down. Thank you, Professor."

Her shoulders sagged as she softly said, "You're welcome."

Whitaker let out a brief sigh. "Now if only we can find some weak spot on the damn Jotnar."

Koosman shrugged. "Maybe let that dragon hang around a little longer in case more Jotnar show up. He did a pretty good job offing those three back in Skien."

"Nice thought," said Whitaker. "But we can't take the chance it'll burn some city to the ground in the meantime. You see it, shoot on sight."

"Yes, sir," McShane and the other Marines replied.

Ylva stared at the screen, gripping her hands.

Whitaker scanned the pilots. "I'll pass your recommendations and theories up the chain. I imagine the groundcrew have your Vipers ready. Hit the head and get back in the air. Dismissed."

The men got up from their chairs. Ylva remained seated for a few seconds, lost in thought, then rose.

McShane entered the hallway when Ylva called to him.

"What's up?" They walked side-by-side.

"Just . . . thinking."

"About?"

Ylva pushed her glasses to the bridge of her nose. "What Lieutenant Colonel Whitaker said, about the dragon burning down a city."

"It certainly has the capability to do it."

"So why didn't it do it in Skien?"

McShane turned to her. "Probably too busy fighting the Jotnar."

"So why not after?" Ylva held her hands out to her sides.

"We had a bunch of jets and choppers in the air. Maybe it didn't want to tangle with us."

"You said it yourself. You shot it with your gun. Not only did you not hurt it, it also made no attempt to attack you."

McShane slowed, forehead wrinkled. "Wait a sec. You're not seriously suggesting that dragon is actually helping us?"

Ylva's mouth hung open silently for a few moments. "I don't know, Makato. But dragons in Norse mythology, English folklore, in most European legends, are portrayed as hostile. If they see a person, they will kill him or her without hesitation. But this one . . . even when you shot it, it didn't attack you."

His eyebrows knitted together, mulling over Ylva's words. Yes, the dragon had only attacked the Jotnar. But like Colonel Whitaker said, who's to say the next time would be different. "Good guy" monsters only existed in movies.

Of course, he used to think all monsters only existed in movies. Same with magic. Now . . .

Crap, could he make any firm declaration about what was real and what was fiction anymore?

"Mack."

His head snapped to the left. Colonel Whitaker had stepped out of the conference room.

"On my way out, sir."

"Don't bother. I just got word from Colonel Esposito. You're not gonna believe this, but we lost sight of that damn dragon."

TWELVE

"Anyone else feel like we're under siege?" McShane scanned the perimeter of the air base at Gardermoen. A mass of reporters, camera operators, and satellite trucks stretched from one end to the other. He counted nearly two dozen news crews doing live reports near the chainlink fence, at least as close to it as the sentries would allow.

"It's the press." Cain scowled. "So hell yeah, I feel like we're under siege."

"A bunch of stone monsters just trashed a city and killed a couple hundred people," said Koosman. "Did you think the media wouldn't show up?"

"I say good." Nunez nodded emphatically. "It's about time something like this got out to the public. This is just the start. Everything's gonna be exposed. Aliens, recovered UFOs, the HAARP project. The world's about to have its collective mind blown."

"And you think that's a good thing?" Johnson's eyes narrowed at the gunner/co-pilot. "Have you seen the news? People are jamming the roads to get out of cities. There was looting in Skien. Everything NATO does is being put under a microscope, and people are coming up with conspiracy theories weirder than anything you've ever thought up. It's a mess. We were better off when we kept this a secret."

"Like hell," Nunez shot back. "People have a right to know about giant monsters stomping around their country. Just like they have a right to know about extraterrestrials visiting our planet."

"How about we deal with the Jotnar and this dragon before we start looking for aliens?" said Hunter.

"What if they're both connected?" Nunez cocked his head to the side in a knowing expression.

Johnson groaned and rolled his eyes.

McShane ignored the argument. It wasn't the first go-around between Nunez and, well, the rest of Hammer Flight about his wacko theories. He continued staring at the army of reporters. Whether or not they were better off keeping all this a secret was irrelevant. No way NATO or anyone else could hush this up after the attack on Skien. If anything, the existence of the Jotnar and the dragon spurred the alliance to go all out in combating this threat. Troops, vehicles, and aircraft poured into Norway, with more en route. Carrier strike groups centered around the *USS Eisenhower* and *HMS Queen Elizabeth* steamed toward the North Sea. While not NATO members, Sweden and Finland mobilized their forces to combat the monsters.

"Looks like we got more company." Tudoran pointed to the sky.

Four sleek Tiger attack helicopters from the German Army approached the runway.

Eastwick swung his torso left to right. "Damn. We got any place to put 'em?"

McShane looked around Gardermoen's runways. He had thought the base crowded when he first arrived. Now it seemed every inch of available space had been taken up by aircraft or DRASHes to accommodate all the additional personnel.

Somehow, the air traffic controllers found room for the Tigers.

"Hope all the extra firepower makes a difference," said Koosman.

"It will," Johnson practically snapped. "Remember what Colonel Esposito said. Hit 'em enough times and we'll kill them. No way they can stand up to everything we're bringing in. No way."

Eastwick and Tudoran groaned. Hunter cocked a thin eyebrow at him.

"Let's hope you're right," said McShane.

The pilots sat under a lone tree near one of the runways, watching the sky for more helicopters or airplanes. None of them had a scheduled patrol and dinner was several hours away. Not much to do except find ways not to be bored. Conversation turned to which of the foreign attack helicopters they would like to fly.

"Those Tigers look sweet," said Hunter.

"Oh yeah." Eastwick grinned. "Heard they're hell'a agile. Good stealth, too. Ain't no one touching me in that one."

"It's got my vote," said Koosman. "What about you, Mack?"

"You guys can go for style all you want. Me . . ." He aimed a finger at a Polish Mi-24 Hind.

"Oh c'mon," Eastwick blurted. "Damn thing's a giant pig with rotors."

"But a well-armored giant pig with a crap-ton of firepower. Besides, it looks cool as hell."

"More like ugly as hell," Hunter scoffed.

"Ugly but deadly." McShane grinned.

"I'm with you, Mack." Nunez's hand shot up. "Hind's my go-to chopper when I play *Air Missions.*"

Hunter shook her head, while Eastwick gave him a dismissive wave.

"Kiss-ass." Koosman smirked at him.

McShane chuckled softly. Banter like this made it easy to forget that somewhere out there lurked stone monsters and an honest-to-god fire-breathing dragon.

"Attention. Attention," a male voice boomed out of the base loudspeakers. "All attack helicopter pilots and crews are to report to the briefing tent at 1430 hours."

McShane checked his watch. They had twenty minutes before the briefing started.

Well, forgetting about monsters was nice while it lasted.

The Marine pilots were among the first at the briefing tent. Rows of folding chairs took up most of the center space. A projection screen, three desks, and a few chairs had been set up in the front, with maps and still shots of Jotnar and the dragon taped to the canvass wall. McShane and his flight grabbed seats in the second row. More NATO pilots filed in, including Colonel Esposito and Lt. Colonel Whitaker, who sat in the front row of the section opposite to them.

Right at 1430, someone in the back said, "Ten-hut."

Everyone stood at attention. Out of the corner of his eye, McShane spotted a lean man just over six-foot with dark hair and graying temples striding down the aisle with a stiff, business-like expression. Commodore Peter Oerlemans, the head of heliborne operations for Allied Joint Force Command Brunssum, the NATO headquarters overseeing what was now dubbed Operation Beast Slayer.

Two aides followed him to the front of the tent. The Dutchman stood at the lectern, scanned the audience for a second, and said, "As you were."

All the pilots sat.

"I am sure you have all seen the footage from the battle in Skien," Oerlemans began. "The Jotnar were deadly enough, but the appearance of this dragon has elevated the threat to Norway, and possibly to the entire continent, to a new level."

There's an understatement, thought McShane.

"While we still have not found a weak spot for the Jotnar," Oerlemans continued, "the same cannot be said for the dragon. After consulting with other NATO officers and members of the research team here at Gardermoen, it is theorized that the dragon's underbelly could be vulnerable to attack."

The corner of McShane's mouth curled. That had been Ylva's theory. He wished the Commodore had cited her specifically, but maybe he was one of those team effort leaders. Or maybe he didn't want to admit the idea came from someone who made a living talking to college students about Thor, Asgard, and mythical monsters. Afraid the other pilots wouldn't take it seriously?

He stifled a grunt. Whatever the case, it irked him Ylva didn't get the credit she deserved.

"There have been many stories throughout the centuries of dragons being killed by a sword to the stomach," said Oerlemans. "Obviously, we do not wield swords anymore. But we do have missiles."

The Dutchman turned to one of the photos of the dragon. "Normally, we would use jets to handle an airborne threat. But there are challenges to that. One, since the creature's airspeed has been recorded at below three hundred kilometers per hour, fighters would have to fly at or below stall speed to engage it. In addition, they would not have the angle to hit its underbelly, especially if the dragon flies at low altitude as it did at Skien and when it retreated from the city. Therefore, it has been decided that helicopters are better suited for an air-to-air engagement with the dragon."

The heads of several pilots swung left and right, looking at those next to them. McShane studied them. Some looked surprised or concerned, or both. Others grinned and nodded, as though relishing the opportunity. Eastwick and Cain were among them. Johnson shifted in his chair, face tight, appearing uncomfortable.

McShane teetered between concern and accepting the challenge. What attack helicopter pilot didn't imagine being in a dogfight? Trouble was, that was chopper-on-chopper, not chopper-on-fire breathing dragon. Also, most pilots like him received little training in air-to-air engagements. It might even be non-existent among pilots from other NATO countries. The focus of Viper, Apache, Tiger, and Hind jocks was blowing up targets on the ground, not in the air.

Commodore Oerlemans went on. "Our helicopters are almost as fast as the dragon. We can operate better at lower altitudes than an F-16 or a Typhoon. We can hover directly underneath the dragon if we have to and fire into its belly. More Sidewinders will be delivered to Gardermoen over the next few days. While the missile obviously wasn't designed for animals, since the dragon breathes fire, it has to generate a heat source. The Sidewinder should be able to lock on to it."

We hope, thought McShane.

Oerlemans stepped up to a photo of the dragon soaring over the Norwegian forests and pointed. "Some of you may be wondering, why not go for the wings? They cannot be as thick as its hide."

McShane wondered that, too. It probably wouldn't kill the monster, but it would take away one of its abilities.

"We considered that tactic as well," said Oerlemans, "but decided if we take out its wings and ground it, hitting its underbelly would prove incredibly difficult. Also, a wounded animal can be more dangerous than an uninjured one. Some on the research team also speculate the wings are thicker and stronger than they appear. It would explain how something that large can stay airborne and fly at the speeds it does."

Okay, makes sense. McShane had wondered how the dragon could actually fly. Even with thick wings, the physics of it should make it impossible.

Then again, giant rock creatures should be impossible, too. So what the hell did he or anyone else know?

"As for the Jotnar . . . ." Oerlemans turned back to the pilots. "It is no secret these monsters are highly resistant to missiles and bombs. But we have only used a few large bombs on them up to this point. The U.S. Air Force is deploying B-52s and B-1s to England and Germany. The massive payloads they carry should be sufficient to destroy the Jotnar. Ideally, we want to strike them in remote areas. Should they attack another city . . . ." He bit his lip for a moment. "The plan is for you to herd them to a less populated area for the bombers to hit them."

McShane turned to Cain, seated to his right, and raised an eyebrow. "Stripes" scrunched his face, the expression screaming, "Is he fucking serious?"

A glance around the rest of the room showed other pilots reacting similarly to Cain.

"I know." Oerlemans held up both hands. "It sounds difficult. It may be impossible. But we must do all we can to avoid collateral damage."

Eastwick leaned over to McShane and Cain and whispered, "And if all those bombs don't work, what then? We nuke 'em?"

"I doubt the Norwegians would like that," McShane whispered back.

"Starting tomorrow," said Oerlemans, "exercises in preparation for air-to-air engagements will begin. The Polish Air Force is sending some of its M28 Skytruck transports here to simulate the dragon. Your squadron commanders will provide you with your schedules. Any questions?"

No one raised a hand.

"Very well. Dismissed, and good luck."

Chairs shuffled as dozens of men and women rose from their seats.

"Hell yeah." Eastwick grinned. "Gonna get me a dragon painted on the side of my chopper."

"Unless I nail it first, Flameout." Hunter gave him a wink.

"Or maybe wait until it kills a few more Jotnar before you shoot it," said Nunez. "I'm not gonna complain if that dragon trims the odds for us."

"Fuck that." Eastwick waved him off. "I get that sucker in my sights . . . bang! Sidewinder through the gut, baby."

McShane's eyes shifted between Eastwick and Nunez. He'd had the same conversation with Ylva and Lt. Colonel Whitaker the other day, and all agreed it was too much of a risk.

But was it worth the risk? If more Jotnar showed up and the dragon fought them, wouldn't it make sense to let it take out the rock monsters before they fired on it?

And what if we miss our chance for a kill shot doing that?

A troubling thought slithered through his mind. How many Jotnar were out there? He doubted the three killed by the dragon in Skien could be the only ones. So the more the dragon got rid of, the better for them. Right?

Hammer Flight had all filed into the aisle when Colonel Esposito approached. Probably to tell them their schedule for air-to-air exercises. Jaw tight, he stared at his CO. If the dragon was the easier of the two monsters to kill, maybe they should save it for last. Maybe they should let it tear through any more Jotnar that popped up. Perhaps that would save more lives than blasting the dragon first.

Was it wishful thinking? Was it a smart plan? Was it something the colonel would seriously consider?

Esposito returned his stare, his face stiff, unsmiling. "Something on your mind, Captain?"

McShane let out a short breath, "No, sir."

THIRTEEN

"Good tone . . . Fox Two, Fox Two . . . Direct hit, both missiles."

"Mm." McShane nodded at Johnson's statement. He eyed the M28 Skytruck as it banked over the forests outside Gardermoen.

Eastwick and Koosman's Viper moved in, also firing a pair of simulated Sidewinder missiles. Both "struck" the twin-prop, twin-tailed transport pretending to be a dragon.

The Polish Air Force plane swung around for another attack run. This time, three of the four missiles found their mark on the aircraft's belly. Same with the third run.

Both misses were by "Koo Koo" Koosman, not Johnson.

"Hot damn." Even though the gunner/co-pilot wasn't facing him, McShane could picture a large, triumphant smile on Johnson's face. "Six Sidewinders, six hits. I'm lovin' that."

"Yup," McShane spoke in a flat tone. "We definitely know we can shoot down low-flying, slow-moving transports if we have to."

"And dragons." Johnson looked over his shoulder. "That's why we're doing this."

"I know, but there's one problem."

"What?"

"Dragons breathe fire, Skytrucks don't," replied McShane.

Johnson let out a long sigh. "Well, it's better than nothing."

"Not by much," McShane grumbled.

Johnson faced forward, shaking his head.

McShane and Eastwick moved their Vipers away from the exercise area, making room for Hunter and Cain to take their shots. The Skytruck returned, flying low, making a slow bank left, then right, trying its best to perform evasive maneuvers. Though smaller compared to the venerable C-130, the Skytruck was still a transport. The plane had been built for hauling shit from Point A to Point B, not speed and agility.

The Skytruck made three passes. All but two missiles from Hunter and Cain's Vipers found their target. They disengaged, giving a flight of U.S. Army Apaches their shot at the transport.

"Good shooting, everyone," McShane radioed Hammer flight, his tone matter-of-fact. They all did shoot very well for not having much practice with Sidewinders. But the exercise was just way too easy.

He didn't want easy.

They returned to base, then gathered for the exercise debrief with Colonel Esposito. The ACE commander listened to each pilot break down their attack runs while going over gun camera footage.

"More than a ninety percent success rate," said Esposito. "That's surprising. I didn't expect so many hits your first time out with Sidewinders."

McShane forced himself not to frown. Talk about a backhanded compliment.

"But you can do better," Esposito continued. "You can't afford misses against the dragon, especially over a populated area. The last thing the Corps wants is bad press because an errant missile took out an apartment complex or a school full of kids. Most of your shots were taken from two miles out or more. For your next exercise, I want you to get closer, within a mile of the target. At that distance, you ought to be able to connect with every shot."

McShane flexed his right hand. The colonel didn't like anyone asking questions until the end of a briefing. But given how things went in the exercise, given what they would face in actual combat . . .

Fuck it. His hand went up.

Esposito froze. Wide eyes locked on McShane, eyes that held a mix of shock and offense. "You have something to say, Captain? Something that can't wait?"

"Yes, sir. I do. I don't believe this exercise was a true reflection of what we can expect next time we meet up with that dragon."

His CO's eyes narrowed. McShane could almost feel heat firing out those slits and burning into his brain. "Is that so?"

Esposito stepped closer to him. McShane stared up at the senior officer, keeping his body rigid. He might be treading on thin ice, but this needed to be said.

"Sir, we've seen the footage of what that dragon can do. There's no way a plane based off a Soviet design from fifty years ago can duplicate the maneuverability or anything else of an actual dragon. It can turn quicker, fly lower to the ground without worrying about crashing and burning, and most important of all, it can breathe fire. We can hit a plodding Skytruck that can't defend itself over and over again, but it won't prepare us for another fight with the dragon."

He glanced at the others. Johnson blinked slowly, face radiating disbelief. Eastwick's mouth fell open, then closed just as quickly. Hunter was her usual, impassive self, but Cain and Nunez's eyes bulged from surprise. Not many would risk such brutal honesty with Colonel Esposito.

His CO stood directly over him, arms akimbo. McShane did not look away from the other man's glare.

"So, you think all this is a waste of time?"

McShane stiffened. How should he answer –

"I asked you a question, Captain," Esposito barked.

"Ye . . . I . . ." He pressed his lips together for a moment. "It's just . . . that Skytruck isn't going to attack us. The dragon will. One quick turn of the head and it could blast a Viper out of the air."

"That's why we have missiles. So we can shoot it from a couple of miles away."

"How do we know its . . . fire breath can't reach that far? Honestly, we don't know much about its capabilities."

Lines dug into Esposito's forehead. "Well since the United States Marine Corps does not have any dragons around that we can send up in the air for training purposes, using the Skytrucks is our best option. Unless you have a better idea. Do you, Captain?"

"Maybe, sir. We can bring in simulators. Program in a dragon to -"

"Program in a dragon that you yourself said we don't know a lot about." Esposito's hand slashed up through the air. "Do you know how long that would take? Not just the programming, but flying Viper simulators from the States to Norway and getting them set up? This whole operation could be over before then."

McShane's jaw clenched. *Yeah, but will it be over with Norway turned into rubble and us dead?*

Esposito's harsh gaze swept over the pilots. "The Skytrucks are our best option to simulate attacks on the dragon, and we will continue to use them . . . without complaint. Is that understood?"

"Yes, sir," they all replied. McShane included, though without much conviction.

"Everyone report back here at eighteen hundred hours," Esposito told them. "We will plan an exercise for tomorrow involving multiple flights attacking the dragon at the same time. Dismissed."

The pilots got up and headed for the exit.

"Captain McShane," Esposito called out. "A word."

He looked back at his CO, shoulders tensing. *Looks like I'm gonna get my ass tanned.*

He caught Eastwick and Nunez giving him supportive nods. Johnson stared at him unsmiling, almost disapproving.

McShane walked back to Esposito while the rest of Hammer Flight left the tent. He stopped a few feet from the colonel, clasping his hands behind his back, staring straight ahead.

Esposito stepped toward him, eyebrows scrunched together. The ACE commander halted mere inches away, getting right in his personal space, lowering his chin to lock eyes with McShane.

He maintained his rigid posture, not looking away. Esposito's shoulders rose and fell in quiet, steady breaths. Time ground to a halt. McShane figured he was waiting for him to wither before him. But he remembered the advice his father had given him for situations like this. Don't flinch, don't swallow, don't stare in another direction. Do nothing to appear intimidated. As Dad said, "Don't give the son-of-a-bitch the satisfaction."

His father would know. He'd gotten called on the carpet more than once in the Army.

Esposito still said nothing. McShane didn't move a muscle.

Deep crevasses dug into the colonel's cheeks and chin. His face reddened.

"Do you think you're the first, Captain?" Esposito finally broke the silence, his voice low but menacing.

"Sir?"

"The first punk ass junior officer who thinks he knows better than Marines who've been doing this job since long before you had your first hard-on?" Esposito bellowed.

Tiny drops of spittle sprayed McShane's cheeks and nose. He did not react in the slightest.

"These exercises are designed to prepare you in the best possible way to destroy one of the greatest threats the Marine Corps has ever faced." Esposito barely dialed back his rage. "They were approved by men and women who have a hell of a lot more experience than you. Do you really think it's your place to question them, Captain?"

"I merely voiced my concerns to my CO, like any good officer should."

Esposito's face contorted, his head shaking slightly. McShane half-expected the man's skull to burst apart.

"You think I'm not a good officer?" he hissed.

So no comment. McShane silently stared straight ahead.

"I'm waiting for an answer, Captain!" Esposito yelled.

Shit. He'd dug himself into a hole now. *Think, Mack. Think.* "You have an eagle on your collar, sir. I think that speaks for itself."

Esposito cranked an eyebrow, as though unsure what to make of the comment.

McShane smiled inwardly. That rather diplomatic answer was something he'd learned from his mother. It would be taken as a compliment by the other person, though not the most endearing of compliments.

Nostrils twitching, Esposito stepped even closer to McShane, to the point he expected their noses to touch. Not a pleasant thought.

"Understand this, Captain. My job is to prepare the pilots under my command for the most difficult and dangerous mission of their careers. I will not have my efforts undermined by a --"

"Sir, I was not --"

"I am talking, Captain! I will not have my efforts undermined by some junior officer who suddenly thinks he's an expert on fighting a monster no one has ever seen before! I will also not have that officer make my pilots doubt their ability to kill that fucking dragon."

Air hissed into Esposito's nose before he continued. "From here on out, you will train the way *I* tell you to train. You will take as many simulated shots at that Skytruck as *I* tell you to, and you will do it without a single complaint. Otherwise, you'll be back at Pensacola in charge of dusting off flight simulators, and whatever family connections you have won't get you out of it."

The skin around McShane's nose wrinkled. He hated it when others assumed his mother could shield him from any trouble.

The corner of Esposito's mouth lifted in a brief, half-smile. Probably satisfied he finally got a rise out of him.

That pissed off McShane more. The son-of-a-bitch had won.

"Is that clear, Captain?" Esposito demanded.

"Yes, sir."

"It better be. Dismissed."

McShane marched toward the exit, teeth and fists clenched. He probably should have known better than to point out his issues over the exercise. Did he really think someone like Colonel Esposito would listen?

He recalled what his father had told him about commanding officers. There were two kinds. The ones that valued the opinions of their subordinates and were not afraid to heed the advice of others – a.k.a. the good kind – and the ones who thought they knew everything about everything and all those under them had the IQ of a gerbil – a.k.a. the asshole kind.

No question which category Esposito belonged in.

McShane grunted as he exited the tent. He halted for a split second in surprise when he found Johnson waiting for him.

"Thanks for the moral support."

Johnson opened his mouth. A moment passed before he spoke. "I wanted . . . permission to speak freely, sir?"

"Go ahead." McShane walked away from the tent, Johnson following. Several seconds passed without his co-pilot uttering a word.

"I said you have permission to speak freely. You gonna use it or not?"

Johnson drew a long, slow breath. "I don't think it was a good idea to antagonize Colonel Esposito like that."

"I wasn't trying to antagonize him. I was bringing a concern I had to his attention." McShane scowled. "For all the good it did."

"Officers like Colonel Esposito don't like being criticized."

"I wasn't criticizing him," McShane replied in a sharp tone. He started to rethink his decision to let Johnson speak freely.

"What if he puts what you did in your official file. It could hurt your chances for advancement . . . yours and other people's."

McShane halted and turned to his co-pilot, eyebrows scrunched together. "And what's that supposed to mean?"

"There are some vindictive officers in the Corps, Mack. A flight leader does something they don't like, it's not just his career that suffers, but those of the men and women under him."

McShane let out a harsh sigh. "And you think you're not going to get those captain's bars because I brought up a legitimate concern over our training methods?"

"I've seen it before. My father." Johnson's cheek twitched in the briefest of scowls. "He commanded a heavy helicopter squadron. But he wouldn't stop making 'recommendations' to his superiors. It pissed them off so much his career stalled and he was forced out of the Corps. And some of the pilots and crews in his squadron got denied choice assignments or had their promotion tracks slowed. If he'd just kept his mouth shut, Dad would have been a bird colonel by now, maybe a general. And those other Marines would have been better off with their careers. No way in hell I'm going to let that happen to me."

"Well, it's nice to know where your priorities lie," said McShane. "Okay, then. If you feel that way, put in for a transfer to another squadron. But you'll have to wait until we're done with our monster hunt . . . if you're still around."

Johnson grimaced.

"Lord knows the last thing I want is to do or say anything that'll keep you from moving up the ladder." McShane strode away.

"If you expect me to apologize for giving a damn about my career, that's not gonna happen."

McShane spun around, glaring at Johnson.

The veins in the co-pilot's neck stuck out. "Um, sir."

With a snort, McShane powerwalked back to Johnson, stopping barely a foot from him.

"If you think I don't give a damn about my career, then you don't know shit," McShane spoke in a low, menacing tone.

Johnson dropped his gaze to the grass.

"But you want to know what I *really* give a damn about?"

"Um, what?" Johnson muttered.

"One. Killing every single one of those fucking monsters out there." McShane stabbed a hand toward the horizon. "And two, making sure we all come home alive."

With that, he stalked off.

FOURTEEN

McShane watched the rain spatter against the windows of the mess hall. Thunderstorms swept over much of Southern Norway. All attack helicopter exercises had been cancelled. Not that he minded. How much more proficient could he and the rest of Hammer Flight become at shooting slow-moving transport planes?

He chewed on his cheese sandwich, shifting his gaze to Johnson on the other side of the table. The co-pilot did not look at him, just focused on his breakfast with a dour expression. He hadn't been too talkative since their confrontation two days ago. The only times they had communicated was in the cockpit of their Viper. Strictly professional, just doing their jobs. Any other sort of socializing . . . well, Johnson had never been the most sociable of people.

Fuck it. He and Johnson weren't buddies. Would never be buddies. Too many differences in their personalities and attitudes. His parents had told him, "You're not going to like everyone you serve with, but so long as the other person does their job, that's all that matters."

Maybe. But he'd seen how unit performance could suffer due to friction between its members. In a situation like this, it could prove fatal.

Well, you're the man in charge. Better do something about it.

"Good morning."

McShane lifted his head to find Ylva standing nearby, tray in hand.

"Morning." His lips stretched into a huge smile.

The other Marines also greeted her, Johnson just giving her a silent nod.

"Do you mind if I join you?" asked Ylva, her eyes drooping behind her glasses.

"Not at all." McShane patted the empty space on the bench next to him. He caught sight of Hunter giving him a wink.

Ylva sat beside him, not much on her tray. Black coffee, some crispbread, and a slice of cheese. McShane had learned that Norwegians typically ate a very light breakfast, sometimes none at all, since lunchtime for them was at eleven in the morning.

She took a big slug of coffee, then another.

"I didn't realize you loved the coffee here so much," said McShane.

"Actually, I need the caffeine." Ylva blinked, her eyelids slow to come back up.

"I thought you looked tired. Not a lot of sleep last night?"

"No. It is my own fault. I received a batch of old Norse texts from the University of Oslo yesterday. Some of the stories date back to the Ninth Century. First-hand accounts of travels and battles. So very interesting."

"And time just got away from you, huh?" said McShane.

"I think it was after three o'clock when I finally fell asleep." Ylva took another gulp from her mug.

"So anything in those books about the walking rockpiles and the dragon?" asked Cain.

"Not that I could find. I still have other books to go through, with more coming in from other universities here and in Sweden. There has to be something about them somewhere. If we have legends of dragons, there must be stories on stone giants. Someone has to have seen these Jotnar."

"Says who?" countered Tudoran. "Look at all the BS stories about Bigfoot, the Loch Ness Monster, and the Jersey Devil. People say they've seen 'em for years. Nobody's ever said anything about monsters made out of rocks."

"First of all, Tooti . . ." Nunez stabbed a finger toward the pilot, "Bigfoot and all those other cryptids aren't BS. They're real. And just because we've never heard stories about the Jotnar doesn't mean no one's ever seen them until now. Maybe some hikers or a bunch of soldiers on maneuvers came across them. But the Jotnar killed them all before they could tell anyone what they saw."

Eastwick whooped. "What'd ya know? Tin Foil actually made a good point. Miracle of miracles."

"Yeah, it was a good point." Hunter sipped her coffee. "Except for the part about Bigfoot and those other monsters being real."

"Oh they are, Clubber." Nunez wagged a finger at her. "You just wait. Now that we know about the Jotnar and dragons, the world's gonna know the truth about other cryptids damn soon."

Ylva's brow furrowed, her eyes darting between Nunez and Hunter. "Tin Foil? Clubber? Are those your nicknames?"

"Call signs," replied Hunter. "All pilots have them."

"Do you get to choose them yourselves?"

"Hell no," said Eastwick. "Where's the fun in that? Sure as hell Nunez wouldn't call himself Tin Foil. He actually believes all that conspiracy theory bullshit."

"I'd rather have that than Flameout," Nunez shot back. "Letting everyone know your luck with the ladies."

Koosman and Cain let out a loud whoop. Eastwick raised both middle fingers.

"And Clubber?" asked Ylva.

"Hunter played softball for some little college no one's ever heard of," answered Eastwick.

"Florida Southern College." She emphasized each word.

"Yeah, that place. She led her conference in home runs twice."

"And was a three-time All-American. Not that I'm bragging."

Ylva chuckled softly. "What about the rest of you?"

"Koo Koo." Koosman raised a hand. "Kinda obvious, given my last name."

"Stripes," Cain grumbled. "Cain. Candy Cane. Some dipshit at flight school thought it was funny and it stuck. Lucky me."

"Mack." McShane shrugged. "Makato McShane. Not the most original of call signs. Used to be Li'l Mac until I became a captain. Kinda hard for the people under you to call you that, so it became just Mack. Rank has its privileges."

"And you two?" Ylva looked at Tudoran and Johnson. The former grimaced, the latter gave her a sideways glance and took a huge bite out of his toast.

"Don't mind them." Eastwick grinned and snapped his hand down. "They hate their call signs. Right, Tooti?"

Tudoran sneered. "I'm a Marine combat pilot, and the jackasses in my first squadron saddled me with a call sign that makes me sound like a five-year-old girl."

Eastwick laughed. "And of course, there's Johnson."

"Please don't." He scowled.

Eastwick ignored him. "The first time Johnson here did a shipboard landing, it didn't go well. He had to go-around three times before he finally touched down. Hence, the call sign Go Around."

Johnson's face scrunched. He bit down hard on his toast.

"That sounds rather mean," said Ylva.

Koosman barked out a laugh. "Whoever said the Corps was nice? Even in these politically correct times."

Johnson ate quietly and quickly, then excused himself when he was done.

One by one, the other pilots finished their breakfasts and left the mess hall, until only McShane and Ylva remained.

"Your friend seemed very upset at his nickname," said Ylva.

"My friend?" McShane cocked an eyebrow. "Oh. You mean Johnson. Yeah, he's pretty sensitive over that call sign."

"Why doesn't he tell them to stop?"

"It doesn't work that way in the Corps." McShane shook his head. "You tell someone to stop using your call sign because you don't like it, they'll use it every chance they get. Honestly, some of it he brings on himself."

"Mm. Lieutenant Johnson does not seem the friendliest of people."

"I'd go more with self-absorbed. His career is everything to him. He's always worried someone is going to screw it up for him. Plus, he wants to prove to everyone he's a better Marine than his father and brother."

"Were they pilots like him?" asked Ylva.

McShane nodded. "His dad flew Super Stallions, our heavy-lift chopper. Got out as a Lieutenant Colonel. Johnson's brother is a V-22 pilot and a captain. I guess he feels he has a legacy to uphold. Probably supersede in his case."

"What about you? Don't you have a family legacy in the military?"

"I do." McShane drained the rest of his now lukewarm coffee. "But I'm not obsessed with outdoing my parents or grandparents. Hell, Great-Grandpop Fujio had a lot more to prove than I ever will, being a Japanese-American fighting for the U.S. Army when my country was at war with Japan. I'm just looking to be the best Marine I can be and not do anything to dishonor my family."

Ylva let out a soft chuckle.

"What?" McShane cocked an eyebrow.

"I'm sorry. It's just when you talked about not dishonoring your family, you sounded like the hero from some mythological tale." She bit her lip and turned away. "Sorry. That sounded stupid."

"Don't apologize. I consider it a compliment."

She returned her gaze to McShane, who grinned at her. "Hey. I can't recall anyone comparing me to someone like King Arthur or Ulysses. Pretty cool, I think."

A shy smile traced her lips. "Thank you. This is what happens when you spend your life wrapped up in myths. You say things like that. Usually people look at me like I need psychiatric help."

"Then that's their problem, not yours. Besides, you can't be serious all the time. That's what my dad told me growing up. Mom never bought into that."

"Your mother is a serious person?"

"Very." McShane tilted his head. "Well, she does have her humorous moments, about two a year."

Ylva laughed. "If you'll forgive me being so forward, it sounds like your mother and father are not very compatible."

"Tell me about it. They're complete opposites. It still baffles me how they got married in the first place, and how they're still together."

"That is not how it is with my parents. Both of them are the most pragmatic people I know. It is one of the reasons I was so interested in mythology when I was younger. They were so normal it was boring."

"So they probably wouldn't like it if some hotshot Marine chopper jock took their beautiful daughter to dinner tonight."

Ylva's cheeks flushed. "No. They would probably disapprove."

"Then let's make them disapprove." McShane gave her a wry grin. "Besides, I did promise to take you to dinner."

"Do you think we can do it tonight?"

"Don't see why not. The weather sucks, so we're grounded. Seems like the perfect time."

Ylva beamed. "Then . . . Yes. Yes, let's do it."

"Great. How about we --"

A sharp wail burst from the PA system, cutting him off.

"Attention all personnel. Jotnar sighted near Kongsberg. All pilots report to your aircraft immediately."

FIFTEEN

McShane gazed at Ylva's face, his heart dropping into a black hole.

But he couldn't dwell on his disappointment. The Jotnar were back and he had a job to do.

"I'm sorry, Ylva." He sprang off the bench.

"Be careful." She grabbed his hand, her chin quivering.

He gave her a reassuring smile, gently squeezed her hand, and rushed out of the mess hall. Cold rain beat down on him as he splashed through puddles on the concrete. His gaze shifted from the line of helicopters ahead of him to the gray skies overhead. McShane grimaced. Not the best flying weather. But the enemy was under no obligation to attack only on sunny, clear days.

The ground crew opened the canopy when they saw McShane and Johnson running toward them. They scrambled inside and quickly went through the pre-flight checklist before starting the engine. Rain pattered against the canopy as Hammer Flight rose into the sky. All around him, more helicopters took off. Apaches, Tigers, Hinds, Hueys. They swung west for the fifty-mile fight to Kongsberg.

Hopefully there'll still be a Kongsberg left when we get there.

He stared ahead, his hand flexing on the cyclic stick. Rain and the swath of gray in front of him reduced visibility to roughly two miles, if that. McShane checked left to right. The other helicopters maintained large intervals to reduce the risk of collision. He eyed the altimeter on his TopOwl's display. It read 1,750 feet. His muscles tightened. He'd like to have a little more room – actually, a lot more room between him and the ground. But with the ceiling under 2,000 feet, no way was he or any other pilot going to fly through the clouds.

At least this part of Norway was relatively flat. He didn't have to worry about smashing into a mountain.

The chopper shuddered. McShane clenched his teeth. Turbulence usually wasn't something to worry about. But on days like this, flying as low as he was, a sudden downdraft or windshear could push a chopper toward the ground without much time for the pilot to recover.

Wouldn't that be a kick in the nuts. To survive Jotnar and a fire-breathing dragon only to be done in by a gust of wind.

The day's still young. A Jotunn or that dragon can still get you.

McShane hoped his luck continued to hold.

The rain didn't let up as they neared Kongsberg. A line of headlights stretched across the highway below. Civilians fleeing the monsters.

Interspersed among them were flashing red and blue strobes. Police, he guessed, trying to keep traffic flowing efficiently. Judging by the slow crawl of the little blobs of light, it didn't appear they were having much success.

"This is Monarch Three," the Czech-accented voice came over the comm. The weapons controller on the NATO AWACS somewhere in the skies over Norway issued combat assignments to the various helicopter flights.

Hammer Flight was ordered to circle the outskirts of Kongsberg to engage the dragon if it showed up.

"Shit," Johnson grumbled.

McShane gave a slight shake of the head. The co-pilot had to be disappointed to not take part in the attack on the Jotnar and prove his outstanding skills to his superiors. "Don't be that way, Go Around. If that dragon shows up, you'll get a piece of the action."

"Yes, sir," he grumbled.

McShane and the rest of Hammer Flight took up position outside the city with a flight of U.S. Army Apaches. He scanned the stormy skies. He couldn't see shit other than clouds and rain. The dragon could be circling above him and he wouldn't know it. At least the AWACS should give them advanced warning if the damn thing popped up. Whether or not their Sidewinders could stop it, who the hell knew?

A flash of movement caught his attention. McShane spotted an F-16 diving toward the city. He shifted his gaze below, looking for any Jotnar. Damned if he could see any.

The jet pulled up without dropping any ordinance. So did a second one. McShane scowled. Without a clear target, no way would they unload bombs or missiles on a city.

His Viper crossed over the river when he caught sight of the beasts. Three of them. Stomping through what looked like a row of houses. McShane traced their path of destruction, clenching the cyclic stick as he took in dozens upon dozens of shattered buildings.

Helicopters closed in and let loose a barrage of missiles. Puffs of orange and black sprouted up and down the Jotnar's massive stone bodies. They only stopped to look at the approaching choppers.

A second wave of anti-tank missiles tore through the air. More explosions leapt off the Jotnar to no effect. One of the monsters ripped a streetlight from the ground and hurled it like a javelin. An Apache shot straight up to avoid it. Another Jotunn chucked a car at the helicopters.

McShane swung to the south, rain blurring the battle below. Dark blobs in the air jerked left or right or up. Choppers avoiding whatever debris the Jotnar flung at them.

One dot spiraled into the ground and burst into a ball of orange. His jaw tightened, thinking of the pilots.

The Jotnar stomped deeper into Kongsberg, still flinging vehicles and debris at the helicopters. A few of the more daring pilots charged right at the giants. Orange flickers spat from rocket launchers or cannons. Explosions and sparks sprang off the Jotnar's heads and chests. The helicopters made sharp turns away from the monsters. McShane guessed they were trying to piss them off and lure them away from the city.

A Jotunn bounded forward and grabbed a large helicopter, a Hind. McShane held his breath as the beast reared the aircraft over its head and slammed it into the ground. Flame and smoke roiled up through the rain.

Another flight of helicopters raked the Jotnar with rockets and cannons before peeling off, trying to goad the beasts into chasing them.

They didn't take the bait. The stone giants stomped and kicked more buildings into rubble.

McShane dipped his chin. It seemed the best they could do was slow the Jotnar's advance and allow the civilians more time to evacuate Kongsberg. The thought made him want to punch something. Marines did not slow an advancing enemy. They destroyed the shit out of him.

But only one thing existed that could destroy the Jotnar, and he had orders to shoot it down.

Hammer Flight circled the outskirts of the city a second time, a third. Missiles and rockets continued to batter the giants. They hurled more debris at the NATO choppers. One of them, an Apache, tumbled through the rain and crashed into the river.

McShane snorted. When they hell was someone going to come up with a way to stop these –

"All forces, all forces, Monarch Three," the AWACS controller blared through the radio. "Bandit approaching Kongsberg from the north, bearing zero two four, forty kilometers out. Size and speed indicate the dragon."

McShane's muscles locked up. He sucked down a breath and scanned the stormy skies. No way would he see the dragon through this soup. He probably wouldn't get a visual on the monster until it was on top of him.

He glanced below, anger boiling as a Jotunn swung its fist down on a three-story building, collapsing it. Two missiles exploded against its back. The creature didn't notice.

But something was coming that the sons of bitches would notice. Something that could kill every damn one of them.

McShane's eyes flickered from the port side wing stub to the starboard one, focusing on the Sidewinders hanging from the wingtip rails. His shoulders sagged. Part of him wanted to tell everyone to stand down and let the dragon take out the Jotnar like it did in Skien. Sure as hell NATO wouldn't be killing any of those giants today.

That wouldn't happen, of course. He had his orders.

"Hammer Flight, Hammer Four," McShane radioed his pilots. "Head east, bearing zero four five. Monarch Three, keep us posted on the dragon's speed and course. On my mark, we're going to swing toward it and attack from the flank."

Everyone acknowledged the order.

"Watch out for its head," he added. "We have no idea how far around it can swing its neck."

Again, the other pilots acknowledged him.

The four Vipers rumbled through the rain, leaving Kongsberg behind. McShane took steady breaths, trying not to imagine tongues of sunset-red flame blasting his choppers out of the sky. Hoping their Sidewinders could bring down the dragon.

Hoping they weren't making a mistake killing it.

"Dragon twenty kilometers from Kongsberg and closing," reported the AWACS. "Same course, same speed."

McShane peered through the rain and clouds. No sign of the dragon. He checked the Target Sight System. Nothing on that either.

"I got something," Nunez blurted. "Extreme sensor range. Gotta be . . . damn. Lost it. Still on same heading to Kongsberg, fifteen klicks out."

"Copy, Tin Foil." McShane did some quick mental math. "Wait till it's ten klicks out, then swing left. Soon as you have a lock, take the shot."

The pilots responded in the affirmative.

Tudoran and Johnson picked up the dragon on their TSS. The AWACS also updated the target's position. McShane flexed his hand on the cyclic stick. Any moment . . . Any moment . . .

"Dragon ten klicks out," announced the AWACS weapons controller.

"Hammer Flight, break left," ordered McShane. "Standby Sidewinders."

The choppers banked left, barreling toward the dragon. McShane kept a close eye on the TSS. Its infra-red systems would spot the beast long before his Mark One Eyeball.

And it did. An elongated blob appeared on the screen, huge batwings propelling it through the stormy skies.

"Hammer Flight, drop to six hundred feet." McShane tensed after giving the order. He didn't like flying so low in a rain storm, but they needed to have a good angle of attack on the dragon's stomach, hopefully its weak spot.

"Watch your altimeter," he added.

"You don't have to tell me twice, Mack," replied Eastwick.

They closed on the dragon, still flying straight and true. No indication it had spotted them.

"Johnson, anything?"

The co-pilot/gunner emphatically shook his head. "Negative. I can't get shit."

"Anyone have a lock?" McShane radioed.

"Negative," answered Tudoran and Koosman.

"No joy," said Nunez.

McShane snorted. The Sidewinders had been designed to pick up exhaust from an aircraft's engine, which was much hotter than the body temperature of a living creature. He wondered if it might be different for an animal that breathed fire. Apparently not.

Unless they had to get closer.

The Vipers pressed on. Still no one could get a lock.

The dragon continued flying toward Kongsberg. McShane eyed its head, that long neck, expecting it to whip around and belch out a stream of flame.

It didn't.

"Got tone!" hollered Koosman. "Fox Two!"

A Sidewinder shot off the right wingtip of Koo Koo's Viper. McShane watched the missile streak toward the dragon, gritting his teeth as it bore in on the underbelly . . .

And flew under it.

"Dammit," Koosman cursed over the radio. "Lost the heat source."

McShane continued the pursuit, keeping below and to the left of the dragon. It paid Hammer Flight no mind as it neared the outskirts of Kongsberg. McShane lifted the Viper's nose, trying to give Johnson a good target. He still couldn't get a lock.

"Got tone!" yelled Nunez. "Fox Two."

Another Sidewinder rocketed through the steady rain. It missed wide.

"We're just not getting a strong enough heat source," said Nunez.

McShane scowled. *So much for all those exercises.* He clamped his jaw to keep the thought to himself. Colonel Esposito would torch his ass if he said it out loud.

"Move in closer. That's probably our best bet."

He pushed the throttle, closing the distance. My God, that thing was huge.

McShane shunted aside his awe and fear, concentrating on his task to give Johnson one good shot.

"Good tone!" Johnson called out. "Fox tw--"

Something crashed down on the Viper. The chopper fell from the sky. McShane glimpsed the contrail of the Sidewinder as he fought with the stick. Alarms blared in the cockpit.

"Holy shit!" Johnson's voice cracked.

"Mack, pull up!" Hunter shouted.

He yanked back on the stick, teeth bared, groaning. The Viper went up, up. Trees and houses flashed past the cockpit, so close it sent a shiver through his body.

The helicopter continued to climb. His heart slammed against his chest. McShane exhaled loudly once, twice, sweat soaking his forehead. Damn turbulence.

He breathed out again, trying to expel his fear and refocus on the dragon.

It soared over the suburbs of Kongsberg.

"Mack, you okay?" radioed Cain.

"Affirmative. Still alive."

"Oh my God," Johnson said breathlessly. "Oh my God."

"Pull it together, Marine," snapped McShane. "Get ready for another shot."

Johnson didn't answer.

"Johnson!"

"Wha . . . Yeah. Yeah, um. Sidewinder."

McShane's heartbeat settled down as he pointed the nose at the dragon. It still made no move to turn him into a cinder or pull a *Game of Thrones* and send a wave of fire through the city. The monster headed straight for the Jotnar.

Do I really want to shoot it down?

Like I have a choice.

"Tone!" Johnson yelled. "Good tone. Fox Two."

Their last Sidewinder flew off the left wingtip. McShane watched the contrail stretch across the sky, drawing closer to the dragon.

A fireball flashed on the monster's underbelly.

"Direct hit!" Johnson cheered.

The dragon kept flying.

"No way!" Johnson blared. "Doesn't anything kill 'em?"

McShane tuned him out, staring at the dragon, expecting it to turn and spit out fire.

It didn't.

He couldn't understand. Their attacks on the Jotnar had been ineffective, but they still retaliated. Why didn't the –

"Mack! Break right!" shouted Hunter.

He yanked the stick right. Something flashed out the corner of his eye. A car? Probably thrown by a Jotunn. He should –

A quake hammered the Viper. The chopper spun wildly.

SIXTEEN

McShane wrestled with the cyclic stick and worked the anti-torque pedals. The Viper kept spinning. Sweat surged out his pores. He gritted his teeth to keep from screaming.

No, no, no. It couldn't end like this. He was just twenty-seven. Too young to die.

He shut his eyes tight, crushing the stick. Faces flashed past his mind's eye. Mom. Dad. His sister Tori.

Ylva.

Tremors shot up his right arm. The cyclic didn't respond. None of the controls responded. This was it.

The world shook. McShane rocked in his seat, the straps preventing him from flying through the cockpit.

He forced his eyes open. The Viper had come to a stop.

What the hell? They hadn't crashed, hadn't exploded. They hung in the air. But how . . .

His chest tightened when he saw the dark red talons surrounding the cockpit.

Johnson gasped and pressed deeper into his seat.

Ice spread across McShane's body. He couldn't keep his eyes off the scaly talons. Had they avoided crashing only to be crushed by the dragon?

They moved forward, the monster's big wings flapping. The Viper trembled, buffeted by wind from the wings.

He opened his mouth, unable to produce any sound. He tightened his stomach, as though trying to force himself to vomit, until words finally escaped his lips.

"Hammer Flight, Hammer Four." His voice was shaky. McShane battled through his fear to project more confidence. "Hammer Flight, Hammer Four."

Only static came over the radio.

"This is Hammer Four. Anyone on this frequency respond."

No one did. The impact must have knocked out comms.

The dragon descended. A soccer field passed beneath them, then several houses. Roofs came up fast. He tensed.

A parking lot appeared. The talons uncoiled. The Viper hit the concrete with a jolt.

McShane sagged in his seat. He watched the dragon fly off. The Vipers of Hammer Flight soared overhead. Tracers spewed from their gatling guns.

McShane stared ahead, pressing down on his legs to stop them from shaking.

"M-Mack?" Johnson stammered.

"Yeah?"

"Did . . . Did that dragon just save us?"

He slowly blinked before answering, "Um, yeah. I think he did."

McShane drew long breaths, trying to slow his hammering heart. He watched the dragon bank left, going after the three Jotnar. One of the giants turned as the dragon angled its wings, going into a dive.

The Jotunn ran forward and jumped into the air.

"Holy shit!" blurted Johnson.

McShane's eyes bulged. He couldn't believe something that large could be so agile.

The Jotunn smashed into the dragon mid-air. Both beasts spun around and slammed into the ground. A tremor shook the Viper.

A second Jotunn rushed over and kicked the dragon. It rolled across a freeway, throwing up trees and debris from buildings. The creature's serpentine neck rose. One of the Jotnar punched it. The dragon's head snapped down and slammed into the ground. Large stone feet pummeled it.

"Get up," McShane hissed, leaning closer to the rain-soaked canopy.

The third Jotunn lumbered over, ready to join in the beatdown. Two Tigers swooped in, launching missiles. Explosions sprang off the giant's back. It didn't flinch, advancing closer to the fallen dragon.

The two Jotnar stomped on the dragon. Its tailed whipped up, but was batted away by a large stone hand.

"Get up, damn you." McShane pounded a fist against his leg. "Get up and fight, you worthless son-of-a-bi--"

A gusher of red flame blasted through the arm of a Jotunn. The stone monster stumbled back, mouth opened wide. The dragon sprang off the ground and swung its front right leg. Talons raked the second Jotunn's chest, carving deep fissures in it.

The third Jotunn charged and drove its shoulder into the dragon's side. It tumbled over a copse of trees, collapsing them, and rolled across train tracks. The Jotunn marched toward it, each footfall sending a tremor beneath McShane's Viper. He backed away from the canopy.

"These guys are getting way too close. Time to bail."

"Sounds good to me," replied Johnson.

McShane opened the canopy. Rain pelted him and Johnson as they jumped out. McShane glanced at the rear of the chopper. The tail rotor had been sheared off.

The pair ran toward a large rectangular building. Could be a good place to hunker down.

A short quake nearly knocked him off his feet. McShane half-ran, half-stumbled, doing a clumsy dance to regain his balance. He glanced over his shoulder. The dragon jumped onto the Jotunn, knocking him to the ground. A crash like a million drums pounded his skull. The ground heaved. Both he and Johnson fell onto the wet, hard concrete.

A second Jotunn arrived and kicked the dragon in its jaw. It flipped over and slammed down on a pair of nearby houses.

McShane pushed himself to his feet and looked across the street. The Jotnar marched toward the fallen dragon. The air stuck in his throat. All those beasts were so close, so immense. It made him feel like a bug staring up at a person.

A Jotunn kicked the dragon's side. It smashed through another house and struck the large building. A shower of aluminum and glass exploded into the air. McShane threw himself on the concrete, covering his head. Small bits of debris bounced off his back and legs.

A quake tossed him a foot into the air. He grunted when he hit the concrete and stared up. The Jotnar stood over the dragon, and towered over him. Fear threatened to paralyze his muscles. If any of them took a step or two to the left, he'd be a big red stain on the parking lot.

Gritting his teeth, McShane pushed himself to his feet. He spotted Johnson nearby, gawking at the battle before him. The dragon's head shot up. A Jotunn wrapped a massive hand around its throat.

"Run!" He slapped Johnson's shoulder.

The two pounded across the parking lot, splashing through puddles. McShane glanced over his shoulder, praying the Jotnar didn't see them.

All their attention appeared focused on the dragon. One Jotunn brought its fist down on the winged monster's back.

McShane and Johnson dashed between a couple of houses and past an auto shop. A shrill blast like a battalion of trumpets tore through the air. McShane swung around. The dragon's jaws clamped down on the shoulder of a Jotunn. Its tail slashed to the right. A storm of rocks burst from the chest of the second Jotunn. It let out a deep wail.

The dragon's head snapped back. The arm of the first Jotunn flipped through the air, hurtling right at them.

"Down!" McShane flung himself onto the concrete, his body tensed. Would that arm fall on him?

A horrendous crash rattled his entire being. He drew a slow breath, as though confirming to himself he still lived. He lifted his head and looked right. The severed arm lay on top of the debris that used to be the auto shop.

Too damn close. McShane let out a shaky breath.

The pair raced through an apartment complex and hopped a fence into the backyard of a house. Two Apaches roared overhead, orange flashes spitting from their rocket launchers. McShane followed the shots. Explosions rippled on and around the monsters. He tensed when sparks and flames erupted off the dragon's back. It showed no sign the explosions affected it.

With a flap of its wings, the dragon pushed off the first wounded Jotunn and swiped at its head. Jagged lines tore across its face. It stumbled back. The dragon climbed higher, roared, and slashed its tail. The spiked tip cut through the Jotunn's skull. A shower of rock flew into the stormy air. The giant stood still for a moment, wobbled, and fell.

"Brace yourself!" yelled McShane, pushing himself against the wall of the house. Johnson did likewise.

The Jotunn hit the ground with a deafening boom. The ground buckled. McShane and Johnson flew off the wall and faceplanted into the damp grass.

Groaning, McShane pushed himself to his knees. The Jotunn with the gashes on its chest grabbed the dragon by the tail and flung it into a railroad terminal. The structure beneath the creature.

The Jotunn took a running jump, hurtling through the air. Disbelief nearly overwhelmed McShane. How could it do that?

Another quake hammered Kongsberg, knocking McShane on his side. He picked himself up as two Hinds unleashed a barrage of rockets and cannon fire at the monsters. The one-armed Jotunn hurled a car at the big choppers. It missed, and the Hinds broke off.

McShane breathed out. The battle was moving away from them. Not that far away, unfortunately. He and Johnson ran a couple more blocks through a tree-lined suburban neighborhood. Moans and trumpeting roars rose behind them. The dragon and a Jotunn gripped one another, spinning around. Two Apaches hammered them with rockets. The two beasts remained locked in their wrestling match.

Satisfied there was something of a safe distance between them and the monsters, McShane pulled the Hook-112 radio from his survival vest. "Any NATO personnel, this is Hammer Four, U.S. Marine Corps, pilot and co-pilot. Chopper is down, but we are safe and uninjured, roughly one mile west from the dragon and the Jotnar."

"Mack?" came the reply from Cain. "Damn, man, you're alive?"

"That's affirmative, Stripes."

"We thought you two had had it. How did you pull that off?"

A tremor sent McShane swaying from side-to-side. He couldn't see the second Jotunn, but the dragon hovered in the rain.

Eyes still on the flying beast, he spoke into the radio. "The dragon caught us, then plopped us down in a parking lot."

"That thing saved you? Unbeliev . . . Whoa!"

Dark red flame gushed from the dragon's maw. Smoke billowed up.

"You see that, Mack?" stammered Cain. "Your new friend just blasted that Jotunn to hell."

"Yes." McShane pumped a fist.

The one-armed Jotunn turned and ran north, away from the dragon.

"Look at that." Johnson pointed. "It's hauling ass outta here."

McShane blinked as rain stung his face, watching the Jotunn run. Did it feel fear?

The dragon was having none of it. It flew after it, mouth open.

What the hell are you waiting for? Blast it.

The Jotunn ran about a mile-and-a-half when a tongue of flame tore through its chest. Arm flying out to the side, the giant toppled to the ground.

McShane watched the dragon fly north, wondering if it needed a bit of time to recharge between . . . fire breaths.

An Apache fired its 30mm chain gun at it. McShane held his breath, praying the dragon didn't attack the helicopter, or the city.

It didn't. He stared at it until it vanished in the gray skies.

McShane threw it a salute. "Thanks, big guy."

SEVENTEEN

McShane and Johnson sat in the back of a Norwegian Army *Geländewagen*. The vents of the boxy vehicle blasted out wonderful warm air while the two pilots drank coffee from thermoses provided to them by the two soldiers who'd picked them up in Kongsberg. McShane's flight suit remained damp, but at least he was no longer cold to the bone and being drenched by rain.

The Norwegians had been quite talkative at first, wanting to know just how he and Johnson survived their ordeal. McShane deliberately gave them short answers, not really wanting to converse on the matter. He was still trying to process everything that had happened. Why had the dragon caught them? Why had it set them down instead of crushing them? Was it actually helping them? Wouldn't that imply some level of intelligence? Was it going off instinct?

He stared out the window at the trees and suburban neighborhoods along the highway. He could come up with twenty theories on why the dragon spared him and Johnson. All could be wrong. Or one could be right. He didn't know. Maybe Ylva would have a better idea.

An image of the pretty Norwegian professor hovered in McShane's mind. After coming so close to death, he desperately wanted to see her again. Do more than just see her.

The sky was gray, but no rain fell when they drove into the air base at Gardermoen. McShane and Johnson thanked the Norwegian soldiers, returned their thermoses to them, and exited the vehicle in front of the dormitory that housed Hammer Flight. All of them congregated by the front entrance. Cain, Hunter, and Nunez were among the first rushing toward the *Geländewagen*.

So was Ylva.

"Makato." She launched herself into his arms.

McShane wrapped her in a hug, squeezing her so tight he feared he might suffocate her. Not that she seemed to mind. She pressed her head against his neck. McShane closed his eyes, savoring the feel of her hair against his cheek, her body pressed to his.

"I couldn't believe it when they told me," said Ylva. "The dragon really saved you?"

"Looks that way."

"It's incredible. Oh, I'm so happy you're okay."

McShane responded with a smile, taking in Ylva's face, her lips. He wanted to –

"Um, 'scuse me, Mack."

He stared over Ylva's head at Cain.

"Sorry, but Colonel Esposito wants to see you and Johnson."

"When?" McShane replied with a slight edge to his voice.

"He said the moment you two got back."

"Of course," he grumbled, then gave Ylva another smile, gently squeezing her shoulders. She smiled back.

"C'mon, Johnson. Don't want to keep our lord and master waiting."

He let go of Ylva, catching Hunter shoot Cain a scathing look. "Stripes" shrugged in a, "What do you want me to do?" gesture.

He and Johnson hiked over to the administration building, the damp flight suit clinging to his body. The chilly air sent goosebumps sprouting across his body. God forbid Esposito let them change into dry clothes before going to see him.

The ACE commander was sat at his desk when they arrived.

"Just what the hell happened out there?" asked Esposito.

McShane fought to keep from scowling. *Yes, we're both fine, thank you for asking.*

"Our helicopter was hit by an object thrown by a Jotunn, took out our tail rotor. The dragon caught us, set us down in a parking lot, and proceeded to take out the Jotnar."

"The dragon just set you down and left you alone?"

"Yes, sir."

Esposito sat back in his chair, unsmiling, dark eyes boring in on him. Did the man not believe him?

"I'm sure the rest of Hammer Flight told you the same story, sir."

"And why would the dragon pluck you out of the sky and put you down safe and sound?"

"I have no idea, sir."

The colonel regarded him stone-faced for a few seconds. "I was told you scored a hit on the dragon."

"Yes, sir, we did." Johnson lifted his chin, projecting an air of pride.

Somehow, McShane stifled a groan.

"So you managed to hit it when everyone else in your flight couldn't. How?"

"Well, sir, I happened to get a strong lock on the dragon and the missile stayed true on target."

"Not that it mattered," said McShane. "The missile had no effect on it."

Johnson turned to him, his lips disappearing in a tight line. McShane wondered if his co-pilot thought he was trying to cut him down at the knees in front of their CO.

"Yes, I know." Esposito scowled. "This after that weirdo Professor Tande told us the underbelly was the dragon's weak spot."

McShane ground his teeth, fury burning throughout him. He didn't bother trying to suppress a glare. If the colonel noticed, he didn't say anything.

"This after all the training we did to shoot down that damn monster," Esposito continued.

"A transport plane is a lot different from a dragon, sir." McShane winced. Should he have said that out loud?

A twitch formed under Esposito's right eye. "Johnson managed to get a good lock. Why the hell couldn't the rest of your flight? Why the hell is that thing still alive after taking a Sidewinder in the gut?"

"Maybe we need to hit it multiple times," said Johnson.

"Maybe. Or maybe Professor Tande's pulling shit out of her ass to make it look like she has any business being part of this operation."

McShane clenched his fists at his side. Rage sent his imagination into overdrive. He pictured himself grabbing Esposito's head and ramming his face into the desk.

"We're going to keep training with the Skytrucks. We're going to talk to the scientists here. *Real* scientists, not someone who wastes her time reading about make-believe bullshit. They should have a better idea where the dragon is most vulnerable than a refugee from a comic book convention. Next time that monster shows up, we're gonna blow its ass out of the sky."

McShane shifted his weight and looked down at the floor. His jaw twitched.

"Do you have a problem with that, Captain?"

He stared back up at his CO, who fixed his narrowed eyes on him. The words, "No, sir," hovered around his tongue. But that wasn't what he said when he opened his mouth.

"Sir, the dragon has not hurt any people."

Esposito's brow furrowed. "Excuse me?"

"At Skien and Kongsberg, the dragon only went after Jotnar. It never deliberately destroyed any buildings or attacked any people. Even when we shot at it, it never retaliated against our aircraft."

The colonel's mouth opened slightly, giving McShane a look that was half-disbelief, half-agitation. "So you think this dragon is one of the good guys?"

"I don't know, sir. All I know is it's killed seven Jotnar. All the missiles, bombs, and rockets we've thrown at them, we haven't been able to bring down one. The dragon's leaving us alone and going after the Jotnar."

Esposito planted his palms on the desk with a *thump*. "And you really believe it's going to keep doing that? Holy shit, Captain, just how fucking naïve are you? Is that Tande chick filling your head with bullshit about good and bad dragons? How do you know when it's done killing Jotnar it won't start killing us?"

"It did save our lives, sir," countered McShane.

"How the hell do you know?" Esposito came out of his chair. "How do you know it wasn't saving you and Johnson for lunch later? This isn't a damn movie, Captain. That dragon is not fighting for us. It poses just as much of a threat as the Jotnar, and our job is to kill that son-of-a-bitch, not make it a pet. So you and the rest of Hammer Flight are going to train your asses off and next time you see that dragon, you're going to pump Sidewinders into it until it stops breathing. Is that clear?"

"Yes, sir," Johnson replied with enthusiasm.

"Yes, sir." McShane kept his voice flat.

Esposito glared at him, then gave a slight nod. "Now go write up your after-action report. Don't leave out a single detail, and sure as hell don't say that dragon saved you."

"You want me to lie on an official report, sir?"

A blood red hue came over Esposito's face. His eyes enlarged. McShane half-expected the man's head to burst.

He took a slow breath before speaking, his tone low yet angry. "Do you have any proof whatsoever that the dragon intentionally saved your lives?"

McShane couldn't look his CO in the face. "No, sir."

"Then leave it out of your report! Dismissed."

The pilots left the office, McShane's face tight, fighting back the eruption he wanted to let out.

"Um, Mack. I don't think --"

He swung around, stopping Johnson in his tracks. "Go Around. I am not in the mood right now."

Johnson swallowed. "Um, yes, sir."

McShane stormed off.

After changing into a dry uniform, he headed to a DRASH on the western side of the base set up for the USMC contingent to write their reports. He sat at a small cubicle, logged on to the secure computer, and just glowered at the screen.

Fucking asshole. He punched the side of the cubicle wall. Why the hell hadn't he pressed his argument that they should let the dragon keep killing Jotnar? Why hadn't he stood up for Ylva? Where the hell did that cocksucker get off calling her useless and a weirdo? And he let him get away with it. Did he leave his balls back in his Viper at Kongsberg?

What was I supposed to do? He's a colonel and I'm a lowly captain.

He could have done something to defend Ylva without being written up for insubordination.

It took several minutes for McShane to settle down and start typing. He put down everything from the time Hammer Flight departed Gardermoen to when they engaged the dragon. How they couldn't get good locks, how their one hit had no effect, how his Viper got clipped by a flying vehicle.

His fingers hovered over the keyboard. *I shouldn't. Esposito would blow like Krakatoa.*

A smile traced his lips. *Aw, fuck it.*

He tapped on the keyboard. *The Viper went into a spin and the controls would not respond. The helicopter suddenly came to a stop in mid-air. I looked out the canopy and noticed the claws of the dragon wrapped around our Viper. The dragon flew for I estimate two miles before it descended and put us down in a parking lot across from a supermarket, preventing the deaths of myself and Lt. Johnson.*

He finished the after-action report and emailed it to both Colonel Esposito and Lt. Colonel Whitaker. McShane went back to his quarters and sacked out on his cot.

Two hours later, a voice wakened him.

"Um, Captain McShane, sir."

He opened his eyes to find a member of Hammer Flight's ground crew standing above his cot.

"What is it, Corporal?" he muttered and rubbed his eyes.

"Message from Colonel Esposito. He says . . ." The younger man winced.

"Well, what does he say?" McShane sat up.

The corporal tensed. "He says . . . get your ass to my office now. His words, sir."

McShane sighed. "Why am I not surprised?"

He threw on his flight jacket and walked to the admin building. When he entered Esposito's office, the colonel held up a sheaf of printer paper, crushing the bottom part in his fist. "What the hell is this, Captain?"

"I'm sorry, sir. I don't follow."

"This." He shook the fistful of paper at him. "I just read your after-action report. Didn't I order you to *not* say the dragon saved you and Lieutenant Johnson?"

"Yes, sir, and I followed your order to the letter."

"Oh you did? Then explain this sentence." Esposito unfurled the papers. "'The dragon flew for I estimate two miles before it descended and put us down in a parking lot across from a supermarket, preventing the deaths of myself and Lieutenant Johnson.'"

He glared up at him. "Well, Captain?"

"Sir, you ordered me not to say the dragon saved us. As I said, I followed that order. But the dragon's actions did prevent the deaths of myself and Lieutenant Johnson. Whether it was intentional or unintentional I cannot say. But the sentence is accurate."

Esposito's brows scrunched together. A thick silence hung between them. The colonel glanced at the report in his hand, then at McShane.

"Captain," he hissed.

"Sir?"

Esposito sucked in a long breath. "Dismissed," the word came out like a curse.

"Yes, sir." McShane turned on his heel and walked out of the office, a wry grin on his lips.

EIGHTEEN

McShane might be stuck on the ground, but he remained busy. He helped evaluate Hammer Flight's exercises against the Polish Air Force Skytrucks. His pilots did an excellent job "shooting down" the transports again and again. Whether that would translate into hits on the dragon he had his doubts. Many doubts. He shared none of them with Colonel Esposito. If he moved up any higher on his shit list, he'd need an oxygen mask to breathe.

Much as he felt the exercise was bullshit, McShane still wished he was in the air with the rest of his flight. But it would be another two or three days before a replacement AH-1Z Viper could be flown over on one of the behemoth C-5 Galaxies.

When not evaluating exercises, he sat in on strategy sessions trying to come up with ways to neutralize the dragon and the Jotnar, either official ones or informal ones in the barracks or mess hall. Hammer Flight conducted one of these informal brainstorming sessions, the pilots sitting on folding chairs or their bunks.

"You gotta figure that sucker's mouth is gonna be way hot after it belches fire," said Eastwick. "Shouldn't be hard to get a sweet lock on it after that."

"Trouble is," Hunter slid forward in her chair, "that means the dragon is attacking something. What if it's some houses or one of us?"

Eastwick shrugged. "I'm just sayin' it's an option. May not be an ideal one, but it's an option."

"It might not just be its mouth," said Cain. "It could be its whole body that gets hotter. We may have to wait for it to get the first shot before we can lock it up with the Sidewinders." He held up a hand toward Hunter. "I know, I agree with you, Clubber. It's not ideal, but we may not have a choice."

Tudoran snorted. "Will it make a difference? I mean, Mack and Go Around nailed it with a 'Winder and it did jack shit."

"It was one missile," Johnson shot back. "We probably need to hit it with more."

McShane stared at his boots. His mind drew him back into the cockpit of his Viper, spinning wildly out of the sky. A chill swept over him. No way should he and Johnson be alive right now, except for the most unlikely of rescuers. A creature that until a couple of weeks ago he thought only existed in myths and movies.

Why? Why had the dragon saved them? Was it some sort of protector? Could Colonel Esposito be right, that it had set them down to eat for later? If so, why did it leave after killing the Jotnar? Why didn't it return for him and Johnson?

"Mack? Mack."

Hunter's voice drilled through his thoughts. "What?"

"You okay?"

"Um . . ." *Shit.* Not a good look for a flight leader to zone out in front of the people under him. "Yeah, just . . . sorry. What was the question?"

Hunter's head cocked to the side. McShane expected her to ask again if he was okay. Thankfully, she didn't.

"We were just wondering if it would be worth the risk to get in close, maybe even fly right underneath it, to get a good shot."

McShane bit his lip for a moment. "It may be something we have to do, probably as a last resort. I'd rather keep my distance from something that can blast us into ash or swat us out of the sky."

"Swat you out of the sky?" Nunez's face scrunched in a doubtful expression. "Man, that thing caught you in mid-air and saved your asses."

McShane nodded. He scanned the other pilots, his insides sinking. How the hell could he talk convincingly about ways to kill this dragon after it had saved him and Johnson? Saved who knew how many people from those Jotnar?

Someone knocked on the doorframe to their quarters. McShane looked up. The breath caught in his throat when he saw Ylva standing there, a black *Naruto* sweatshirt nicely hugging her frame.

"Ylva." He got to his feet. "Hey. What's up?" Out the corner of his eye, he noticed Hunter grinning.

"I'm sorry if I'm interrupting, but I have some news about the dragon and the Jotnar."

McShane squared his shoulders. The other pilots all stared at her, interest and curiosity radiating from their faces.

"What d'you got?" McShane waved her in.

"I overheard some of the scientists talking." Ylva walked over to the group, stopping next to McShane. "I assume they will let everyone know soon, but I wanted to let you know first." She looked at him when she said that last line.

"Always nice to have the inside scoop." Koosman nodded. "What'd you hear, Professor?"

"After studying the burn marks on the Jotnar, estimating the temperature of those burns, and taking radiation readings, they are convinced the dragon is not breathing fire, but superheated plasma."

McShane drew his head back, digesting the information. "Well I didn't think ordinary fire could burn through rock like that. I know plasma is way hotter than regular fire."

"It can be hotter than the core of the Earth," said Ylva. "I did some research after I heard this. A plasma torch can get as hot as twenty thousand degrees."

Eastwick and Johnson's jaws dropped, while Cain's eyes widened.

Nunez raised a hand. "Um, is that Fahrenheit or Celsius?"

"Does it matter?" asked Eastwick. "Either way it's really, really fucking hot."

"Sorry," said Ylva. "It is Celsius."

"So how the hell can this dragon shoot out something that hot without melting itself?" asked Koosman.

"Apparently, at least in the case of plasma torches, there are certain gasses that cool the torch head so it does not melt." Ylva frowned. "Unfortunately, much of what I heard from the scientists and read online was hard to understand. But one of the biologists sounded shocked by the news. He said it is not possible for a living creature to produce heat that intense."

"Well the dragon apparently can do it," said Hunter. "So what's his explanation for that?"

"That the dragon cannot be a product of nature."

Johnson's face scrunched in puzzlement. "So what does that mean?"

McShane glanced at his co-pilot. "It means someone made that thing."

"What?" Johnson looked even more confused. "How do you make an animal?"

"Scientists have been doing it for years," said Nunez. "Ever heard of Dolly the Sheep? Get some skin cells, use 'em to grow an embryo inside a surrogate mother, and bang. Clone. They've done it with deer, cats, mice, pigs."

"All of them existing animals," Cain pointed out. "Whoever made that dragon had to do it from scratch."

"Who's to say dragons didn't already exist?" Nunez held his arms out to his sides. "Maybe someone caught one and cloned it."

"No." Ylva shook her head. "That would mean the original dragon was part of the natural world."

"Okay, so someone actually created a brand new monster," said Eastwick. "Who in the world has the technology to make their own fire breathing dragon?"

"I do not think anyone on this world can do it." Slowly, Ylva tilted her head to the ceiling.

"Aliens!" Nunez nearly jumped out of his chair. "Ha! I knew it."

"C'mon. Seriously?" scoffed Tudoran.

"You think the Chinese or Iranians or Russians have the capability to do it?" Hunter turned to him. "Or any other country?"

"I knew I'd turn you into a believer, Clubber," Nunez beamed.

She rolled her eyes. "I'm saying it's the most likely explanation in this instance. Don't expect me to jump on the alien conspiracy theory bandwagon for the pyramids, Stonehenge, and Roswell."

"I second that," said McShane. "Whoever made that dragon is far more advanced than we are."

Cain looked at Ylva. "So if aliens made that dragon, is the same true for the Jotnar?"

"That is what the scientists believe. They have done examinations on the dead Jotnar. Autopsies have not gone well. Many drill heads have been broken trying to cut into them. Ground-penetrating radar has been more successful. The Jotnar do have a brain, and the chest has what appears to be some central organ. They're hesitant to call it a heart, since they have not found any evidence of a circulatory system."

"Whatever it is, it's a weak spot," said McShane. "Whenever the dragon blasted a Jotunn in the chest, it went down for the count."

"Be nice if our stuff could blow a hole through its chest, too," muttered Tudoran.

"So if aliens made these things, does that mean this is an invasion?" The veins in Koosman's neck stuck out.

"Then it's a pretty strange invasion when one of your weapons is attacking another one of your weapons," said Cain.

"Maybe it's not one race of aliens," suggested Nunez. "Maybe we're dealing with two different ones. One side uses the dragon, the other the Jotnar."

"Well, nice to know we've got good guy aliens versus bad guy aliens," Eastwick chimed in.

"Who says that's the case?" McShane folded his arms. "It's possible both sides are bad guys."

"If that's true, why did the dragon save you and Go Around?"

McShane stared at Eastwick, trying to come up with an answer. He couldn't.

"Whatever the case, guys. . ." Koosman looked around, "...we got an actual alien invasion on our hands. Shit, there could be a bunch of lizard people orbiting Earth, letting these monsters soften us up before they come down and turn us into slaves or eat our brains or whatever."

"Honestly, I don't think this is an invasion."

All eyes turned to McShane.

"I think we're all in agreement that it's gotta be aliens who made those monsters," said Tudoran. "They've wrecked a couple of cities. Sounds like an invasion to me."

"Every time the Jotnar have attacked, there's never been more than three of them," said McShane. "It'd be like us saying we're going to invade Iran and plop down only six M1 tanks. Yeah, they'll do some damage, but eventually they'll be overwhelmed. And no way can you hold territory with just six tanks, or six Jotnar."

"Good point." Hunter nodded. "If this was an invasion, why not send thousands of Jotnar, or millions. We wouldn't stand a chance."

"Maybe . . ." Johnson straightened in his seat. "Maybe it's to test our military. See our capabilities first hand."

"They can probably find that out with standard reconnaissance," Hunter countered. "If they have the technology to travel from one solar system to another and make monsters, I don't think it would take them long to realize our weapons are inferior to theirs."

Johnson's eyes narrowed and he lowered his head. McShane figured he didn't like having his idea go down in flames.

"All right, so this isn't an invasion," said Eastwick. "Then how the hell did these things wind up on Earth?"

No one spoke. Probably thinking, guessed McShane. He gazed at the floor, turning the question over in his mind. Giant alien weapons – living weapons – roamed Norway. They're not here for an invasion. What else would bring them to Earth?

"What if they were lost?" He raised his head.

"What?" Johnson's brow wrinkled. Most of the other pilots also gave him perplexed looks. So did Ylva.

"What if these aliens were traveling past Earth, something happened, and they lost those monsters?"

"But we're not talking about a rifle or a knife," said Johnson. "The Jotnar and the dragon have to be some of the best weapons in their arsenals. How do you lose something like that?"

McShane answered, "Back in 1965, a Skyhawk rolled off the deck of the *USS Ticonderoga* and fell into the ocean about seventy miles off the coast of Japan. The plane was carrying a hydrogen bomb. To this day, that bomb is still missing."

Ylva grimaced. "Well that is a scary thought, knowing a hydrogen bomb is lying at the bottom of the ocean for anyone to find."

"So maybe a spaceship crashed on Earth, let these things loose, and the aliens searched but never found them," said Cain.

"Maybe." McShane nodded. "But remember, we're likely dealing with two races. So it could be both of them had a ship in our solar system, they got into a firefight and were so badly damaged they either crashed on Earth or made emergency landings."

"But if those ships were transporting a bunch of Jotnar and dragons, they'd have to be enormous." Eastwick held his hands far apart to emphasize the point. "You'd think someone would have found something like that by now."

"It depends on where they crashed," explained Hunter. "Those ships could have come down in the Arctic and got buried under the ice. Or they could have crashed in some remote part of Siberia, or in the ocean."

"Whatever the case, that would make these things really old," said Nunez. "I mean, there've been legends about dragons and giants for thousands of years. That has to be where they came from. How the hell could they live for so long?"

Ylva turned to him. "It could be the creatures we're seeing now were not awake when their ships crashed."

Koosman cocked an eyebrow. "What do you mean?"

"Who knows how far these ships traveled? Even if they could travel at light speed, or faster than light, it would still take years to reach our solar system. It is likely the crew and the creatures would be kept in suspended animation. The resources needed to sustain and care for everyone aboard would be huge, far more than even a large ship could carry. Having them in suspended animation would reduce the amount of supplies needed for such a long trip."

Cain leaned forward. "So the ships crash, some of the monsters wake up, get loose, and start the myths of dragons and giants. But some of them stayed in suspended animation."

Ylva nodded as Koosman spoke, "And now the ones that stayed asleep for thousands of years are waking up."

McShane let out a long breath. "Now comes the scary question. If these ships were as big as we think, how many more Jotnar and dragons have woken up?"

NINETEEN

An electric charge of joy shot up and down McShane's body as the Viper lifted off. Damn, but it felt good to be in the cockpit again. It had been almost a week since his previous chopper went down in Kongsberg. Too long to be stuck on the ground, especially with his flight and many others buzzing over Gardermoen.

His elation faded after the second go-round with the Polish Skytruck. The transport pilots did their best to throw off his aim, but a lumbering aircraft could only do so much in the maneuverability department. Johnson easily locked on his Sidewinders.

"Another hit," stated the co-pilot/gunner in a flat voice. A far cry from his enthusiastic responses when these exercises first started, McShane noted. Maybe Johnson was finally starting to realize this was bullshit.

When they returned to base, Sergeant Tamargo, the chief of the Viper's ground crew, told McShane, "Colonel Esposito scheduled a briefing for 1330."

An hour from now. McShane wondered what the CO wanted with them. Maybe he'd come up with another useless exercise.

Hammer Flight headed for one of the briefing rooms several minutes before 1330. Everyone was in their seats and conversing when Colonel Esposito and Lt. Colonel Whitaker entered.

Standing in the front of the room, Esposito surveyed the pilots before speaking.

"I've called you here to inform you of a new tactic to incapacitate the dragon and the Jotnar. Since our weaponry has had some difficulty penetrating the skin of the monsters . . ."

Some difficulty? Try utterly failed. McShane wanted to roll his eyes. Did Esposito think they were so stupid to believe some less negative-sounding wordage would make the situation better?

"While their torsos may be well protected," Esposito continued, "one area that should be vulnerable is their eyes."

McShane pressed back in his seat, eyeing the colonel. Was he going to ask them to put a Sidewinder or Hellfire into the monsters' eye sockets? Even with precision-guided weapons, that would be a difficult shot, especially against moving targets.

Esposito pressed the remote in his hand. The screen showed a twin-prop aircraft with a Q-tip shaped fuselage and no cockpit.

"This is the Boeing Phantom Eye unmanned aerial vehicle. While normally used for reconnaissance, there is a version the Air Force has been testing that carries a megawatt laser. Even though it's still in the testing stages, the Pentagon has approved its use for Operation Beast Slayer."

McShane spotted a few pilots shifting in their seats or widening their eyes, looking either surprised or impressed. He was certainly intrigued by this development.

"It's not known if this laser is powerful enough to burn through the dragon's skin or that of a Jotunn," said Esposito. "But that's not what we will be attempting. Our target is the eyes, to try and blind them. The Geneva Convention on Conventional Weapons prohibits the use of lasers to permanently blind people. Luckily for us, it says nothing about using lasers to blind dragons."

The corner of his mouth curled in something akin to a smile. Esposito glanced around the room. Seconds of silence ticked by. Was the man waiting for everyone to laugh at his lame-ass joke?

An F-35 pilot let out a half-hearted laugh. Johnson gave a barely audible guffaw. McShane looked at him, eyebrow raised. He expected a much more enthused response from his brown-noser of a co-pilot.

Esposito scowled as the rest of the room sat quietly. Blowing out a loud, short breath, he continued. "Once we are able to blind the dragon, we'll try to use other weapons to finish him off. As for the Jotnar, again, we will try to push them toward unpopulated areas where B-52s and B-1s will be cleared to drop their payloads. Those things may be able to survive hits from one or two bombs; I doubt they'll be able to withstand dozens of bombs."

The colonel ran down the specifications for the Phantom Eye. The UAV ran on liquid hydrogen fuel, could reach a max speed of 200 knots, fly at 65,000 feet, and remain airborne for four days.

Heck of an aircraft, thought McShane, especially with a laser hanging from it. He wondered if it could burn out the retinas of the dragon.

He also wondered if that was a good idea.

The briefing ended, the pilots heading back to the barracks. Many talked in excited tones about the addition of the Phantom Eye to the fight.

"Four days in the air," commented an F-35 jock. "Damn, these UAVs are getting more impressive all the time."

"Yeah," Tudoran chimed in. "One day they'll be so impressive they won't need people like us in the cockpit anymore."

"Not gonna happen." Cain shook his head. "There's always going to be a need for pilots on the front line. The person flying the drone in some shack on another continent doesn't have the situational awareness that we do."

"But the laser sounds kick-ass," said Eastwick. "Wonder when they'll get around to putting stuff like that in our Vipers. How about it, Mack? The world's first laser helicopter."

"Huh?" McShane looked up from the pavement, Flameout interrupting his thoughts about laser beams and blind dragons.

"A laser-armed Viper, Mack. C'mon, how awesome would that be?"

"Um, yeah. Pretty awesome."

Eastwick screwed up his face. "Damn, I thought you'd be more amped about something like that."

"Leave him be, Flameout," said Hunter. "Mack has his mind on something else, and I think I know what it is."

McShane looked over his shoulder at her, brow furrowed.

"You're finally going on your big date with Professor Tande." Hunter grinned.

"Um, yup." McShane forced a grin. "That's exactly what I was thinking about."

***

"You look nice." McShane smiled at Ylva as she stood in the doorway of her quarters.

"Thank you." She glanced down at her attire, biting her lip. "It was the best I could do. I never expected to go on a date here."

He was totally fine with Ylva's best. The mythology professor wore a red sweater, light gray slacks, and black flats. Her hair was done up and she had just the right amount of lipstick. She looked gorgeous.

McShane wore a woodland camouflage MARPAT uniform. As he was technically in the field, he had no dress uniforms on hand. It was either this or his flight suit.

At least he'd ironed the MARPAT before his date.

"Shall we?" He held out his elbow.

Ylva smiled and slipped her hand around his arm. They headed out of the dormitory and to the main gate.

"What the hell?" McShane's forehead wrinkled as he stared at the sight across the street.

"What are they doing?" asked Ylva.

They slowed, McShane studying the crowd of about forty people. Nearly all of them shouted. What exactly they said he didn't know. It all merged into a wave of angry noise. Several men and women held up signs, some in Norwegian, others in English. McShane focused on the ones in English.

JOTNAR HAVE RIGHTS TOO.

JOTNAR AND HUMANS CAN LIVE TOGETHER.

AMERICAN JOTUNN KILLERS GO HOME.

"Are you fucking kidding me?" McShane shook his head.

Ylva let out a gasp of disbelief. "Don't they know how many people the Jotnar have killed?"

"Maybe they do and don't care. I guess even monsters get their share of sympathizers."

The pair crossed the street. McShane hoped to give the crazies a wide berth. Unfortunately, the bus stop was about fifteen feet from the protestors. He glanced down at his MARPAT, which certainly gave him away as an "American Jotunn killer."

McShane positioned himself between Ylva and the protestors, just in case they tried anything. He glanced across the street at the main gate. Four sentries had been posted. He doubted the Jotnar lovers would attack him and Ylva with heavily armed soldiers watching from the other side of the street.

They didn't try anything physical, but they did yell at them, in both English and Norwegian. So many hollered at once McShane couldn't pick out more than a few words in his language.

One woman bounded to the forefront of the group. She raged away in Norwegian, stabbing a finger at McShane.

"What's she saying?" he asked Ylva.

"She says you are a typical American that must kill anything different from you. She also called you a Nazi and a Jotunnphobe."

"A what?" McShane wondered if he heard Ylva correctly.

"I swear, that is what she said. Jotunnphobe."

He turned back to the woman, who had her hands on her hips, nodding with confidence.

"How do you say, 'You're a fucking idiot' in Norwegian'?" McShane asked Ylva.

She grinned, *"Du er en jaevla idiot."*

He had her repeat it once more, just to make sure, then looked back at the smug female protestor.

"Du er en jaevla idiot."

The woman's mouth opened wide, as did her eyes. She stood still for several seconds, then shrieked in fury, waving her arms.

McShane chuckled to himself. Typical of people like that. They loved to insult others, but throw an insult back at them and they lose their little minds.

The bus arrived a minute later. The woman still screamed and flung her arms in all directions as McShane and Ylva got on board. They rode into town, getting off at a shopping center. McShane had gotten a few suggestions on restaurants in the area from the Norwegian personnel stationed at Gardermoen. One thing stuck out to him as they strolled down the sidewalks.

"I didn't realize you Norwegians loved pizza so much." He'd counted six pizza places, and they couldn't have walked more than a mile.

"Well we cannot eat fish and reindeer all the time," Ylva chuckled softly.

After passing another pizza place and two Japanese restaurants, they settled on a casual restaurant and bar. Both ordered local beers, with McShane ordering the *Torsk*, poached cod with boiled potatoes, and Ylva getting potato dumplings with ham. She sipped her beer, then looked around the restaurant, which was three-quarters full. Several seconds passed without her saying anything.

"Something wrong?" asked McShane.

She swung her head back to him. "Oh no, nothing is wrong. Just . . . looking at all these people eating dinner, being here with you. It's all so . . . ordinary. There are stone monsters attacking the country and people are still going about their everyday lives."

"Even in a crisis, people have to eat. But yeah, after having your life revolve around Jotnar and dragons for the past few weeks, it's kinda hard to think about people going to work or school or restaurants while all this craziness is going on."

He let out a long breath. "I remember when I got back from my first tour in Afghanistan. I was looking around at people in convenience stores and coffee shops, or just walking past me with their eyes glued to their phones, wondering if they had any clue what was going on over there. Wondering if they felt grateful they could go back to their homes and families safe and sound every night, while we were in the middle of nowhere, far away from our families with a bunch of psychos prowling around wanting to kill us." He stared quietly at the brown wooden surface of the table.

Ylva shifted, looking left and right. "Um, was it . . . was it bad over there?"

A dark cloud of guilt weighed down on him. His mind pulled him out of the restaurant and back into the cockpit of his Viper. The pickup sped down the road below him. He just watched it, helpless. Then the explosion, then . . .

"Makato?"

He lifted his head. Concern radiated from Ylva's eyes.

"Are you all right?" she asked.

"Um, yeah. Yeah. Just . . . thinking back."

Ylva bit her lip. "I'm sorry if I made you think about . . . any bad things."

"No. That's okay. I mean, other Marines and soldiers had it worse than I did. My chopper got hit by small arms fire a few times. That'll get your attention to say the least. But the Viper has good armor, so I wasn't in danger of going down. My base came under mortar attack a couple of times. Luckily the Taliban had shit aim. The groundpounders had it a lot worse. I slept in a bunk every night while they had a rock for a pillow. I got hot meals while they suffered with MREs. They had bullets and RPGs whizzing around them while I was up in the air in an armored cockpit. I know it made me glad to be a helicopter pilot."

"Is that what you always wanted to be?" Ylva sipped her beer.

"Pretty much," McShane replied. "It was either that or follow in my mom's footsteps. But I figured reading reports and studying photographs twelve hours a day wasn't as fun as zipping around in an attack helicopter like Dad did."

Ylva laughed.

McShane took a swig of his beer. "What about you? Was it your dream to be a mythology teacher?"

"No. I never imagined I would do that. I never imagined I would be a teacher at all. I was really shy when I was in school. But I knew I did not want to have boring jobs like my parents, and I liked history and mythology, so I became a teacher."

She leaned back in her seat, a half-smile on her lips. "I will never forget the first class I taught. It was at a lower secondary school in Kvaløysletta. I was so nervous, stuttering my way through my lessons. After a week I thought I made the biggest mistake of my life becoming a teacher."

"I assume you got over it, since you're a university professor."

"I did, thanks to a couple of other teachers who helped me. They said that if I'm really interested in something, I should enjoy talking about it. That's how I got over my nervousness. When there was an opening for a history and mythology teacher at Tromsø, I applied for it and got it."

"And look where it got you. A consultant's gig in a battle with stone giants and dragons." McShane lifted his beer mug and took a gulp.

"Yes, but it seems like everything I have ever known about dragons and giants, or thought I knew about them, is not helping much."

"The more we deal with them, the more we'll learn."

"That is true. Of course . . ." Ylva rubbed a finger back and forth on the table.

"What?"

Ylva sighed. "The one thing we know about the dragon is that it has killed Jotnar and has not attacked any people."

"Yeah, I've noticed that, too." McShane nodded.

"And everyone still wants to kill it." Ylva leaned forward. "You heard about this plan to blind it?"

"Yeah. They're bringing in a Phantom Eye UAV armed with a laser."

"It is stupid. We have not been able to destroy any Jotnar, but the dragon can. Why is everyone so eager to kill it?"

McShane steepled his fingers. "Well, I guess they're afraid the dragon might attack people once it's done with the Jotnar."

"Do you believe that?"

"Um . . . I don't know." He took a long swallow of his beer.

"You do not sound very sure of yourself," said Ylva. "What will happen if we blind the dragon?"

"We'll hit it with everything we've got until it's dead."

"And you will shoot at it, too?"

McShane's shoulders sagged. "Yes. Yes I will."

"But why?" Ylva flung her hands out to her sides. "Why, if it is fighting the Jotnar?"

"Because those are my orders."

She let out an exasperated breath. "That's it? Because someone told you to do it?"

"That's how it works in the Marine Corps."

"And you agree with those orders?"

"They are lawful orders from my superiors."

"That is not what I asked," said Ylva.

McShane looked away, slowly rubbing his hands together. "I admit, I have some doubts about it. A lot of doubts, actually."

"Then you need to tell your superiors that," Ylva's voice rose a pitch.

"I tried. Colonel Esposito didn't buy it."

Ylva's face stiffened. "So you are still going to shoot the dragon?"

"Yeah," McShane spoke in a low tone.

"Even after it saved your life. You can still shoot it?"

"Those are my orders," he muttered, not looking her in the eyes.

"Even though you know it's wrong."

"Right or wrong doesn't matter." He jerked his hands in front of him for emphasis. "I swore an oath to follow the lawful orders of my superior officers. Same as my parents, my grandparents, and Great-Grandpop Fujio. We can't pick and choose what orders we follow. No military on Earth could survive like that."

He softened his voice. "It's not the first time I've had to follow orders I don't like." He gritted his teeth, thinking about the pickup and the explosion. "It sure as hell won't be the last time."

Ylva's stare hardened behind her glasses. "Do you know how many people died in Skien and Kongsberg?"

"Yeah. Over eleven hundred."

"Do you think more would have died if the dragon had not killed those Jotnar?"

He glanced away for a second before answering. "Yeah."

"Do you think the Jotnar will slaughter more people if we kill the dragon?"

Another pause by McShane. "Yeah, I do."

"And you are still all right with killing the dragon?" Ylva demanded.

"I didn't say I was all right with it. But I don't have a choice in the matter."

A sharp breath escaped Ylva's nose. "No. No, I guess you don't." She pressed her back into her seat, not looking at him.

Their food came, and they ate in relative silence. McShane tried to get some conversations going about anything not related to the dragon or the Jotnar. Ylva responded with short, clipped answers before going back to her dumplings and ham.

The bus ride back to Gardermoen Air Base was also done with few words between them. McShane walked her back to her dormitory.

"Good night." He forced a smile, almost saying, "I had a good time." He didn't, as both knew it would be a lie.

"Good night." She gave him a quick nod and headed inside. No long, parting kiss. Not even a peck on the cheek.

"Shit." McShane trudged back to his dormitory. He'd been so looking forward to dinner with Ylva, hoped they could have a very enjoyable time after they'd finished eating. Instead, his date turned into a bust.

If only he could convince Ylva why he had to follow orders, even if he disagreed with them. It didn't matter that the dragon saved him and Johnson. It didn't matter how many Jotnar the thing took out. The men and women way above his pay grade deemed it a threat. He had a feeling the dragon would not attack people, but feelings were not proof. Could he truly say the dragon wouldn't incinerate Oslo or some other city on a whim? No, he could not. He had to have faith that the colonels and generals above him knew better.

McShane wondered how he could convince Ylva of all that when he couldn't even convince himself.

TWENTY

"Attention all personnel. Jotnar advancing toward Drammen. All pilots to your aircraft."

McShane and the rest of Hammer Flight were in the briefing room reviewing their latest air-to-air exercise with the Skytruck when the alert blared through the P/A. They jumped out of their seats, racing for the door.

Drammen. Dread slithered through his insides. Ylva's parents lived in Drammen.

Ylva. Disappointment gnawed at him, thinking about their date last night.

They dashed toward the runway. Groundcrew swarmed their Vipers, refueling and rearming the attack helicopters. McShane climbed into the cockpit and started the pre-flight checklist.

"All pilots, all pilots," the air controller's voice came through his headphones. "Six, repeat, six Jotnar approaching Drammen from the north."

McShane paused on his checklist. Six? That was the most they'd ever deployed in an attack. An escalation? Could it be these were the last of the Jotnar from the alien ship? That is if his SWAG – Scientific Wild Ass Guess – was correct.

No word on the dragon. Part of him wished the beast would come to take out the Jotnar. Another part was glad it stayed away so the Phantom Eye wouldn't melt its pupils.

His mind replayed the argument with Ylva. Yes, he agreed with her the dragon had been a huge help to them against the Jotnar, whether intentionally or not. But he didn't take orders from her. He took orders from Colonel Esposito, and every other colonel and general. Sure as hell none of them gave a damn about his feelings.

If they said shoot, he'd shoot, whether he wanted to or not.

He finished the pre-flight checklist and got clearance for takeoff. The rotors roared and the Viper lifted off. McShane pointed the nose southwest, the rest of Hammer Flight forming up behind him. He pushed aside all thoughts of his dinner with Ylva.

"Hammer Flight, Monarch Three," radioed the Czech weapons controller on the distant AWACS.

"Hammer Four. Go Monarch."

"Hammer Flight, you are to circle the perimeter of Drammen in the event the dragon appears."

McShane's jaw tensed.

"Hammer Four, do you copy?" asked the Czech.

"Hammer Four copies, Monarch. Circle perimeter of Drammen in case the dragon shows up."

Johnson glanced over his shoulder. "Everything okay, Mack?"

"Oh yeah. Everything's fucking peachy."

The co-pilot stared at him for another second or two before facing forward.

Dark blobs zipped across the sky near the horizon. Jets. A ball of orange and black roiled up from the ground. Another followed. He wondered if the bombs had any success against the Jotnar.

They didn't. McShane counted six of the stone giants smashing through a residential area when he reached the outskirts of Drammen. An F-35 streaked down on one of the Jotnar, dropping a JSOW glide bomb. The swept-winged, cylindrical projectile struck the monster in its thick chest. Smoke, dust, and fire erupted from its torso.

The Jotunn marched forward, stomping a house flat. McShane noticed ruts and burn scars on its chest, but no wounds that would prove fatal.

Tanks and infantry fighting vehicles lined a road south of the neighborhood, firing main guns and missiles. Further south, across the river, self-propelled artillery pounded away. Explosions burst from the Jotnar's bodies.

The barrage did not slow the monsters.

The tanks and IFVs swung right and raced down the main road. The Jotnar broke into a run. McShane's gut turned cold as the distance between the beasts and the armored force grew shorter.

Apache helicopters tore through the sky, Hellfires streaking off their rails. Blobs of flame blossomed from the heads and chests of several Jotnar. They ignored them, bearing down on the armored vehicles.

McShane grimaced when a giant stone foot slammed down on a tank. A kick by another Jotunn sent two IFVs spiraling through the air. Both crashed into houses.

Another tank got crushed. Another. One Jotunn grabbed an IFV and heaved it into the air. It splashed down in the river.

"Holy shit," muttered Johnson as a Jotunn lifted a Leopard II tank over its head. It reared back and flung it skyward. The tank crashed into an Apache. A mass of flame and jet black smoke enveloped both. Fiery pieces of helicopter rained down on Drammen. The Leopard tumbled through the sky, gushing fire.

McShane felt hot blood rushing to his face. Once again, the best weapons that NATO could field did jack shit to stop the Jotnar.

Two of the giants kicked a row of houses. A storm of debris shot into the air. McShane eyed the main thoroughfares running through the city. Traffic moved at a crawl. Ant-like dots scurried through the stalled vehicles. How many would get away safely? How many would die? Would Ylva's parents be among the dead?

"Monarch Three," radioed the AWACS. "We are tracking a large bandit moving toward Drammen. Size and speed matches the dragon. Approaching from the northwest, heading three two two, thirty klicks out."

"Monarch Three, Delta Six," replied General Tellefson, the operational commander back at Gardermoen. "Vector in Phantom Eye for laser attack. Move in helicopter flights for air-to-air engagement."

"Roger, Six."

McShane drew a slow breath as he heard the Czech air controller guide the drone toward the dragon.

"Hammer Flight, come to heading three one zero and take up station at following coordinates. Await attack orders."

A line of GPS coordinates from the E-3 AWACS popped up on McShane's helmet-mounted display. He stiffened before replying, "Monarch, Hammer Four. Proceeding to new coordinates."

The four Vipers skirted the suburbs of Drammen and circled over what appeared to be a ski resort. Tension knotted McShane's shoulders, waiting to hear the order to fire the laser. Waiting to hear the order for his flight to finish off the blinded dragon.

"Tally on the dragon," reported Cain.

McShane scanned the horizon. The winged, serpentine form glided over the treetops.

"Phantom Eye, come to heading two five eight," ordered the AWACS.

"Phantom Eye copies," replied the drone pilot back in the U.S. "Heading two five eight."

McShane glanced back at Drammen. The six Jotnar stomped through the city. His teeth clenched at the trail of crushed houses and fallen trees behind them. Hundreds more houses lay before them. So did hundreds of vehicles jamming the main roads, filled with desperate Norwegians. Did that include Ylva's parents?

Two Tiger attack choppers dove at the giants, firing anti-tank missiles. Explosions sprouted from the heads of two Jotnar. It did not faze them.

"Phantom Eye, come twenty degrees to port," ordered the AWACS.

"Roger. Twenty degrees to port."

McShane looked at the dragon, then the Jotnar, then the packed main roads of Drammen. Hundreds, thousands of people were at risk of being crushed. No missile or shell or bomb could stop the Jotnar, but . .
.

He swung the Viper around and gunned the engine.

"Mack, what are you doing?" blurted Johnson.

"Mack?" radioed Cain. "Mack, what's going on?"

"Hold your positions," snapped McShane. "I . . . I gotta do this."

He put the nose right on the dragon.

"Mack?" Johnson pushed himself into his seat. "Mack, you're going straight at him."

"I know. Trust me on this."

"Hammer Four, Monarch Three." The Czech controller's voice held a mix of urgency and surprise. "Return to your position at once."

McShane did not respond.

"Hammer Four. Hammer Four, respond," demanded the Czech.

Again, McShane kept silent.

The dragon grew larger by the second. Sweat flowed from every pore. Part of him feared a blast of superheated plasma would turn the Viper into ash.

No flame gushed from the dragon's mouth.

"Mack, are you out of your mind?" Johnson hollered. "You're gonna get us killed!"

He ignored the co-pilot and swung the Viper right. G-Forces pressed against him as he whipped the chopper into a tight turn. He pushed the throttle, bringing the aircraft alongside the dragon, parallel to its head. He stared into the ink black orb of its eye, holding his breath. Was the creature staring back at him? Would it attack?

The dragon left him alone, maintaining its course to Drammen, to the Jotnar.

"Hammer Four," an angry voice pierced his ears. Not the Czech weapons controller. It was General Tellefson. "Hammer Four, what are you doing?"

McShane didn't respond.

"Hammer Four, you are in the Phantom Eye's line of fire. Break off, now."

He pressed his lips together. Should he tell them? Would it matter?

Screw it. "General, there are thousands of people stuck in Drammen. We can't stop the Jotnar, but the dragon can. We blind it, those people don't stand a chance."

"Hammer Four, you will break off and return to base," ordered Tellefson. "That is an order."

"Dammit, General. Do you want to be responsible for a massacre? Let the dragon --"

"You are placing everyone in that city at risk, Captain. Break off, now."

McShane's lips slowly parted. Could he actually say it?

He squared his shoulders. "I'm sorry, sir. I cannot follow that order."

"Captain McShane." A new voice came over the headphones. Colonel Esposito. "Unless you want to spend the next ten years in Leavenworth, you will break off and return to base now. That is a direct order."

McShane said nothing. He just kept pace with the dragon.

"Lieutenant Johnson," Esposito blared.

"Yes, sir."

"Captain McShane is relieved as flight leader and aircraft commander. Take control of the Viper and RTB."

"Yes, sir." Johnson looked over his shoulder. "Captain, give me control of the aircraft."

"Sorry, Lieutenant. Not happening."

"Mack. The colonel just relieved you. You have to hand control of the chopper to me."

"You deaf, Go Around? I said that is not happening."

Johnson's mouth hung open for a few moments. "Um, Colonel. Captain McShane will not relinquish control of the helicopter to me."

"Dammit, Johnson. Make him do it."

"How, sir?"

"Use force!" Esposito yelled.

"Force? How?"

"You have your pistol, right?"

"Yes, sir," said Johnson.

"Then use it!"

Johnson sat frozen. McShane's gaze shifted from the dragon to his co-pilot. Would he really –

"Johnson!" screamed Esposito.

The co-pilot pulled out his Beretta and swung around. McShane tensed as Johnson leveled the barrel at his chest.

TWENTY-ONE

"Sir, give me control of the aircraft." The gun in Johnson's hand didn't waver.

McShane's eyes narrowed behind his visor. "You really want to do that?"

"I have my orders."

"You want to fire that thing in a confined space? Maybe hit some vital electronics? Or the engine?"

Johnson's hand trembled slightly.

"Or maybe you do hit me," said McShane. "Maybe I jerk the stick and we crash into the dragon before you get control."

The co-pilot's mouth opened. A couple of seconds passed before he spoke. "I . . . I have my orders."

"And I have to do what's right, and that's make sure the dragon doesn't get blinded and can fight the Jotnar. The same dragon that saved your ass and mine."

Jaw stiff, Johnson stared at the winged beast. Several seconds passed before he turned back to McShane. "C'mon, Mack. This --"

"Johnson!" Esposito hollered over the radio.

"Yes, sir?"

"Do you have control of that Viper?"

The veins in his neck stuck out. "Um, no, sir."

"Dammit, Lieutenant! I don't care what you have to do, take control of that helicopter right the hell now!"

Johnson inhaled and straightened his arm. "Captain. Give me control of the aircraft or . . . or I will shoot you."

McShane's insides went cold. Had Johnson been a friend, it would have been easier to talk him out of it. But the pair were anything but friends, and with Johnson's desire to always please his superiors, could he convince him otherwise?

"You really think you can do it?"

Tension radiated from Johnson's face. "Colonel Esposito said to do whatever it takes."

"Then you're gonna have to shoot me." McShane fought not to swallow. But he couldn't help wonder if he'd just signed his death warrant.

The pistol did not go off, but Johnson kept it pointed at him.

"Easy to kill someone in a tank or an APC. We never see the people in them. Up here they're just big hunks of metal." McShane shoved back his visor. "But it's a hell of a lot different doing it up close. Can you do it, Johnson? Can you look someone in the eye and pull the trigger?"

Johnson locked gazes with him. He bit down on his lower lip.

"Can you?"

Again, silence from both Johnson and the Berretta.

McShane inched forward. "Can you?"

Johnson's shoulders rose in a slow breath. He lowered his eyes, then his pistol.

McShane's entire body went slack. "Thank you, Scott." He couldn't remember ever calling his co-pilot by his first name.

"Johnson, do you have control of the aircraft?" demanded Esposito.

The co-pilot just stared out the cockpit window at the dragon.

"Johnson? Johnson!"

He remained quiet.

McShane glanced at the dragon, then scrunched his brows together. "What the hell?"

Another Viper took up position on the dragon's right side. Eastwick's Viper. Flying above and behind it was Hunter's chopper. McShane checked his mirrors to find Cain on his six.

"What the hell are you guys doing?"

"Making sure that Phantom Eye doesn't have a clear shot at the dragon," replied Eastwick.

"Are you nuts? You're gonna get court-martialed, all of you."

"So will you most likely, Mack," Cain responded.

"I go down that's one thing. I'm not letting you guys screw up your careers, too. Get back to your station. That's an order."

"Sorry, Mack," said Hunter. "Like you told the general, this dragon's our best shot of stopping the Jotnar and saving everyone in the city. So we're with you, whether you like it or not."

Part of him was moved that his pilots thought so much of him they'd risk their careers to help. Another part wanted to kick all their asses for being so stupid.

But they were adults. They knew the score and were putting everything on the line to help the civilians down there.

"All right, you dumbasses," said McShane. "Stick close to the dragon's head. Don't give that drone a good shot at the eyes. And keep the hell away from its mouth in case it wants to use its fire breath."

The rest of Hammer Flight answered with, "Roger."

McShane pushed down his visor and checked to the left. The Phantom Eye circled just outside Drammen. So far the higher-ups did not want to risk blinding him or his pilots. But would that last? Would they decide they couldn't risk the lives of thousands of Norwegians over those of eight Marines – insubordinate ones at that – and four helicopters with a combined price tag of 124 million dollars?

The Phantom Eye did not fire its laser. The dragon soared over Drammen, drawing a bead on the six Jotnar. Its maw opened wide.

"Uh-oh," said Eastwick. "I think it's about to go nuclear blowtorch."

"Back off a bit," ordered McShane.

He drew the cyclic stick left, sliding about fifty feet between his Viper and the dragon's head. He still paralleled the monster, preventing a clean shot by the Phantom Eye. Below, the Jotnar crashed through more houses, sending debris cascading into the streets. One Jotunn brought its massive fists down on a six-story office building. Brick and glass exploded around it. Another giant rammed its foot into an apartment complex. Half the building collapsed, spewing a cloud of dust.

Red flame shot from the dragon's mouth. For an instant, McShane feared it would blast through an entire neighborhood, proving his theory about the dragon wrong. Dead wrong. Literally.

But the flames ripped through the shoulder of a Jotunn. Its severed arm dropped to the ground. The stone monster jerked back, smoke billowing from its stump.

The dragon pulled up, flapped its large wings, and dropped onto the wounded Jotunn. It bit into the stone neck. The Jotunn swung around, trying to swat the dragon with its remaining hand. It missed every time.

Another Jotunn rushed over to help its comrade. The dragon lashed out with its tail. The spiky tip cut through the Jotunn's stone chest, driving it back.

The dragon dug its claws through the first Jotunn's neck. Dozens of stone fragments tumbled down its body. Soon, its entire head followed.

Crouching, the dragon leaped off the falling Jotunn, aiming for another giant. It wrapped the dragon in a bearhug and body-slammed it onto an entire block of houses. McShane cringed, feeling the creature's pain.

Two Jotnar marched toward the fallen dragon. It rolled onto its side, raising its neck. McShane expected another fiery blast.

The Jotunn that had body-slammed the dragon kicked it in the back. Its long neck whipped around and snapped at the giant. The other two Jotnar brought down their fists. The dragon jerked from the hammer blows to its side. It tried to scramble to its feet, swinging its tail. The spikes grazed the upper leg of one Jotunn. Its partner punched the dragon in the head, while the third Jotunn kicked it in the side.

The dragon jumped away from the melee attack. It landed on a field of kindling that used to be houses and swung around. Fire surged from its gullet. The blast burned through one Jotunn's shoulder and half its head. It threw out its one good arm and collapsed on its back, crashing down on a pair of houses. The monster did not get up.

McShane glanced at the Phantom Eye, still on the outskirts of the city. Between Hammer Flight hovering around the battle, and the battle itself, he doubted the drone operator could target the dragon's eyes.

An Apache raced in and launched two Hellfires. Both missiles exploded on the dragon's back.

"Dammit," McShane hissed, switching to general frequency. "All units, all units, this is Hammer Four. Do not, repeat, do not fire on the dragon. Let it fight the Jotnar."

"All units, this is Delta Six," radioed General Tellefson. "Disregard all orders coming from Hammer Four. Engage all targets of opportunity. Hammer Flight, return to base immediately."

McShane maintained his orbit over the battle. So did Cain, Eastwick, and Hunter.

"Hammer Flight, acknowledge my order," Tellefson demanded.

None of them did.

The dragon leapt at a Jotunn, raking its massive chest with its claws. A second Jotunn lowered its shoulder and rammed into the dragon. It cleaved through an apartment house, throwing up a mass of debris, and crashed on the street. The remaining two Jotnar kicked it in the neck and the stomach. The dragon tried to slither away from the attack. Stone feet and fists hammered it. One Jotunn clubbed it with a light pole.

"Damn," Eastwick blurted. "They're beating the crap out of that dragon."

"Then let's take some heat off our big buddy," said McShane. "Target the Jotnar. Hopefully they'll shift their attention to us."

The others acknowledged his order.

"Johnson. Two Hellfires on the Jotunn to the left."

No response.

"Johnson? Johnson!"

"Y-Yes?"

"Two Hellfires. Jotunn on the left. Do it."

He made no move to the fire control. "It's over. Our careers are done."

"Then they're done. So go down fighting."

Johnson glanced over his shoulder.

McShane looked below. The Jotnar continued to hammer the dragon with a flurry of fists and feet. Its right wing was bent awkwardly.

"Listen to me, Lieutenant. We're in a fight. That dragon needs us. The people down there need us. So either be a Marine and launch those missiles or spend the rest of your life thinking about how you sat on your ass and did nothing when a bunch of monsters were tearing apart this city. What's it gonna be?"

Johnson's shoulders rose in a sharp breath, then another. He reached for his console. "Hellfires One and Six, locked on."

"Fire."

The two missiles flew off the rails. Both exploded against the Jotunn's shoulders.

More Hellfires blasted off from the other Vipers. Rocket barrages followed. Mini-orange suns sprouted across the bodies of the Jotnar. Two of them looked their way.

"I think we got their attention," said Cain.

Johnson sent two more Hellfires at a Jotunn. Both exploded under its chin.

Two Hungarian Hinds barreled toward the monster brawl. Their wing stubs lit up with missile and rocket fire. More explosions sprang off the Jotnar's hides. Two Apaches and Two Tigers did strafing runs on the stone giants. McShane wondered if the pilots actually heeded his advice or if they were going with General Tellefson's order to engage targets of opportunity. Maybe a combination of both, with the pilots deciding they had a better opportunity against the Jotnar than the dragon.

McShane grinned.

Three Jotnar turned to face the helicopters. One snatched up a piece of wall from some wrecked building and reared back to throw it.

Orange lines zipped away from the rocket pods on Hunter's Viper. At least three hit the Jotunn's hand, blasting the wall into concrete splinters. The monster gawked at his smoking palm. McShane swore the thing wore an incredulous look. It almost made him laugh.

The dragon clamped its mouth around the fourth Jotunn's leg. It yanked its head back, ripping out a chunk of rock. The giant teetered to the left. Its leg snapped off at the knee. The Jotunn fell on its side.

The dragon swung around sluggishly. It brought up its right foreleg and swung down. Talons ripped through the back of the Jotunn's skull. The dragon swatted at the other monster until it severed the stone head just above the nose.

Another Jotunn turned toward it. The Vipers unleashed more Hellfires. Smoke and fire sprouted along its huge body. One missile exploded against its thigh. The Jotunn took a stutter step, and turned back to the helicopters.

The dragon's mouth opened wide. A stream of fire roared from it and blew through the Jotunn's chest. It toppled onto its stomach.

The remaining two Jotunn looked at one another, then turned and ran toward the forests bordering Drammen. The dragon pushed itself up on all fours. McShane grimaced, noting how shaky the beast looked. It flapped its large wings, flew a few feet, then crashed back to the ground.

"I think its flying days are over," said Eastwick. "Look how messed up that one wing is."

Another rush of flame flew from its mouth. The blast roared between the fleeing Jotnar. They stomped on houses, then crashed through numerous trees. Helicopters and jets chased after them. Missiles and rockets burst on and around the monster. A British Typhoon dropped a pair of small diameter bombs. One sent a geyser of fire and smoke up from a Jotunn's back. Another exploded near the monster. Both stone creatures kept running.

Two planes rocketed over the city, stubby with long wings. SU-25 Frogfoots of the Bulgarian Air Force. McShane sucked down a breath and held it as he watched them dive at the dragon. A blazing orange streak stretched out from the lead Frogfoot's starboard wing. An anti-tank missile. A fireball burst from the dragon's side.

"No!" McShane shouted. He was about to yell into the radio to stop attacking the beast, but stopped himself. Tellefson had already told the other pilots to disregard anything he said. He doubted they'd disobey the orders of a general over a captain they didn't know.

Flames flashed under the nose of the second SU-25. Tracers of 30mm fire laced the dragon's side. McShane tensed as the Russian-built attack jet shot over the monster. He expected it to incinerate the two planes.

That didn't happen. Instead, the dragon reared back on its haunches and jumped . . . right at a roadway packed with cars. McShane pushed himself deeper into his seat, shivering. He waited for the massive bulk of the dragon to come down on dozens of vehicles and people.

It missed the road and landed in a parking lot, grazing the side of a large office building. Debris rained down onto the ground. The dragon leaped again, diving headlong into the river. An enormous wall of blue and white stretched into the air.

"Damn," blurted Nunez. "That thing can swim, too?"

"Apparently," said Cain.

Waves surged over the river banks, drenching buildings along the shoreline. Two Norwegian Hueys hovered over the water, searching in vain for the submerged dragon. They'd probably have to bring in choppers equipped with sonar to find it. McShane hoped by the time they arrived on station, the dragon would be long gone.

"What now, Mack?" asked Eastwick.

McShane sighed. "Might as well follow our last order and RTB."

"Guess we have to face the music sooner or later," Hunter added in a flat tone.

Grunting an acknowledgment, McShane wheeled the Viper to the northeast. The others fell in behind him. His adrenaline subsided with each passing minute. His emotions settled and gave him a chance to reflect on his actions. He'd completely fucked his career, he knew that. But his actions had saved hundreds, maybe thousands of people in Drammen, hopefully Ylva's parents among them. He could live with that.

But what about the next attack?

Worry flared within him. Could the dragon fend off another assault by the Jotnar? If it tried, who would be there to keep the Phantom Eye from blinding it? Answer, no one.

All his muscles felt heavy. Had he just delayed the inevitable?

No way could he convince any of his superiors to not attack the dragon. If they hadn't listened to him before, they sure as hell wouldn't after what he'd just done.

He straightened when the realization hit him. There might be one person he could convince. McShane was hesitant to do it. It was someone he'd never wanted to ask a favor of for the sake of his career.

Not your career, but for the war effort. For everyone in this country, maybe on the entire continent.

The four Vipers soared over Oslo. McShane gazed down at the sprawling city. He caught sight of a white circle with a red "H" in a parking lot.

"Hammer Four," he radioed. "Everyone maintain your heading back to Gardermoen. I need to make a pitstop."

"What's going on, Mack?" asked Cain.

"Hopefully I can do something to help that dragon. I'll see you back at base."

McShane banked the chopper toward the ground. Johnson looked up at him. "Won't this get us in more trouble?"

"After what I pulled back in Drammen, what's one more infraction? Might as well go for broke."

McShane circled the hospital once and touched down on the helipad. He removed his helmet and jumped out of the cockpit. A few people stood or sat by the main entrance, nearly all with their cell phones. A few took pictures or videos of the Viper. It would have been much more convenient if he had his own cell, but combat pilots didn't carry them on missions. If shot down and captured, they didn't want the enemy to have access to their personal information. Not that the Jotnar would capture him and poke around his cell, but it was standard operating procedure, and engrained in all pilots.

The glass doors slid open. McShane strode inside and up to the front desk, where a pretty young blond sat, gaping at him. She muttered something in Norwegian.

"Do you speak English, ma'am?"

"Y-Yes," she nodded, eyes unblinking.

"Good. Captain Makato McShane, United States Marine Corps. I need to place an emergency long distance call to America."

TWENTY-TWO

"Do you think you're special? Do you think you can disobey a superior officer whenever you feel like it?"

McShane kept his face stiff and his hands clasped behind his back as Colonel Esposito yelled from behind his desk. To his right stood an unsmiling Lieutenant Colonel Whitaker.

"You prevented the use of the Phantom Eye," raged Esposito. "You jeopardized the lives of every civilian in Drammen and every service member deployed to protect them."

"I saved lives, sirs."

Esposito's cheeks glowed crimson. "Are you really that arrogant, McShane? Where do you get off thinking you and you alone know best how to deal with these monsters?"

"The dragon has only attacked the Jotnar. It hasn't attacked any civilians. It even saved me and Lieutenant Johnson."

"Is that it? You think you owe that thing? Are you telling me you're more loyal to that dragon than you are to the Corps? To the United States of America you swore an oath to protect?"

"I know I disobeyed a lawful order from my superiors, sir," replied McShane. "But I did what I felt was right."

Esposito slammed a fist on his desk. "You do not get to decide what's right and wrong! The Marine Corps decides that. The Supreme Allied Commander Europe decides that. The President of the United States decides that. Not you!"

McShane did not say a word. Esposito could scream all he wanted. It would not change his mind.

"You are done, McShane," Esposito lowered his voice, which made his tone even more menacing. "You are beyond done. Not only will you and your flight be charged with failure to obey an order, I'll make damn sure you're charged with mutiny."

Worry drilled through him. Mutiny was an offense punishable by death under the Uniform Code of Military Justice. But he couldn't recall a time since the 19th Century when any service member was executed solely for that charge. In fact, no military executions had been carried out since 1961. So he and his flight were likely safe from the needle.

A long stay at Leavenworth, however, was another matter.

"Sir, my intention to protect the dragon was mine and mine alone. At no time did I ask for or encourage anyone in my flight to help me. I ask that they be given leniency."

Esposito's eyes bulged. "You are not in a position to demand leniency or anything else. You and your pilots are confined to barracks, under guard, until you are flown back to the States to await a general court martial. Whatever family connections or legacy you have will not get you out of this." He stared past McShane's shoulder and hollered. "You two! In here now!"

A pair of MPs entered the office.

"Take Captain McShane back to his dormitory." Esposito turned his glare on him. "You're a disgrace to the Corps. Get out of my sight."

"Sir." McShane saluted before the MPs led him away.

He walked straight, chin up, the whole way back to the dorm, trying to mask his worry. Not so much for himself. He knew what he did at Drammen would end his Marine career. He accepted that. His worry was directed more toward the rest of Hammer Flight, and the dragon. Hopefully, the phone call he made at the hospital would help them.

Two more MPs waited outside the four-bed dorm he shared with Johnson, Cain, and Nunez. McShane entered, one of the MPs shutting the door behind him. Cain and Nunez laid on their bunks, looking up from the magazines they were reading. Johnson sat on the edge of his bed, staring at the floor.

"So how did it go?" Cain jumped off the top bunk.

"About as bad as you'd expect," said McShane. "The words 'mutiny' and 'disgrace' and 'Leavenworth' came up. I did plead for mercy on your guys' part, but Colonel Esposito wasn't having any of it."

"Well thanks for trying, Mack. Speaking for the rest of the flight, we all appreciate it."

His eyebrows pressed together. "I wouldn't have had to ask that if you all would have backed off like I ordered you to."

"Yeah, but we didn't," Cain retorted. "You're not the only one who thought knocking out the dragon was a dumb idea. Yeah, let's blind and kill the only thing that's been able to kill the Jotnar. I'll probably never fly in the Corps again, probably wear an orange jumpsuit for a while, but what we did saved the lives of thousands of civilians. I'm okay with that."

McShane glanced over at Nunez. The co-pilot got to his feet and shrugged. "Hey, I've always dreamed of being a malcontent. At least I did it for a good cause."

McShane shook his head. "I don't know whether to thank you for having that kind of faith in me or call you both dumbasses for flushing your careers down the toilet with mine."

Cain grinned and held up a hand. "Semper Fi, Mack."

He grinned back and clasped Cain's hand. "Semper Fi, Stripes."

He exchanged a handshake and "Semper Fi" with Nunez before looking at Johnson. He still stared at the floor. McShane sat next to him.

"For what it's worth, I'm sorry I got you into this mess."

Johnson turned to him. McShane expected his co-pilot to launch into a tirade blaming him for screwing up his career, berating him for not following orders. Instead, he remained silent.

"Look," McShane continued, "I know we don't get along great. You've got your way and I've got mine. Still, you're in my flight, and if you go to court martial, I will go to bat for you."

"I don't know if . . ." Johnson clamped his mouth shut for a moment. "Um, thank you, Mack."

"I think I know what you were about to say. Yeah, I don't know how much weight the word of a captain charged with mutiny will carry, but I'll give it anyway. For you and everyone else."

Johnson nodded. "Thanks, Mack."

McShane nodded back and stood.

"I don't know . . ." Johnson clenched the side on his bunk.

"Don't know what?" asked McShane.

"I don't know . . ." Johnson's shoulders sagged. "What I did, what they wanted me to do. Shoot you. I mean . . ." He looked away for a moment. "You were right. Killing someone with a missile a mile or two away is a lot different than doing it up close, especially when it's a fellow Marine you're looking at. I couldn't . . ."

He drew in a long breath before continuing. "And I think you're right about the dragon. I mean, if it wasn't for him, I wouldn't be here, neither would you. I don't know how, but the more I think about it, the more I'm starting to believe it really is trying to help us."

"Hah!" Nunez barked and slapped Johnson on the leg. "I knew you weren't a total douche, Go Around. Welcome to the right way of thinking."

Cain rolled his eyes. "You are a master of the compliment, Tin Foil."

McShane chuckled and climbed onto the top bunk, stretching out.

The four "inmates" chatted, read magazines or paperbacks, did pushups and sit-ups – Cain especially, fitness freak that he was. Meals were brought to them. MPs escorted them to the latrine.

Sleep proved difficult for McShane. Along with wondering about a possible future behind bars, he also thought of Ylva. He hadn't seen her since their dinner date that ended so badly. Had she heard what happened to him? Probably. Gardermoen wasn't that big a base, and news traveled fast on military installations, especially bad news. Had she asked to visit him? If so, had Esposito denied her request?

He frowned, staring up at the darkened ceiling. He doubted he'd see Ylva before getting shipped back to the States. His insides deflated. A relationship with an incredible woman over before it began. Maybe she could be his pen pal while in prison. Though letters couldn't take the place of being with her in the flesh.

Those were some of his last thoughts before drifting off to sleep, Ylva in the flesh . . . bare flesh. Damn, what could have been.

The four woke up the next morning, escorted to the latrine by the MPs, then served their breakfast. Reading, exercising, chatting, more exercising, and more chatting passed the time for the rest of the morning.

Shortly after one in the afternoon, Lieutenant Colonel Whitaker came into the room. All four pilots stood at attention.

"As you were." The XO's mouth pressed into a tight line. His gaze landed on McShane.

He maintained a stoic expression, though some regret crept through him. He could see it in Whitaker's eyes. The senior officer felt that McShane had broken the faith, betrayed the Corps by his actions. That bothered him more than he expected. He genuinely liked Whitaker. Not only was he a good XO, but a good guy. Someone who treated the men and women under him fairly. Someone whose respect McShane felt he earned.

Not anymore, apparently.

He braced himself for the expected announcement to board a C-17, layover at Camp Lejeune, and final destination Leavenworth, Kansas.

Whitaker grunted. "This comes straight from the Commandant."

McShane's eyebrows went up. So did everyone else's. The head honcho of the entire United States Marine Corps himself had weighed in on this matter?

"All charges against the pilots of Hammer Flight are hereby dismissed."

Johnson gaped. So did Nunez. Cain let out a quiet breath. McShane closed his eyes, fighting the urge to sag in relief.

"Furthermore," Whitaker continued, "all pilots are restored to active flight status and to their previous positions in the air combat element effective immediately. Also, per orders from National Command Authority . . ."

Again, McShane cranked an eyebrow. National Command Authority meant the man himself, the President of the United States.

"... the Secretary of Defense, and Supreme Headquarters Allied Powers Europe, no combat action is to be taken against the dragon unless it engages in direct hostile action against the civilian population or the forces of NATO and its military partners. From this point on, we are to let it engage and destroy any Jotunn it comes across. Is that understood?"

"Yes, sir," they all replied.

"McShane, Johnson. You have patrol with Hunter and Tudoran. Mission brief in one hour."

"Yes, sir," the pair replied.

Unsmiling, Whitaker stepped toward McShane until his face was inches from his. "Apparently, the higher ups think court martialing the man who convinced them the dragon is an ally wouldn't be prudent. Might be bad for morale. For the public image of the Corps. But understand this, Captain. You used up your one get out of jail free card. Don't think you can pull this shit again." He turned to the others. "Any of you."

Whitaker refocused on McShane. "I don't care if you thought you were right or you felt you owed a debt to that dragon for saving your life, you disobeyed a lawful order. That is not something I am going to forget. Discipline and the chain of command exist for a reason, meaning you do not get to decide which orders to follow and which you don't. You may have gotten a reprieve here, but your stunt is going to follow you for the rest of your time in the Corps. Every CO you have from here on out is going to have second thoughts on whether or not they can trust you. Your promotion track is going to be severely derailed by this. Is this all sinking in, Captain?"

"Yes, sir."

"It better, because if you ever do something like this again in my battlespace, I will make your life worse than that of a day one recruit at Parris Island before anyone can save your worthless ass. Is that clear?"

"Yes, sir."

Whitaker grunted and turned on his heel. "Mission brief. One hour. You better not be late."

The XO exited, waving for the MPs to follow.

"Oh man. Thank God," Johnson spoke in a hushed, relieved tone.

"I guess that phone call you told us about paid off," said Cain.

"Yeah, nice to have family in high places," added Nunez.

McShane nodded. It violated his rule about asking family for favors, but he figured he could make an exception this time, as it benefitted his pilots and the dragon, not him.

He and Johnson changed into their flight suits and set out for flight ops. They approached the entrance to the two-story white building when a voice called out from behind. "Makato."

He spun around. Elation washing over him as he laid eyes on Ylva. She strode up to him and right into his arms. He closed his eyes, delighting in the feel of her body against his.

"I heard what happened," she said. "I asked if I could see you, but they would not let me. I . . . I . . . ." Her lip quivered. "I'm sorry if I got you in trouble."

"What?" McShane's forehead wrinkled.

"When I told you you shouldn't kill the dragon. I didn't think . . . you could have gone to jail."

"Hey." He gently grasped Ylva's shoulders. Out the corner of his eye, he saw Johnson wince, nod toward flight ops, and walk away.

McShane stared back into Ylva's eyes. "Don't blame yourself. You had nothing to do with what I did. The truth is, even when you were telling me we shouldn't kill the dragon, I was already having those thoughts. It hadn't attacked any people, it saved me and Johnson, it killed a bunch of Jotnar. I thought of all the people in Drammen, including your parents, how they might be killed or injured if we didn't let the dragon do its job. I couldn't let that drone blind it. But that wasn't the only reason I did what I did."

He bit his lip for a moment. "Remember at dinner, when you asked if anything bad happened to me in Afghanistan?"

"Yes."

"Well, something did." McShane's shoulders drooped. "I was patrolling outside Baghran and spotted a pickup racing down a road, heading right to one of our checkpoints. Didn't even attempt to slow down. Thing had suicide bomber written all over it. I radioed for permission to take it out. They ordered me to hold my fire. They didn't want to risk killing civilians by mistake. I didn't think any civilian would be flooring it toward a checkpoint, but I kept my finger off the trigger."

He lowered his head, squeezing Ylva's hand. "The pickup crashed into the checkpoint and exploded. Four Marines were killed and four others were injured."

Ylva's mouth fell open. "Oh, Makato." She squeezed his hand back. "I'm so sorry."

"I knew what was coming, felt it in my gut. But I didn't do a damn thing to stop it. I followed orders like a good little Marine. I'm sure that'll mean something to the families of the dead and wounded."

McShane looked up at Ylva. "I have four deaths on my conscience because I blindly followed orders. I wasn't about to add hundreds more to it, so that's why I did what I did."

He put a hand on Ylva's cheek. She shuddered, in a good way. "It was all my decision. Don't feel one bit guilty, okay?"

"Yeah. Okay." A smile spread across her face.

"Your parents okay?"

"Yes. They were in a traffic jam trying to get out of the city, but they are fine."

"I'm glad to hear it."

She took hold of his hand, still on her cheek. "How . . . how did you get out of trouble? Clubber told me you could have gone to jail for years. All of you could have."

"You have my mother to thank for that."

She cocked her head, deeper into his palm. "How?"

"I told you she's a big deal in the intelligence community. After I kept the Phantom Eye from blinding the dragon, I knew there wasn't going to be anything to stop it from happening next time. So I landed at a hospital and called home, pleaded my case to Mom about sparing the dragon, letting it fight the Jotnar. Looks like I convinced her, and she convinced the powers that be in Washington and NATO."

McShane bobbed his head back and forth. "I also asked her to make sure my guys don't pay for what I did. Looks like she managed to get them out of trouble, and me, not that I asked her to do that."

"She is your mother."

"Yeah, but when I went into the Corps, she made it clear I was not to use her position to advance my career, and she wouldn't use her influence to help me get ahead . . . or bail me out of trouble. Looks like she went back on that."

"As I said, she is your mother," said Ylva.

"You don't know my mother."

"I hope I get to meet her and thank her for keeping her son from going to jail." She gave him the warmest smile he'd ever seen.

McShane gazed into her face, heart thumping. Last night he thought he'd never see this wonderful, beautiful woman again. But God had smiled on him big time, given him a second chance like no other. He was not going to waste it.

He leaned in and kissed her, savoring the softness, the moistness of her lips. When he pulled back, he noticed Ylva's eyes half-closed, pure joy radiating from her face.

"I'm sorry," he said. "For our date. For sounding stubborn when we were arguing about the dragon. I should have told you I was thinking along the same lines."

"It's okay." Ylva smiled, her hand gliding down his cheek.

They kissed again, much deeper the second time around, McShane pulling her into his body. What he wouldn't give to keep this going, but . . .

"Much as I hate to say this, duty calls. I have a mission brief to get to."

"I understand. Be careful."

After another kiss, Ylva waved as he turned away, beaming.

He stopped when he saw Hunter leaning against the wall of flight ops, arms folded, a wry grin on her lips.

"'Bout damn time, Mack."

He gave her a faux scowl. "Shut up, Clubber."

She chuckled.

So did he.

TWENTY-THREE

McShane and Hunter were assigned the sector near the lakeside village of Tuddal. Nearly two hours of searching turned up no sign of Jotnar or the dragon. Concern crept through him. His big buddy got one hell of a beatdown at Drammen. Could it recover? What if it didn't? Could they stop the Jotnar on their own? Would they need to drop nukes on the ugly bastards?

He scanned the lush forests and blue lakes below. Norway had some gorgeous scenery. He didn't like the idea of having to wipe it out with radioactive fire. McShane bet the five million-plus people who called this country home wouldn't like it either.

They headed back to Gardermoen, McShane thinking about spending his downtime with Ylva. Thinking about kissing her again . . . doing more than simply kissing her.

He'd been back on the ground barely an hour when word came down of a Jotunn sighting. A patrolling British AW159 Wildcat helicopter spotted the monster making its way along a fjord near Lampeland, fifty miles west of Oslo. McShane and Hammer Flight were ordered back in the air, joining more than a dozen other attack choppers.

They searched up and down the fjord, employing night vision, thermal sensors, and spotlights. No one spotted a single stone giant. McShane and his pilots returned to Gardermoen, topped off their tanks, and headed back to Lampeland.

An hour later, the search was called off. McShane grunted as he wheeled around his Viper. When they got back to base and headed to flight ops for the mission debrief, Lieutenant Colonel Whitaker stood at the front of the room, a sour look on his face.

"False alarm, Marines. The pilot who radioed in the alert saw a big rockslide go into the fjord and for whatever reason thought a Jotunn caused it. Dumbass gets spooked and we waste a bunch of time and fuel. I hope his CO rips him a new one."

So did McShane. All this time wasted was time he could have spent with Ylva. By the time they finished the mission brief and planned for tomorrow's patrol, it would be approaching midnight. Ylva would probably be asleep by then. Lord knew he needed sleep himself after this long-ass day.

The next morning was shit-shower-shave, calisthenics, breakfast, then mission brief. Hammer Flight had been assigned the area of the

Finnemarka Forest, minus Eastwick and Koosman. Their chopper had to be grounded when a malfunction with the Target Sight System cropped up.

Two hours flying back and forth over thousands of acres of forest yielded nothing. After a short debrief, McShane made his way to the building that housed the research group. His steps grew quicker the closer he got to the entrance. He couldn't wait to see Ylva.

She sat at her desk in the far corner of the room, wearing a *Sword Art Online* sweatshirt. An old book lay open in front of her. She jotted something down on a notepad.

"Good morning, Professor."

Ylva's head snapped toward him. A huge smile brightened her face. "Makato."

She practically jumped out of her seat, threw her arms around him, and planted a kiss on his lips. The disciplined side of McShane said this sort of PDA in a work environment was unprofessional. Every other side of him didn't care.

"I'm so glad to see you," she said.

"After what you just did, I'm glad to see you, too."

Ylva smiled and kissed him again. "Perhaps I should say there is a second reason I'm glad to see you."

"What is it?"

"I was about to go find you when you came in. I think I know where the Jotnar and the dragon came from."

His eyes widened. "Where?"

She sat down and pointed to the open leather-bound book. "This is one of the books I received from the Cultural History Museum in Oslo. It's a collection of stories from the Viking Age published in 1870. At the time it was one of the most comprehensive accounts of Viking culture. It took the author a long time to compile all these stories. Aside from poetry, Vikings themselves had very few written records of their history and culture. Most of it was passed down orally. It was usually traders, missionaries, even their enemies who kept written accounts of the Vikings."

"So those stories could be second or third-hand," said McShane. "Though after a thousand or so years, probably twentieth or thirtieth-hand."

Ylva chuckled. "Yes. Normally I would be suspicious of believing every single word from any of these stories. Until I came across this one." She pointed at the open page.

McShane glanced at it. "Yeah, you're gonna have to help me with the Norwegian."

She grinned. "It was originally written by a missionary in 1033. Much of it was meant to be disparaging of Viking culture in order to justify the spread of Christianity through Norway. He used several mythological stories to show, in his mind, how unsophisticated the people of the region were and how imperative it was to extinguish paganism. One of the stories he cited caught my attention."

McShane sat on the corner of the desk as Ylva continued. "The missionary spoke to a child in a village in the Telemark region. He told of how his father and a few other men went out hunting and encountered a giant. They described it as brown in color, with a head that reached to the clouds."

"That sounds like that Mok . . . Mokar . . ."

"Mokkurkalfi."

"Yeah, that monster you mentioned before."

Ylva nodded. "This story could have been the basis for that myth. Anyway, the missionary wrote that the child told him his father and the others attacked the giant. It ran from them and into a river. That's when they report it vanished in, and I quote, 'The time it takes for the blink of one's eyes.'"

"The giant they're talking about could be a Jotunn," said McShane. "My big problem with the story is how the Vikings say they chased it off. We can barely hurt the Jotnar with missiles and shells. I doubt one of them got scared off by a few guys with arrows and battleaxes."

"Ah . . ." Ylva held up a finger. "But this is where you take the story literally. These are men we're talking about. Men of the Eleventh Century. Big, strapping, tough men who dared not look weak in front of anyone. What I believe is when they saw the giant, they hid and observed it until it disappeared. But they could not admit that to their fellow villagers, so they made up a story of how they fought it and drove it off."

"And everyone could keep believing they were total BAMFs."

Ylva scrunched her face, confused.

"Sorry. Badass Mother Fuckers."

She grinned at that. "Yes. But more than the encounter itself, it is the statement of how the giant disappeared I find most intriguing."

"Well, the Jotnar do seem to do that. Smash up a city, run back into the forest, and we can't find a trace of them. I know your country has lots of forests they can hide in, but with all the aircraft we have up there you'd think we would have spotted some of them by now."

McShane cocked his head. "You think there are some tunnels they use? Maybe ones that lead to a spaceship."

"I have another theory, but first," she grabbed a printout of a map of Southern Norway, "I checked the bibliography, read up on this particular missionary, and located the village where he talked to the boy. It was not far from present-day Nome."

"That's where we tracked the Jotnar after their attack on Drangedal. We spotted footprints on one side of the river, but not the other, like . . . like they disappeared into thin air."

"I did more research on the area," said Ylva. "I checked cryptozoology and paranormal websites for any stories about giants in Telemark, but did not find anything. Then I looked into missing persons reports. There are several for that specific area."

She picked up her notepad. "1797, 1822, 1835. Three different reports of farmers who said they were going fishing at that river, but never returned. In 1913, two brothers went for a swim and were never seen again. In 1942, two German soldiers went into the forest with two women from Nome. None of them ever came back. The Germans thought the resistance might have killed them and executed twenty innocent people in the town. More recently, a teenage couple who went there for a swim in 1964 were reported missing, as well as a father and his young son in 1982. Those last two I confirmed through police records and the report from World War Two came from the Norwegian Resistance Museum."

McShane nodded. "So the Jotnar's home is probably somewhere near that river. Maybe they popped up when those people were there and killed them."

"I think it is more than that. In all the human disappearances, nothing was ever mentioned about large footprints, felled trees, or any other evidence of a Jotunn attack. All of them vanished without a trace. Then there was the encounter the Vikings had in the Eleventh Century. They could clearly see the giant and it disappeared right in front of them, in an instant."

"Some sort of teleportation?"

"I do not think so." Ylva shook her head. "I think our theory that they are of alien origin is wrong. I think the Jotnar, and likely the dragon, come from a place much closer."

"Where?" asked McShane.

"I think these creatures originate from a parallel world."

TWENTY-FOUR

Ylva's explanation did not stun McShane. Jotnar and dragons existed, likely created by . . . someone. So how far-fetched was it to talk about the existence of parallel worlds?

He also thought about the footprints he discovered after the Drangedal attack. They had been on one side of the river, but not the other. The water had not been deep enough for them to sink completely, so if they had not crossed it, where had they gone?

"So you're saying there's some kind of . . . gateway along that river."

"Yes." Ylva nodded.

"Those disappearances you mentioned date back centuries," said McShane. "How come more people haven't stumbled across it?"

"That part of the river is in a remote location. I doubt many people go there, and it's not an area where boats travel."

"So how did this gateway form?"

"Maybe whoever made the Jotnar or the dragon also created a portal to our world. Or it could have formed naturally. Portals to other worlds is one theory to explain mysterious disappearances in areas like the Bermuda Triangle, the Devil's Sea in the Pacific, the Alaska Triangle, and the *Untersberg* Mountain in Austria."

McShane stared at the floor in thought. "Well, it certainly would explain why the Jotnar and the dragon seem to just vanish." He smiled and clutched her shoulder. "See, I told you you'd find out where these things come from."

Ylva grinned and patted his hand. "Thank you, but it is just a theory."

"Then how about we go prove your theory is correct."

***

McShane submitted a request to Colonel Esposito to search the river outside Nome for the gateway to another world. He expected it to be shot down. Along with the idea sounding preposterous – at least to someone like his CO – it wasn't like Esposito thought highly of him even before his disobedience at Drammen.

So it surprised him when the colonel approved the mission.

"He probably did it just to get you out of his hair," Cain theorized when McShane told him.

Fine by him. McShane didn't care what Esposito's true reasons were, just as long as he got permission.

With Eastwick's Viper still grounded for maintenance, he picked Hunter for his wingman. He also would not have Johnson as his co-pilot/gunner. Taking his seat would be Ylva. Her expertise in mythology could come in handy with whatever they might find on the other side of the gateway, if it existed.

He helped her into the front seat and gave her a quick rundown of the TopOwl helmet before she slid it over her head. He then connected her to the ICS so they could talk in flight.

"You good?" he asked.

"Yes." She took a quick breath, her face ablaze with excitement. "This is the first time I've ever been in a helicopter."

"I promise no puke-inducing maneuvers." He gently patted the top of her helmet and climbed into the rear of the cockpit.

McShane's Viper lifted off, followed by Hunter's. The two choppers swung south to begin their 100-mile flight to the river. Ylva constantly moved her head left and right, apparently scanning the scenery below, especially when they left Oslo behind and forests and hills stretched out before them.

"The view is incredible," she said.

"Yes it is," replied McShane. "And it never gets old."

"You doing okay over there, Professor?" radioed Hunter.

"I am, Clubber, thank you. I was just saying how beautiful the scenery is from up here. And I love this helmet you get to wear. All the displays you have are amazing. It's better than any video game I've played."

"Glad you're enjoying the flight," replied Hunter. "And you're certainly in good hands with Captain McShane."

"Yes I am." Ylva turned and flashed him a smile. He smiled back.

The levity and sightseeing ended when they approached Nome. It was all business at that point.

They found the part of the river the Jotnar had traversed. The large, rectangular footprints remained, though partially worn away by recent weather.

"Well, there's no big glowing portal like you see in Marvel movies," said Hunter. "So how do we find this thing?"

McShane circled the river, thinking the same thing. No aircraft had disappeared while searching for the Jotnar or the dragon in this area. Probably because they were hundreds or thousands of feet off the ground. So this portal probably did not extend too high into the sky. He guessed it had to be at least forty feet in height to allow the Jotnar to pass through it. As for the width, the dragon's wingspan was about seventy feet, so maybe seventy-five or eighty feet for the portal.

Or maybe smaller. Maybe the dragon had to fold in its wings in order to enter and exit the portal.

"So do we just fly down the river until we go through the portal?" asked Ylva.

"No way." McShane shook his head. "Our rotor diameter is forty-eight feet. If that portal's forty-five or forty-six feet across, that won't be good for us."

"Oh. Good point. I didn't think of that. Sorry."

"No problem. We'll just have to come up with another way."

"We could fire a Hellfire along the length of the river," Tudoran suggested. "If it disappears, there's our portal to . . . wherever."

McShane was about to sign off on that idea when a thought struck him. "I don't like the idea of wasting ordnance we might need in a fight later. Plus, we don't know what's on the other side. What if that missile keeps going until it hits a village or a hunting party or a group of hikers? I don't want to be responsible for an international incident . . . or inter-dimensional incident with a race of people we've never met."

He continued to circle the river, thinking. Using missiles or rockets was out. Maybe land and throw rocks ahead of them? But if a Jotunn came through the portal, they had no means to make a fast escape.

What else could they do? What could they send through the portal that wouldn't be lethal to any innocent parties on the other side?

"Flares."

"What?" Ylva looked over her shoulder.

"We carry flares as counter-measures for heat-seeking missiles," replied McShane. "We can use those. Yeah, having one fall right on top of your head won't be good for your health, but it's less risky than firing an anti-tank missile to who knows where."

He glanced at the other Viper. "Clubber, Tooti. Cover me in case any Jotnar pop up."

"Copy, Mack," replied Hunter.

McShane hovered over the river where the footprints entered the water. Ylva dug a GoPro camera out of her pack and started recording as the Viper slowly descended. McShane halted fifty feet above the river, pointing the nose to the west bank, the rotorwash kicking up circular ripples in the water. He toggled the switch for manual control of the counter-measures and triggered a short burst. Bright orange flares streamed out the starboard side of the chopper.

"Cool," Ylva blurted. "It's like a miniature fireworks show."

The flares arced through the air and dropped toward the water and the bank. None of them vanished in thin air.

"All right. Second attempt."

McShane moved the Viper further down the river. He punched out another round of flares. He watched as they soared over the water, Ylva tracking them with her GoPro.

Four of the flares just vanished over the river.

McShane gawked at the spot of air. No, they had not burned out. They wouldn't have done that so quickly. They just . . . disappeared.

"Utrolig," Ylva spoke in a whispered tone. Maybe the Norwegian version of "My God" or "incredible," McShane thought.

"Clubber, Tooti. You guys see that, too?"

"That's affirmative, Mack," Hunter replied in an awed voice.

"Double affirmative," added Tudoran.

McShane looked down at the front seat. "Congrats, Ylva. Looks like your theory was spot on."

"It appears that way." She continued to point the GoPro at the portal. "But we will not know until we go through it."

"Before we do that, we need to figure out the size of this thing. Clubber, Tooti. Track my flares and calculate the height and width of this portal."

The pair acknowledged the order.

McShane moved back, up, and forward, firing off short bursts from the flare dispenser. He didn't care how many of the things he punched out. Jotnar did not use heat-seeking missiles.

Several flares vanished. Others soared into the river or the ground on the other side of the portal. He'd nearly exhausted his supply of flares by the time Tudoran made his calculations.

"Okay, Mack. From the center of the river, the portal is fifty feet in height, and sixty-five feet wide."

"Copy, Tooti." He gave a satisfied nod. They had enough clearance to fly the Viper through.

He glanced at the digital readout in his TopOwl helmet, checking his fuel status. "Okay, I have enough fuel for an hour of recon on the other side. If I'm not back in that time --"

"We'll come get you," said Hunter.

"Negative. Return to base and tell them about this place. No sense in losing two helicopters in there."

Ylva turned to him. He couldn't see her eyes through her visor, but the stiffness around her mouth radiated nervousness. As if his words showed her this was no longer some exciting adventure. This was deadly serious. A pang of regret went through him, but he'd be damned if he was going to lie and say there was no risk in traveling to another world no one ever imagined existed.

He gave her a reassuring nod. She tensed, but nodded back and faced forward, still recording with her GoPro. He smiled. The lady was a trouper.

McShane swung to the west bank of the river and fired a rocket into the ground, then did the same on the east bank. The craters would give him a visual reference on the boundaries of the portal. He then settled over the middle of the river and aimed the nose directly ahead.

"You ready for this?" he asked Ylva.

She exhaled. "Yes. Yes, let's do it."

McShane clenched the cyclic stick, eyes aimed straight ahead. "Go for broke."

The Viper shot forward.

TWENTY-FIVE

McShane didn't think he had gone through the gateway. There had been no science- fiction-like glow or weird lights or anything unusual like that. A forest still stretched before them. There wasn't any dramatic difference in the landscape.

Except . . .

"Makato?" Ylva leaned closer to the canopy. "Does it seem there are more trees out there?"

He scanned the forest. The trees did appear more plentiful than just a few seconds ago. He couldn't find any sort of clearing.

"You're right. The forest is thicker." McShane raised his head. "We also had clear skies a minute ago. Now look."

"It's . . . it's cloudy." Ylva's voice was nearly a whisper.

McShane gazed at the overcast sky for a few moments, then looked back at the ground. The river remained, cutting through the thick forest, staying straight for about a half-mile.

But instead of veering right as it had, it now curved left.

"No doubt about it, we are on another world." His words came out slowly as he tried to wrap his mind around this new reality.

"Utrolig," Ylva whispered in awe. She swept the GoPro left to right.

"Ma . . . s Club . . ." The words filtered out his headphones, wrapped in static, " . . .d me . . . ck . . . opy?"

"Clubber?" replied McShane. "Clubber, do you read me? We made it through. We are in some parallel world. Repeat, we are on a parallel world. Do you copy?"

More static and chopped words echoed in his helmet, ". . .py you. Ca . . . ference. Trying t . . ."

"Clubber? There's too much static. I can make barely make out what you're saying."

"Maybe the portal is interfering with the radio," suggested Ylva.

McShane grunted, then said, "Clubber, if you can hear me, we're all right and we're beginning our recon. See you in an hour."

He fired a rocket at each side of the river bank to again mark the edges of the gateway, then put the Viper into a climb. McShane leveled out at two thousand feet. Nothing but forest lay before them.

Well, I guess just pick a direction and see what we find.

McShane flew east, and by force of habit checked the GPS in his helmet-mounted display. It read "unavailable."

What did you expect? If there was some advanced civilization on this world, they might have their own version of a Global Positioning System, though one probably not compatible with the Viper's.

He'd have to navigate the old-fashioned way, checking his compass and noting prominent landmarks. Along with the river, there was a pair of humpback hills and a large lake several miles beyond. He shouldn't get lost.

McShane double-checked his gun camera and flight recorder to make sure both were functioning and continued east. Where the town of Nome should be, he and Ylva found nothing but dense trees. More forest lay ahead, along with another large lake.

"I think that is Lake Norsjø." Ylva pointed to it. "There should be all sorts of towns around it."

But there weren't. Just more trees.

After five minutes, McShane headed east. Neither he nor Ylva saw any signs of civilization. They also saw no Jotnar or dragons. So far, the first known exploration by humans on a parallel world had been uneventful.

The heavy forests continued. After five minutes McShane turned north and found more of the same. He groaned. There had to be something more than just trees here. He cursed himself for not attaching auxiliary fuel tanks to the chopper. They could have covered a lot more of this alternate Norway.

He tried to comfort himself with the fact that just discovering a gateway between his world and this one was remarkable enough. Still, he wanted to bring back more to the intel weenies than just miles and miles and miles of pristine forest.

McShane prepared to swing the Viper west when something caught his eye on the horizon. Something tall. Not a tree, but . . .

More objects appeared, rising above the trees. His eyebrows scrunched together.

"Ylva. Up ahead. Do you see that?"

"What?" She leaned forward. "Are those buildings?"

"I think so."

His anticipation spiked as they got closer to the buildings. Then concern gripped him. If this civilization could create rock monsters and dragons, they had to have some kind of sensor system that had detected his Viper. Would they scramble jets or some other sort of craft to intercept him? Would they just shoot him down?

When he was a few miles away from the buildings, those worries vanished.

The Target Sight System revealed large cracks and broken windows in all of the high rises. Several had massive chunks of the façade missing.

The forest thinned out. An entire city stretched before them. Or rather, what had been a city.

"My God," Ylva spoke in a hushed tone. "Look at this."

"Oh believe me, I am."

McShane took in the scene with unblinking eyes. The city had to be as large as Oslo. But no traffic circulated through its network of roads. He doubted any vehicles could navigate the streets as they were all choked with weeds, fallen trees, and other debris.

He saw other skyscrapers, or what remained of them. The top halves of several had been sheered off. Some had collapsed, along with many smaller buildings. What appeared to have been residential neighborhoods had been razed, save for a few dome structures that might fall in on themselves any moment. Several vehicles dotted the numerous streets, most oblong in shape. None of them moved. Judging by the rust, faded paint, and in some cases crumpled frames, they hadn't moved in many years. A large river weaved through the eastern section of the city. McShane counted three bridges, or at least, what would have been their entry and exit points. Twisted metal that should have been the spans poked out of the water.

One thing McShane didn't see was people. Not a single one.

"What happened here?" asked Ylva.

"No idea. But at least we know there's some civilized society that lives on this world . . . Or did."

"Could all their cities be like this?"

"I don't know."

"Maybe . . . maybe there was a war," said Ylva.

"That'd be my first guess," replied McShane. "If they can make Jotnar and dragons, who knows what other weapons they developed. If two sides like that fight an all-out war, well, it would probably end the same way a war between the U.S. and the Soviet Union would have back in the day."

Ylva gasped. "You mean they might have used nuclear weapons here?"

McShane's gut twisted at the thought. My God, had he flown them into a world ravaged by fallout? Were they being bombarded by radioactivity right this moment?

He closed his eyes and took a breath, recalling his mother's basic advice when it came to intelligence collection. "Rid yourself of fear and worry, then observe and analyze."

McShane stared at the ravaged cityscape. "I don't think so. If they used nukes, there'd probably be a big ass crater around here. And I don't think the forests would look as lush as they do with so much radiation around. I think we're good."

Ylva let out a breath. Her shoulders relaxed.

He relaxed as well, though a paranoid voice whispered in the back of his mind that he was wrong. McShane certainly couldn't call himself an expert in nuclear weapons.

He ignored the voice and continued flying, passing the outskirts of the city. Several miles away he spotted another structure. Several, actually. Some sort of complex with a number of rectangular buildings. But the most prominent feature had to be the five clamshell-shaped humps.

"What do you think that is?" Ylva pointed at it.

"I don't know. It's outside of the city. Maybe an industrial complex. Or a military base."

"Let's go see."

McShane checked his fuel status and ran some calculations in his head. He had enough in the tank to get back to the gateway. He'd have to refuel at Nome to make it back to base. Worth it if he could bring back good intel on this world.

He flew toward the complex and circled it. Two of the buildings had massive holes and piles of bricks and mortar around them. McShane guessed they took some hits in the war. The walkways and the parking lots had been overrun by weeds. Several oblong vehicles remained where their owners had parked them before whatever had happened, happened.

McShane hovered over the clamshells. Two of them were marred by holes and scorch marks. He ran his eyes up and down the structures. Seventy, maybe eighty feet in length.

"They look like some kind of . . . silos," he thought aloud. "But they don't look like they're for ballistic missiles."

Ylva straightened in her seat. "Dragons."

"What?"

"What if they are for dragons? They are large enough to accommodate them. Perhaps they grow them here and launch them if the Jotnar attack."

McShane stared at the clamshells. "Only one way to find out, and that's to do it at ground level."

"Cool." Ylva bounced a little in the front seat. McShane could sense her excitement. He couldn't blame her for the feeling. Down below could hold the secrets of the origin of monsters she believed to be only myths all her life.

McShane found a clear patch of ground on the east parking lot and set down. He retrieved a flashlight, canteen, first aid kit, and a couple of protein bars from his survival pack. Next he pulled out his Beretta and Ka-Bar, and let out a frustrated grunt. He should have foreseen doing recon on foot and requisitioned an M4 rifle or a Mossberg shotgun. What if they ran into some post-apocalyptic band of rape-happy cannibals? Or a bear or wolf or whatever sort of dangerous wildlife existed on this world? What good would a pistol and knife do against them?

He grunted again. Nothing he could do about it now. He had to go in with what he had. If serious shit went down, he'd do what Marines had always done since their inception: Adapt and overcome.

He opened the canopy and slid out, followed by Ylva. She clipped the GoPro to her jacket and looked around, eyes wide with amazement. Her mouth hung open for a few moments before she spoke. "We're actually standing on another world."

McShane stood still, letting the fact sink in. Another world. A place no one imagined existed. The place where the dragon and the Jotnar had come from, along with the civilization that created them. What had been their history? Why had there been a war? Was every city on the planet like this one? Surely there had to be pockets of survivors somewhere. Would they be human, human-like, or something else?

He shook off the thoughts. Speculation would get them nowhere. Searching the complex would.

They walked across the parking lot, the weeds coming up well past their ankles. Ylva stopped at one of the vehicles, checking it over.

"Look. It has no wheels."

McShane gazed at the bottom. Indeed, there were no wheels. "Maybe it uses some sort of maglev technology." He used the term for magnetic levitation.

Neither of them found a discernable hood. They moved on, glancing at the other abandoned vehicles. They also had no wheels. McShane and Ylva headed toward the clamshells.

"Makato?"

"Yeah?"

"I'm curious. What did you mean, what you said before we entered the gateway?"

"Huh?" His forehead wrinkled.

"The phrase you used. 'Go for broke.' What does that mean?"

"Oh. That was the motto for my great-grandfather's unit. Basically, it means to put it all on the line to accomplish something."

"I guess we certainly did that." Ylva looked around. "We really had no idea what would be waiting for us on the other side."

"That's for damn sure."

The pair reached the clamshells, which rose about sixty feet in the air. The holes in the two silos were much too high for them to reach, and neither he nor Ylva could find a ladder.

"Looks like we'll have to go through the buildings," said McShane.

They cut a path through the high weeds toward the nearest building. Some of the windows had been busted out. The walls bore chips and scars, but the structure was made out of solid marble, so McShane didn't worry about it collapsing.

He stopped at the door, staring at . . .

"A doorknob?"

"What about it?" asked Ylva.

He shrugged. "I don't know. I guess I've watched too much *Star Trek*. I figured a really advanced civilization would have all sliding doors."

McShane tried the knob. It twisted fully. He guessed locking a door hadn't been important for people trying to escape an apocalypse.

That got him thinking of post-apocalyptic boogeymen.

He waved Ylva to move to the side, then brought up his pistol. He glanced over to her. "Ready?"

She grinned. "Go for broke."

McShane flashed her a smile, turned back to the door, and kicked it in.

TWENTY-SIX

McShane peeked around the doorway, Beretta up, and stared down the corridor. Nothing. He swept his pistol to the right, then leaned around the frame and checked to the left.

"Clear."

He moved forward, followed by Ylva. The room was spacious, with a number of boxes and containers. All were open and empty, several laying on their side.

"Looks like some kind of supply room," said McShane. "Stripped bare."

"I wonder what was in these boxes?" asked Ylva.

"Could be anything from parts to a time machine to something as mundane as office supplies."

They crossed the length of the room to another door. McShane opened it and checked the corridor. Deserted. Not even so much as a rat skulking about. He and Ylva went through, finding a row of doors on either side, all of them open. Faint sunlight spilled out of the rooms. Probably from windows.

They looked through the first doorway on the left. A curved desk was planted near the window, with a chair knocked on its side. McShane and Ylva went inside. The desk had nothing except a thick layer of dust. All the drawers had been left open, emptied of whatever contents they had contained. To their left was a narrow door, opened to some sort of closet. It, too, contained nothing.

The second office they went to was in a similar state. Same with the third. Though each one did have placards on the door with some sort of writing. Sharp lines, a few waves, and half-ovals.

"Any idea what all this is?" he asked Ylva.

She stepped closer to the placard. "They appear similar to Norse runes. But not like any I have ever studied."

The next four offices they searched also contained nothing of consequence.

"Maybe whoever was here evacuated before the complex was attacked and took everything with them," suggested Ylva.

"Or it could have happened after the war. There had to have been some survivors. They would have ransacked any building left standing for anything useful."

The next office they checked had also been picked clean. Same with the next one.

But not the one after.

"What's that?" Ylva wondered aloud as she walked toward the desk.

McShane gazed at the object that interested her. It resembled one of those square china dishes found in fancy restaurants, only with a clear surface. At least, it would have been clear it not for all the dust. The . . . thing was perched on a square base that had a small, plastic-looking bulge protruding from its front.

"It looks like a dish," said McShane. "But I have a feeling this thing wasn't made for food."

"I think so, too." Ylva aimed her gaze at the bulge. She reached out her finger, hesitated, and tapped it.

Nothing happened.

She grabbed the sides of the object, strained and lifted. It rose out of the desk, leaving a small, square-shaped gap in the middle. McShane used his hand to sweep away the dust that had accumulated in the gap. The sides and the bottom were made of some clear plastic-like substance.

"I'm wondering if it's some kind of device," he said.

"That is possible." Ylva stared at the gap. "It might have received its power from the desk itself. Or it could receive power through wireless means."

"Yeah. I guess a civilization that can make dragons and stone giants advanced beyond wires and power strips."

Ylva stuck the device in her pack. Hopefully some scientist back on their world could figure out what the hell it did.

The desk drawers were empty, like in all the other offices. The closet door had been left open. Unlike the others they had checked, this one was not empty. Someone had installed a small bookcase inside with four books, all leather-bound.

Ylva removed one of them, kicking up dust particles from the shelf. She walked near the window and opened the book. The sunlight flowing in showed lines of runic writing similar to the placards on the doors. She sighed and shook her head. "I cannot make out any of these symbols."

"Then let's take it back with us," said McShane. "Hopefully there are linguists around who can translate these scribbles."

Ylva tucked the book into her pack, then grabbed another one out of the closet. McShane took the remaining two.

They trekked deeper into the complex, finding more offices, along with what appeared to be research or engineering stations. Some had tubular chambers and large aquarium-type structures. Equipment too big to be moved in a hurry or salvaged by bands of post-apocalyptic survivors. As to their purpose, McShane couldn't begin to guess.

He and Ylva descended a flight of stairs, heading for the sub-levels. That meant no more windows, no more sunlight. Both got out their flashlights. McShane held his in his left hand, keeping the pistol in his right.

They played their beams back and forth along the wide corridor. A musty odor hung in the air. A carpet of dust lay at their feet. McShane again tried to estimate when this world had gone into the shitter. Twenty years? Fifty? A hundred? Longer?

The pair found another room with three rows of tables and some kind of filthy crystalline circle embedded in the wall. A screen? Some sort of control room? Security station?

Twenty feet down the corridor they discovered another room with a steel door. Or rather, it used to have a steel door. It now lay on the floor, the hinges cut off by something. McShane shined his light inside, gritting his teeth at what he found.

"Shit," he muttered.

"What is it?" asked Ylva.

"Advanced society or not, I know weapons racks when I see them."

Ylva winced. "And they are all empty."

He nodded, concern clawing at him. He could only imagine what sort of small arms this sort of civilization could produce. Weapons perhaps in the hands of people desperate to do anything to survive.

McShane sensed the pistol in his hand. How inadequate he felt with it. Once again, he cursed himself for not bringing an M4 or a shotgun. Or a SAW. Or a grenade launcher. Hopefully whatever band of wasteland mutants might have taken those weapons had long since moved on, or got wiped out by another band of wasteland mutants who also had long since moved on.

They continued down the corridor, McShane shining his flashlight behind them, just in case. The beam picked up nothing but empty space.

He and Ylva entered another room. A dust-covered table and three chairs took up the center. A sofa had been set up against the wall to his right. To his left was a bar top counter. Could be a breakroom, he guessed.

A large, rectangular object stood behind the countertop, its door open. A refrigerator? Nothing inside it, of course. Anything that might have contained food would have been cleaned out long ago.

McShane started toward it when Ylva called out, "Makato, look at this."

He followed her flashlight beam along the wall, adding his a second later.

"Whoa." His eyes widened.

Drawings covered the wall. All the walls. Very detailed ones. McShane settled his beam on one image in particular, a round man with a snow-white beard and intense dark eyes, hands raised. Above him were three dragons.

He examined the other drawings. Dragons diving out of the sky, flame shooting from their mouths. Fire consumed a group of people and a six-wheeled vehicle McShane guessed was some sort of infantry fighting vehicle. His brows scrunched together when he noticed something else about the scene. There were people sitting on the dragons, flying them.

More drawings wrapped around the four walls. His light swept over scenes of dragons and Jotnar engaged in battle, of destroyed cities, of elaborate cities with domes and needle-like towers, and dragons soaring over them. Protecting them, he wondered?

"Looks like a mural," said McShane.

"I think it is more than that. I think it is part of their history." Ylva walked over to the wall on her left, slowly moving her flashlight back and forth. McShane joined her.

"See that man." She pointed. "The one with the white beard. He appears three times along this wall. Here with dragons flying over his head, here pointing at dragons on the ground, and here directing dragons, dragons being flown by one group of people attacking another group."

Ylva turned to McShane. "Who does the white-bearded man remind you of?"

"A badass version of Santa Claus."

Ylva softly chuckled, then said, "Think Norse mythology."

McShane straightened. "Odin." He moved the flashlight back and forth over the drawings of the bearded man. "You're saying Odin, or the person he's based on, created dragons?"

"I do not think this person created them. This looks more like he is training them."

Her mouth hung open wordlessly before looking back at McShane. "I think dragons are, or maybe were, actual creatures on this world. I mean, part of the natural order."

"So first the people here trained them to become weapons, then years or centuries later, they could genetically engineer them to make them more powerful."

"Possibly." Ylva turned back to the wall. "My God," she spoke in an amazed whisper. "We could be looking at the foundations of Norse mythology right here."

She whirled around to face him. "Remember the reports I told you about people who had gone missing in the forests near Nome?"

"Yeah."

"What if not all of them disappeared? What if some people stumbled through the gateway, but found their way back to our world?"

"Bringing back stories of a big white-bearded guy commanding an army of dragons." McShane aimed his flashlight at the image of the combat vehicle. "And if that . . . IFV is any indication, the people here were hundreds of years more advanced than the Vikings. Skyscrapers, motorized vehicles, maybe planes and computers."

"That person's mind would not be able to comprehend such things," Ylva continued for him. "Their only explanation would be magic."

"Making the people wielding that sort of magic gods. The Norse Gods."

Ylva nodded, then swept her light across the next wall, and the one after that. The dragon images no longer had riders. This was probably the point in their history when the beasts had been genetically modified, apparently able to seek out the enemy on their own. Like a living smart bomb.

"Look at these images." Ylva's flashlight lingered for a few seconds on three drawings, each one depicting dragons breathing fire at Jotnar. In all three, groups of people sheltered behind the dragons.

The beam then settled over a pair of images, with two armies battling it out with rifles, saucer-shaped vehicles with two big guns – tanks, McShane figured – and manta-shaped craft that could be this world's version of fighters. Both scenes also showed dragons and Jotnar fighting.

"Notice how in the images where people are riding dragons," said Ylva, "they attack the people from what appears to be an enemy nation. But in the later ones, where the dragons fight by themselves, they only attack Jotnar."

"Mm." McShane stared at the mural, thinking. Given what an effective killing machine their dragon was, why only limit it to taking out Jotnar? It could just as easily destroy aircraft, armor, troop formations, bunkers.

"They didn't want to risk fratricide."

"What?" asked Ylva.

"Friendly fire." McShane looked at her. "Think of all the NATO troops you've been around the past few weeks. American, Norwegian, British, German, Dutch. How different are all our uniforms?"

"Not very. You all seem to wear the same splotches of green, brown, and black."

"Exactly. We all have different patterns to our camo, but to Joe and Jane Civilian, all our fatigues look the same. So how do you get a dragon to differentiate between two sets of uniforms?"

"Perhaps train it somehow to recognize enemy uniforms." Ylva gazed up at the darkened ceiling in apparent thought. "Actually, a civilization capable of this level of genetic engineering might be able to program some kind of uniform recognition into its brain."

"Maybe, but you've heard the phrase 'fog of war' before?"

"Yes."

"Combat is chaos. Noise, explosions, smoke. It could be taking place at night or in bad weather. It can be hard to tell who are the good guys and the bad guys, especially from the air. During the First Gulf War, one of our A-10s blew up a couple of LAV-25 armored vehicles and killed eleven Marines. In fact, a quarter of our KIA in Desert Storm was due to friendly fire."

Ylva gasped. "My God. I had no idea."

McShane turned back to the wall. "At this stage in their timeline, it looks like the dragons act as autonomous weapons. Let 'em loose, fly around, and engage any Jotnar they come across. You wouldn't want it accidentally mistaking a group of your troops for the enemy."

"So instead of programming them to not attack certain humans, they programmed them not to attack *any* humans." Ylva shined her light on one of the scenes with people sheltered behind dragons. "Asimov."

"What?" McShane's brow furrowed.

"Isaac Asimov. You are familiar with *I, Robot?* The book, not the terrible movie."

"I never read the book, but I know about his robotic laws. Robots can't harm people or allow people to be harmed, and they can protect themselves so long as they don't violate those two tenants."

Ylva nodded. "The people here probably programmed similar commands into the dragons. It is probably why our dragon saved you and Lieutenant Johnson before your helicopter crashed."

"It would also explain why it didn't attack us when we were shooting it," said McShane. "I guess the dragon really is on our side."

Ylva tsked. "We do need to give it a proper name. We cannot just keep calling it the dragon."

"You're the mythology expert, so I'll leave that up to you."

Ylva smiled before they headed back into the corridor. They followed it to a T-junction, turned right, and found a rectangular opening. Sunlight poured down from the open clamshell doors above, washing over an immense, empty aquarium tank.

"Looks like we were right," said McShane. "This must be where they kept the dragons when they weren't at war." He gazed up at the clamshell doors. "When the balloon went up, they launched them from here. Kinda like our ICBMs."

The pair moved down the corridor to the other silos. All the doors had been left open. The tanks in the second and third silos were empty.

Not so the fourth one.

Ylva gasped at the skeletal remains of a dragon lying in a dark yellow liquid.

"What happened to it?" she asked.

"Who knows? Maybe some malfunction that kept them from launching it."

Squaring her shoulders, Ylva walked toward the tank, McShane next to her.

"I wonder if this liquid keeps the dragon in suspended animation," she said. "When this place was abandoned, there was no one to maintain its operation and it died."

She pinched the GoPro between her thumb and index finger and angled it up, probably to get a better shot of the tank and the remains within. McShane ran his gaze over it. The beast seemed smaller than their dragon. Forty, forty-five feet or so. He wondered how many such facilities were scattered around this version of Norway, or this entire world. Could other dragons be out there, alive and well, carrying on the fight against the Jotnar despite their human masters being gone? If so, NATO needed to find them so –

Something growled.

McShane's pistol came up. He stared into a darkened corner on the far side of the silo.

"You heard that, too?" whispered Ylva, her eyes wide with fear.

McShane nodded. He lifted the flashlight, the beam penetrating the shadowy corner.

Two blazing yellow eyes stared back at him.

TWENTY-SEVEN

Terror punched through McShane's gut. He locked eyes with the wolf. Not a normal wolf. It had to be more than twice the size of any such animal he'd ever seen at a zoo, with thick, matted black fur. Its jaws opened, revealing rows of sharp teeth.

He fired his Beretta three times. Ylva jumped.

The wolf roared.

"Run!" McShane pushed Ylva ahead of him. They sprinted toward the door.

The wolf unleashed a chilling howl and bounded after them.

He and Ylva rushed into the corridor. They bolted toward the T-intersection, McShane looking over his shoulder.

The wolf pounded across the dusty floor, teeth bared.

McShane fired twice. The beast didn't slow down.

Piece of shit, he thought to his pistol and dashed into the next corridor.

"In here." He grabbed Ylva's arm and pulled her into the break room.

McShane slammed the door shut and raced over to the couch. With Ylva's help, they pushed it across the floor and against the door.

A horrific *thump* shook the door. It cracked in the middle. The couch got propelled back a few inches. McShane shoved it back in place.

"I don't think that will keep it out," said Ylva.

"I also don't think we can outrun it."

The door buckled again. A hole appeared in the middle. The wolf growled.

He waved Ylva to follow. They ran around the countertop and behind the refrigerator. Both shut off their flashlights and sat against it. Ylva pressed against his shoulder. He could feel her shaking. Dammit, why did he bring her here? If anything happened to her . . .

The door shattered. Ylva flinched.

McShane leaned close to her face, a finger against his lips. She swallowed and nodded.

"We're gonna get out of this," he said as softly as possible, putting a reassuring hand on her knee.

Her face stiffened and she nodded.

Now you just gotta come up with a plan. He held his breath as the wolf's big paws thumped against the floor. It let out a low growl.

What the hell could he do against this thing? His pistol was useless. The only other weapon he had was his Ka-Bar. He didn't like his chances going knife to claw and teeth with that mega-wolf. There was nothing in the breakroom he could use as a weapon.

The paws thudded closer to the refrigerator.

His head snapped up. He looked at the fridge. Maybe . . .

McShane peeked around the corner. The wolf stalked around the countertop, those evil yellow eyes aimed right at the refrigerator.

He twisted around, got in a catcher's crouch, then turned to Ylva, keeping his voice low. "When I tell you, push with everything you've got."

Drawing quick breaths, she looked up at the refrigerator, then back to him, and nodded. She also got into a crouch, both hands on the fridge.

McShane poked his head out as far as he dared. The wolf growled and angled to the right.

"Now."

McShane pushed. So did Ylva.

The refrigerator toppled over. The wolf snarled.

The fridge crashed on top of it. The beast let out a half-bark, half-whine.

"Go!" he shouted.

Ylva ran past. He followed, staring back at the wolf. It was sprawled on all fours, hacking, trying to push itself up. The refrigerator rose a couple of inches.

Flashlight beams bouncing along the floor and walls, McShane and Ylva sprinted down the corridor and up the stairs.

"Did we kill it?" Ylva asked over her shoulder.

"Not even close. We just stunned it. Barely." Hopefully enough to give them time to reach the Viper.

They made it to the first floor and turned down the hallway of research rooms.

A howl rose from the sub-level.

He and Ylva ran faster.

They dashed past the offices when another howl echoed off the walls. Lungs burning, he and Ylva hurried across the supply room and through the door leading outside. McShane's eyes flickered from the stationary Viper to Ylva. Her mouth hung open and she breathed heavily, but she kept going.

The two reached the helicopter. McShane threw open the canopy and half-shoved Ylva into the front seat. She pulled on her TopOwl helmet, pressing a hand against her chest and panting hard.

McShane slammed the canopy shut and started the engine. The rotors slowly turned.

"Ma-Makato," Ylva blurted as best she could, pointing a shaky finger.

The wolf charged through the door, heading straight for the Viper. McShane stared up at the rotors. The spinning picked up, but nowhere near enough for liftoff.

The wolf didn't break stride. McShane had no doubt the damn thing could crash through the canopy and rip him and Ylva to shreds.

At least now, he had a far better weapon than a pistol.

He brought up the crosshairs for the 20mm gatling gun in his helmet-mounted display, pointed directly ahead.

The wolf was just to the right of it, running full out, less than thirty yards away.

McShane moved his head right. The three-barreled gun, slaved to the helmet, slewed with it.

Ylva pressed herself against her seat when McShane pulled the trigger. The gatling gun buzzed. The wolf's head, its entire front half, vanished in a volcanic blast of red. What remained of the body collapsed on its side.

McShane let out a long exhale and fell back into his seat. He closed his eyes, willing his heart to slow down. They were alive. He'd saved Ylva.

"You okay?" he asked her.

"Yes, I . . . I think so." She pressed a hand against her chest. "I don't think I've ever been so scared in my life."

"Yeah, this is definitely in my personal top five." McShane stared out at the bloody chunks that used to be the mega-wolf. "Well, at least there's one monster on this world we can kill without the dragon's help."

His focus switched to Ylva below, still breathing hard. He reached down and gripped her shoulder. She rested her chin against his gloved hand. McShane closed his eyes, relishing the feeling, wanting to take Ylva in his arms and never let go of her.

Hard as it was, he pushed down his thoughts and desires. They were still on a hostile world. Who knew how many other threats lurked?

"Any objection to going home?" he asked.

"None." Ylva shook her head. "None at all."

The rotors finally spun fast enough to give him the lift he needed. The Viper rose.

"I wonder . . ." Ylva paused.

"What?"

"That wolf. I wonder if it, or rather its species, was the basis for the legend of Fenrir."

"The wolf that ate Odin?" McShane looked at the bloody pile of black fur below. "Doesn't look like much of a badass now, does it?"

He scanned the wrecked facility, checked to his right, then his left. "Makato! Jotnar!"

He guessed Ylva saw them the same time he did. Two rock giants, standing on a hill half-a-mile from the complex. They stared at him as the Viper climbed higher. Thankfully, they were well beyond their effective tree flinging range.

The monsters retreated down the reverse slope of the hill. McShane observed them as they ran through the forest, knocking down pines.

He cocked his eyebrow. Why hadn't they charged at him, tried to get closer for a tree shot? Why run without a fight?

Could they be . . .

McShane swung the Viper in the direction of the fleeing Jotnar.

"Where are you going?" asked Ylva.

"I got a feeling about those two."

He continued to fly higher. Four thousand feet. Five thousand. McShane didn't plan on attacking them, just observing. No need to be in their throwing range for observation.

The Viper reached 5,500 feet when he caught sight of something in the distance. Rows of jagged brown. He leaned closer. Were they moving?

He aimed the chopper at them. Within a minute, the mass of brown took on more distinctive shapes. He zoomed in with the Target Sight System.

"Oh my God," Ylva stammered. She must have seen it on the TSS in her helmet display.

All of McShane's muscles tightened as the camera swept over the gathering of Jotnar. Well over a hundred. Maybe well over two hundred. He tried to clamp down on his shock and fear as he kept the Viper level.

"Look at them," awe filled Ylva's voice. "If they all come through the gateway . . ."

"Yeah. It's gonna be a bad day for Norway. Maybe all of Scandinavia, all of Europe."

McShane took another look at the image of all the stone giants, imagining Oslo in ruins with dozens of wrecked tanks and helicopters scattered about the rubble.

"I think we've got enough footage for the intel weenies. We need to get back and warn NATO what's coming."

He swung the Viper around, flying over the city and descending toward the river. He followed the snaking line of water, checking his fuel. They had more than enough to reach the gateway, but would have to refuel to make it back to Gardermoen. Nome had a small airfield. McShane could top off there no problem.

He turned down another bend, dropping to treetop level. Not long before he was back in his world.

McShane pointed the nose straight down the middle of the river, descending lower. The gateway lay just ahead.

"Oh shit." His eyes widened.

On each side of the river bank where the gateway was located stood two Jotnar.

TWENTY-EIGHT

Muscles tight, McShane stared straight ahead. Whole squadrons of attack helicopters had not been able to put down a single Jotunn. Now here he was, a lone Viper against two of the monsters, blocking the only way back to his world.

"What are we going to do?" Ylva's voice cracked.

"Only one thing to do . . . fight."

He armed the Hellfires and rocket pods as the Jotunn to his right tore a tree out of the ground. McShane tagged its face with the laser and launched a Hellfire. The missile rode the beam right into its nose. Smoke and flame leapt off the giant's face.

Yellow streaks flashed from the rocket pods. A string of explosions burst across the Jotunn's body. The top half of the tree it held blew apart, flaming chunks of wood spiraling through the air.

McShane veered right and sent another volley of rockets into the head and shoulders of the second Jotunn. Ylva gasped as he threw the chopper into a hard right turn. It was the best plan he had. Shoot them, hopefully piss them off, and get them to chase him through the forest. He'd lure them a mile or two from the river, turn around, and make for the gateway. No way could they catch up to the Viper before he made it back to his world.

He checked behind him. One of the Jotnar tromped through the forest after him.

"Shit," he hissed, noticing the other one remained at its post. Did they do that intentionally, make sure at least one of them blocked the gateway? Just how smart were these fucking monsters?

A tree soared toward the Viper. McShane slammed the stick right. The tree flew harmlessly past. He zigzagged to throw off the Jotunn's aim, glancing at his fuel gauge. Combat maneuvers ate up gas, and he'd already gone through a lot of it getting to Nome, then flying recon on this world. If he didn't end this fight soon, they'd be crashing in the forest or in the river. Should he and Ylva survive, they'd be sitting ducks for the Jotnar.

He continued flying away from the first giant. It threw another tree, missing. A little farther, then he could circle back and only have one Jotunn to fight at the gateway instead of two. But even one Jotunn would be difficult, maybe impossible to defeat by himself.

McShane flew on for another minute before checking the Jotunn behind him. It had to be about two miles from the river. Good enough. He banked the chopper right and headed back to the gateway. The Jotunn launched another tree through the air. It came nowhere close to his Viper.

"Clubber, it's Mack," he said into the radio. "Do you read me?"

His only reply was static.

"Clubber. Clubber, respond. We are under attack by two Jotnar. One of them is standing in front of the gateway. If you can hear me, fire every Hellfire you have through the gateway."

Again, "Clubber" Hunter did not reply.

McShane hissed in frustration. No back up from the other side. It was all on him.

The Jotunn remained in front of the gateway, a pine tree in each of its massive hands. It made no move to hurl the trees at him. It just stood there, almost daring him to get past.

McShane flew down the river, right at the son-of-a-bitch. He locked on a Hellfire and sent it flying. A ball of orange and black erupted from the Jotunn's neck. It didn't even flinch.

The monster raised the tree in its left hand. McShane fired a short burst from the rocket pods. The pine exploded, flaming wooden debris falling to the ground. Another volley blew up the tree in its right hand. The Jotunn turned, reaching for another tree along the river bank. McShane thumbed the fire button. Flame spat from the rocket pods. Some projectiles missed, throwing up geysers of water or vanishing into the gateway. Others struck its side and shoulder without harm.

Two rockets exploded against its left knee. The Jotunn staggered.

McShane's brow furrowed. He stared hard at the giant's knee, smoke curling off the stone skin. He thought back to other battles with the Jotnar. Hadn't there been a couple of times when they'd taken a stutter-step after getting hit in the leg? Or a specific area of it?

His mind took him back to his hand-to-hand combat courses, to something one of his instructors said. A new plan formed.

He broke away from the Jotunn. It flung a tree at him. McShane dodged it. He circled around as the giant ripped out another tree and threw it. Ylva gasped as he banked left to avoid it. McShane pointed the laser designator at the Jotunn's left leg and mashed the fire button.

Please let this work.

A Hellfire shot off the right wing stub. McShane held his breath as the missile closed with the Jotunn.

An explosion tore through its knee. The giant stumbled, nearly collapsing.

"You hurt it!" Ylva jumped in the front seat.

McShane didn't respond. He lined up for another shot and fired. A second Hellfire exploded against the Jotunn's knee. It staggered and sank to the ground. He zoomed in with the TSS as the Jotunn struggled to get back on two feet. The left knee was shredded, barely connected to the lower leg.

He fired a third Hellfire. The knee vanished in smoke and fire. The lower part of the left leg fell away. The Jotunn fell on its side.

"You did it!" Ylva shrieked.

"Oo-rah!" McShane barked. "I had a hand-to-hand combat instructor who told us the knee is one of the most vulnerable parts of the human body. Looks like it applies to Jotnar, too."

"Speaking of Jotnar." Ylva pointed.

The remaining stone giant charged through the forest, tree held high in its hand. It reared back and threw the wooden missile.

McShane banked right. The tree missed him by twenty yards. He swung the Viper's nose at the monster, readying another Hellfire.

"Makato! The other Jotunn." Ylva stabbed a finger toward the ground.

The one-legged Jotunn pushed itself up to a kneeling position, its left hand flat against the ground to balance itself. It reached out with its right hand and grabbed a tree.

McShane's jaw tightened. He only had three Hellfires left. He glanced at the small craters on either side of the river marking the location of the gateway. Could he fly straight through it without one of these monsters knocking him and Ylva out of the sky?

Before he could decide, another Viper suddenly appeared over the water.

"Clubber?" he blurted.

"Mack?" she radioed back. "You --"

"Jotunn on your left!" McShane hollered. "Jotunn on your left!"

The monster wrenched another tree out of the ground, eyeing Hunter's helicopter.

"Shit." She lifted the Viper's nose and shot into the sky. The Jotunn reared back with the tree.

McShane fired a volley of rockets. They exploded along its chest and face. The Jotunn redirected its hollow, dark eyes toward him. He banked hard right as the tree soared over the river, missing him.

"Clubber. Knee. Go for the knee."

"Say again, Mack?"

"Aim for the knee. That's their weak spot. Three Hellfires will blow off its leg."

"Copy, Mack. Tooti?"

"Just bring us around and I'll lop off that bastard's leg," replied the co-pilot/gunner.

McShane swung around his Viper in time to see the one-legged Jotunn fling its tree. It was off-target by so much he didn't have to evade. He painted the monster's right knee with the laser designator and fired a Hellfire. The missile blew off chunks of rock. McShane let fly a second Hellfire. Out the corner of his eye, he caught an explosion on the left leg of the other Jotunn.

His second missile hit, throwing up a cloud of orange and brown. The Jotunn trembled and fell to its side. The right leg barely clung to what remained of the knee.

Tudoran's next two missiles found their mark. The other Jotunn's leg fell away, trailing smoke. It threw out its arms and toppled forward, its face and shoulders crashing into the river, sending up walls of water.

"Time to get the hell outta Dodge," said McShane. "Clubber, you first. I'll cover you."

"Copy, Mack. Heading out."

Hunter flew over the river. McShane's eyes flickered between the two monsters. The Jotunn he'd attacked had rolled onto its stomach and was clawing at the ground, either trying to push itself up or crawl away. The second one pushed its face out of the water.

Hunter's Viper disappeared.

McShane swung his chopper over the water and barreled toward the gateway. He passed the craters on either side of the river, then looked behind him. The Jotnar were not there.

"We're clear." His muscles uncoiled.

Ylva let out a loud sigh of relief. "Thank God."

"Heading east to Nome for refueling." McShane turned to Hunter's Viper, flying off his starboard side. "Clubber, Tooti. Thanks for the assist."

"No problem, Mack. We were orbiting the area when we saw some rockets go through the gateway. Thought you needed a hand."

"And now we know how to take those bastards down," added Tudoran.

"We still can't find a way to kill 'em with our weapons." McShane turned his Viper toward Nome, glancing at the fuel gauge. Just enough gas to get to the town. "But they're not gonna be much of a threat if they can't walk."

"So how did the recon go?" asked Hunter.

"We found an advanced civilization that created the dragon and the Jotnar," blurted Ylva. "Or I should say, we found the ruins of it. It looks as though they destroyed themselves in a war."

Hunter huffed. "Too bad they couldn't take all the Jotnar with them."

"Speaking of the Jotnar, we've got big trouble," said Mack.

"How big?" asked Hunter.

"It looks like they're done with raids. They're prepping for a full-scale invasion of Norway."

TWENTY-NINE

Two days. That's how long NATO intelligence personnel, scientists, and researchers took to debrief McShane and Ylva. They went over every frame of footage from his gun camera and her GoPro, asked endless questions, bandied about more theories than he could count. No one could say for certain how long ago the parallel world's apocalypse occurred, if anyone there might be controlling the Jotnar or the dragon, or how exactly the monsters had been created.

One thing everyone agreed on, the Jotnar were done messing around. The next time they came through the gateway, it would be a full-scale assault.

As soon as the debrief officially ended, Colonel Esposito ordered McShane to join Hammer Flight at an FOB – Forward Operating Base – in Nome. No time to rest or be with Ylva. They wanted him there yesterday.

He walked to his Viper, Ylva beside him. Holding his hand, squeezing it as hard as she could. They slowed as they neared the runway. Ylva pressed her lips together. Tears glistened in her eyes.

"Be . . . Be careful. Please."

"I will." McShane gave her hand a reassuring squeeze. "Who knows? Maybe our dragon will show up to give us a hand when the Jotnar come through."

"You mean Tuzvihar."

McShane's face scrunched. "Tuz-a-what?"

"You told me to come up with a name for the dragon, so I did. Tuzvihar. It's Hungarian for Firestorm."

"Why Hungarian?"

"I experimented on Google Translate for possible names. I thought Tuzvihar had a mythological ring to it."

McShane bobbed his head from side to side. "Yeah, it kinda does. Tuzvihar it is, then."

He took both of Ylva's hands, gave her a long kiss, then wrapped her in a crushing hug.

"Be careful." Her warm breath washed over his ear.

"I will."

They kissed again. With a final squeeze of her hand, McShane headed to his Viper. Johnson was already strapped into the co-pilot/gunner seat. They went through the pre-flight checklist, started the engine, and lifted off. He looked down at Ylva and waved. She waved back.

Swallowing against the lump in his throat, he turned the helicopter southwest.

***

McShane landed at a small airstrip several miles outside Nome proper, where he had refueled after returning from the other world. Then it had been home to three Alouette III scout helicopters from the Portuguese Air Force. Now it had grown significantly with dozens of helicopters and DRASHes spread out far beyond the little strip. Fuel trucks were lined up near the tree line. A pair of Marine LAV-25s, two Slovakian BVP-2 infantry fighting vehicles, and two Norwegian M113s, all packing anti-tank missiles, provided security.

He learned that was a pittance of the forces arrayed in and around Nome. The FOB's operations officer, a Norwegian Air Force major, showed him and Johnson the disposition of NATO forces. Three defensive lines had been set up, staggered six miles apart, made up of tanks, IFVs, self-propelled guns, and field cars and infantrymen with anti-tank weapons.

The major informed them that every airfield within a hundred-mile radius, from little dirt strips to large civilian airports, had been packed with combat aircraft from every NATO country. U.S. B-52 and B-1 bombers were already in the air or on standby at bases in England and Germany. Out in the North Sea, the carriers *USS Eisenhower, HMS Queen Elizabeth,* and Spain's *Juan Carlos I* were ready with their F/A-18s, F-35s, and Harriers.

"We have also sent squads of *Jegerkommandos,* U.S. Marine Force Recon, and German KSK to the other world, which is now designated World Bravo."

McShane managed to not roll his eyes. *Wow. What a creative name.* Why not call it Asgard? Especially if Ylva was right and it was indeed the birthplace of Norse mythology.

The major continued, "These units will provide us early warning should the Jotnar approach the gateway. They can communicate with each other by radio on World Bravo, but cannot get a signal through to our world. We are getting around that problem by stationing a squad of *Jegerkommandos* near the gateway to act as a relay unit. When one of the reconnaissance squads alerts them of Jotnar movement, they can quickly return to our world with the message."

"Good." McShane nodded. At least they'd have a heads up before a Jotnar attack.

He also learned Nome's entire population of 6,600-plus had been evacuated. With more than two hundred Jotnar expected to charge through the portal, no one wanted civilians anywhere near this battlespace. Given the raw power of the monsters and the massive NATO arsenal arrayed against them, there was a good chance Nome would be wiped off the map.

The briefing ended around dinner time. McShane and Johnson headed for the mess tent, where they found the rest of Hammer Flight.

"Mack. Go Around." Eastwick threw them a big wave. "We were wondering if we'd ever see you again."

"I thought you'd be gone even longer," added Hunter. "I figured every acronym agency in NATO would grill you."

"They did." McShane sat at the table. "Even I thought it would take longer given all the footage Ylva and I brought back from Asgard."

Tudoran and Cain's brows knitted together in confused looks.

"That's what I'm calling that other world." McShane cut into his meatloaf with his fork. "Sounds a lot cooler than World Bravo."

"I'm down with that." Nunez nodded enthusiastically. "That's the problem with all those staff POGs." He used the term for Person Other than Grunt. "No imagination. They can't even come up with some cool name for the dragon."

"Ylva did. Tuzvihar."

Koosman drew his head back. "Da'fuck?"

"It's Hungarian for firestorm," said McShane.

Eastwick's face wrinkled in a doubtful expression. "She couldn't come up with something easier to pronounce?"

"Enough with talking about names." Nunez snapped his hand in a dismissive wave. "You and the prof were actually on a freakin' parallel world."

"Hello." Hunter turned to him. "So were me and Tooti."

"Yeah. For, like, two minutes." Elbows on the table, Nunez leaned toward McShane. "You did the full tour, man. We need details."

All the other pilots aimed their gazes at him. He spent the next twenty minutes talking about the ruined city, the complex where the dragons were apparently made, and the Fenrir-like wolf that chased him and Ylva.

"So now we've got monster wolves to worry about, too?" Koosman shook his head. "What the hell else are we gonna find over there?"

"Let's worry about the Jotnar for right now," said Cain. "They're the ones getting ready to storm Norway."

"Stripes is right." McShane sipped his coffee. "Any other monsters over there, we can deal with later." *If any of us are still around.*

"At least we know how to take 'em out now," said Tudoran. "Tough to fight when you don't have any legs."

"I heard we're getting reinforcements from the States." Johnson looked around at the others. "Two more carrier groups are headed here. So's the First Cavalry Division."

"This thing might be over by the time they get here." Hunter stabbed a boiled potato with her fork.

"Tanks and carriers? That's nothing," scoffed Nunez. "There's stories going around that us, the Brits, and the French got missile subs out in the North Atlantic. We can't stop the Jotnar, they're gonna nuke Norway off the map."

"Oh, come on," blurted Johnson. "There's no way we'd do that."

The corner of Cain's mouth curled. "I don't know. If these things start marching across Scandinavia and threaten the rest of the continent, we may not have a choice."

Hunter's shoulders sagged. "Well if they want to attack the rest of Europe, that means they'll have to go through Russia, and that means a whole new set of problems."

"You mean like the Russians launching nukes at the Jotnar." Cain grimaced. "Probably before they set one foot on their soil."

McShane pressed his fork on his meatloaf, staring at it, pondering various scenarios. What would the response be if the Russians dropped a nuke on Norway? Or even non-aligned countries like Sweden or Finland? Would NATO brush it aside as part of the fight against the Jotnar? Make a strongly-worded diplomatic protest? Or would one of those SSBNs in the Atlantic Nunez mentioned drop a missile on Moscow?

He held his breath. Would a war with the Jotnar ignite World War III?

***

McShane and Eastwick drew patrol for 2200 to 2400. They flew in a racetrack pattern twenty miles from the gateway. In the distance, red and white lights blinked in the nighttime sky. Two Dutch Apaches and two German Tigers also circled the forests outside Nome. High above, a pair of F/A-18s from the *Eisenhower* and two Norwegian F-16s fighters roamed. All of them ready to pounce if any Jotnar appeared.

So far, none did.

It only served to keep McShane on edge. Any second, he expected someone to radio that the Jotnar were approaching the gateway. Instead, the comms remained silent, except for routine check-ins with air controllers. Even Eastwick didn't seem up for his usual jovial banter. Tension weighed on everyone. When the Jotnar would attack, who the hell knew? NATO certainly couldn't intercept their communications like a human enemy. If those moans and groans they emitted were some sort of language, no one on Earth knew what the hell it meant. All they could do was wait for the special ops guys on Asgard to signal the Jotnar were on the move.

McShane looked in the direction of the gateway. Part of him almost wanted the monsters to invade. At least in combat he could focus on fighting the enemy. All this waiting gave him too much time to think, to concoct scenarios, most of them ending badly. He thought of his family, of Ylva, wondering if he'd ever see them again. He thought of the Jotnar advancing across Scandinavia and into Russia, of nukes exploding across Europe.

Nothing remotely exciting happened the entire patrol. He and Eastwick headed back to the FOB, letting the next patrols go round and round over the darkened forests of the Telemark region. The two men and their co-pilots headed back to their heated DRASH, stripped out of their flight suits, and climbed into bed.

McShane shut his eyes, his entire body tense. Would a klaxon sound during the night? Would they be able to stop the Jotnar? Would the dragon – Tuzvihar – come to help them? How was Ylva doing?

Somehow, he managed to fall asleep.

The flight awoke at 0500 and assembled with the Viper groundcrews for morning PT. Cain, fitness freak that he was, put them through his usual insane amount of pushups, crunches, burpees, and squats, followed by a three-mile run. The sky had become a brilliant canvass of purple, pink, and orange by the time they finished. McShane sucked down lungfuls of cool air, his olive-green physical training uniform soaked with sweat. He started back to his DRASH with the rest of the pilots, looking forward to a shower, breakfast, and a day of sitting on his thumb and spinning wondering when the Jotnar would –

Klaxons screamed throughout the FOB.

THIRTY

McShane froze for a split-second. His heartbeat kicked into high gear.

This is it.

He raced to his DRASH with the rest of Hammer Flight. McShane stripped off his sweaty PTUs, pulled on his flight suit, and hurried to the flight line. Other NATO pilots ran for their helicopters. He nearly vaulted into the cockpit of his Viper, Johnson joining him seconds later.

The rotors began spinning when one of the air controllers announced over the radio, "All pilots. All pilots. Jotnar spotted approaching gateway. Fifteen miles and closing. Estimated number between one hundred-and-eighty and two hundred."

"Oh man," Johnson muttered over the ICS.

"C'mon, Johnson," McShane replied. "We know how to hurt these fuckers now. If anything, they should be scared of us."

The co-pilot gave a brief chuckle. "I hope so."

McShane stared down at him, more than a little surprised. Johnson had actually laughed at a joke. Not much of a laugh, but still, there might be hope for the guy.

The air controller cleared Hammer Flight for takeoff. Other helicopters rose into the air, including the little Portuguese Alouette IIIs. Though primarily used for scouting, the choppers could be fitted with TOW missiles. With around two hundred Jotnar bearing down on them, everything that could fly and fight had to be pressed into service.

They soared over the forests, lakes, and fjords. Ten miles from the gateway, the air controller handed them off to Ironhide One Three, the command post in charge of the first line of defense. They stacked the helicopters in a snaking line toward the gateway, all hovering in place, waiting.

McShane sat still, gaze aimed at the gateway, he and Eastwick third in line behind four Apaches, two from the U.S. Army, two from the Royal Netherlands Air Force. Strobe LED lights had been set up around the craters his rockets had made along the banks of the river, indicating the edges of the gateway.

He glanced to the left, then the right, hoping to see a serpentine form with bat wings. But there was no sign of Tuzvihar.

Looks like we're on our own for this one. Much as he wanted the dragon here, at least NATO was fully prepared to meet the Jotnar. Armored vehicles and anti-tank crews stretched across the field below, backed up by two dozen attack helicopters and several jets. They also had a great tactical advantage. The Jotnar had only one way to enter this world. At best, they could only send two at a time through the gateway. If they could kneecap the first few, that would bottle them up and maybe, just maybe, force them to retreat.

Something moved near the gateway. McShane held his breath, eyeing the ant-like form near the edge of the river.

"Mack." Johnson pointed.

"I see him. Probably one of the guys from the *Jegerkommando* relay team. I think shit's about to get real."

Johnson said nothing, just responded with a slow nod.

The man stood there for a few seconds, then ran back to the gateway, vanishing.

"All personnel," a voice blurted in McShane's headphones. "All personnel, this is Ironhide One Three. Enemy force less than one mile from gateway. Prepare to engage."

McShane closed his eyes, sent out a quick prayer, then radioed the others. "Hammer Flight, you heard the man. Arm all weapons."

Everyone acknowledged the order, Nunez adding, "Time for some payback."

"Amen to that, Tin Foil," said Cain.

McShane nodded as Johnson reported, "Hellfires armed. Rockets armed. We're ready."

"Copy." He stared straight ahead, taking slow breaths to settle himself.

Any minute now . . . any minute . . .

A Jotunn suddenly appeared. It waded through the river, the water sloshing just above its knees.

Fiery contrails leaped off the wing stubs of the first two Apaches in line. Geysers of water and smoke burst on and around the Jotunn's legs. The monster threw out its arms, its mouth open wide. Three more Hellfires exploded around its legs. It pitched forward and crashed into the water, waves surging over both banks.

"Oo-rah!" hollered Eastwick. "One down."

A second Jotunn appeared. The Apaches launched their remaining Hellfires, then switched to rockets. The creature collapsed on its side as a third rock monster emerged.

The U.S. Apaches broke off, giving way to the Dutch attack helicopters. Another salvo of anti-tank missiles blasted into the water. Chunks of rock flew off the Jotunn's legs. It swung its arms trying desperately to maintain its balance when a fourth one appeared. The giant looked at its fallen comrades in front of him. It shuffled left and right, trying to find a gap between the wounded Jotnar. Another Jotunn came through the gateway, bumping into its buddy.

The Dutch Apaches let fly their remaining missiles. The Jotun stumbled, its hand slamming down on the river's eastern bank. It dragged itself from the water, the right leg gone, the left one still attached.

The Apaches banked away.

"We're up, Flameout." McShane moved his Viper forward. "Take out the one with the one good leg. I've got the other."

"Copy, Mack."

"Johnson, fire when ready," McShane told him.

"I'm locked on. Firing."

Three missiles flashed away from the Viper. Two exploded against the Jotunn's right leg. The other tore out a crater along the western bank.

"Shit!" Johnson barked.

"You missed," said McShane. "Get over it and keep firing."

Two more Hellfires rocketed away from the Viper as a gusher of smoke and flame sprouted from the wounded Jotunn's remaining leg. Curtains of water shot up around the other monster's right leg. It staggered and toppled face first into the water.

Another Jotunn tromped through the gateway. It reached down and tried to push aside one of the wounded creatures when Johnson launched the rest of the Hellfires. Water and smoke erupted around the Jotunn's left leg. It teetered from side to side, but remained standing.

"All missiles expended," announced Johnson. Koosman repeated the statement a second later from Eastwick's Viper.

"Break off. Stripes, Clubber, you're up."

McShane swung his Viper left, taking up a flanking position on the western side of the river, just in case any Jotnar made it out of the river. Hellfires streaked away from Stripes and Clubber's choppers, throwing up huge fountains of water around the fifth Jotunn's legs. Another one appeared behind it. The monster he and Johnson wounded pulled itself out of the river. It planted both hands on the ground, trying to push itself up to its one leg.

Smoke coughed from the barrels of the tanks. Contrails from anti-tank missiles soared over the ground. Flame, smoke, and shards of rock jumped off the Jotunn's leg. One of the American Apaches charged forward, yellow streaks zipping from its rocket pods.

The lower leg dropped away. The Jotunn collapsed on its stomach.

The other wounded Jotnar crawled out of the river as two more marched through the gateway. McShane snorted. While they could blow off their legs, they still couldn't kill the damn giants. Even a legless, crawling Jotunn could be dangerous.

Polish Hinds and German Tigers sent volleys of anti-tank missiles at the newly appeared Jotnar. One tumbled into the water. The other stalked onto dry land, wobbling, its right kneecap torn. An American Apache swooped in and launched two Hellfires. Both hit the right leg, blowing it off. The Jotunn fell on its side. Tank guns and missiles from the ground forces pummeled the monster's left leg.

The legless Jotnar crawled forward, their fingers digging large indentations in the ground.

"Ironhide One Three," radioed the command post. "All helicopters without anti-tank missiles, use rockets on the wounded Jotnar. Go for the elbow joints."

"Hammer Four, Copy One Three," McShane replied, hoping the elbows were as vulnerable as the knees.

He hovered over one of the crawling Jotnar, Eastwick's Viper taking up position on his right. Orange flashes rippled from their rocket launchers. Flames and spouts of dirt sprang up around the Jotunn's left arm. Two American Apaches blasted the right elbow with more rockets.

McShane glanced at the river. Another Jotunn emerged from the gateway. TOW missiles soared away from the Portuguese Alouettes. Gushers of water shot up around the monster's legs. The bulbous little helicopters broke off, making way for two Apaches. Hellfire missiles exploded against the Jotunn's knees and the water around them. It crumpled into the river.

He turned back to the wounded Jotunn as Johnson let loose another volley of rockets. A thick cloud of smoke and dust settled over the monster.

"Cease fire," ordered McShane. "Cease fire. Don't waste ammo."

He peered at the mass of brown and black that had settled over the Jotunn, trying to detect any movement. He spotted none.

The dark cloud started to dissipate. More of the Jotunn became visible. It flung out its right arm, scarred and pockmarked from rocket hits. The left arm lay limp at its side, barely attached to the elbow.

"It's working!" The words burst from McShane's mouth. "The left arm's almost gone. Hit it again."

Rockets streaked away from his and Eastwick's Vipers. The Apaches kept up their fire on the right arm. The smoke and dust soon cleared, revealing stumps where the Jotunn's arms had been.

"Hammer Four! We just blew off its arms." McShane didn't bother hiding the elation from his voice. "Repeat, elbows are vulnerable."

"Ironhide One Three copies, Hammer Four," came the reply from the CP. "All personnel, concentrate fire on knees and elbows. Repeat, knees and elbows."

Dozens of smoky contrails tore through the air. Rockets exploded around other Jotnar crawling toward the NATO lines. Smoke belched from tank guns. Anti-tank missiles raced over the field. Another Jotunn appeared from the gateway. Two Tigers blasted its legs with missiles. The monster fell on its side.

Yet another Jotunn emerged from the gateway. It swept its head slowly from left to right, its mouth open wide. McShane's forehead wrinkled. Was it his imagination, or did the thing look shocked?

Two missiles from a Tiger slammed into its right knee. It stumbled, staring at the helicopter. Another missile burrowed into the river, missing its legs but throwing up a gusher of water.

The fourth missile did not miss, striking the Jotunn's left leg. It stood still for a moment, then turned and vanished through the gateway.

McShane's eyes bulged. Did it just –

"They're retreating!" someone hollered over the radio. "The Jotnar are retreating!"

McShane could barely move, astonishment freezing his muscles. Three wounded Jotnar flailed in the water as they fought to drag themselves back to World Bravo. Missiles and rockets fell around them. Several shots missed, others exploded ineffectively against their heads and backs.

One Jotunn blinked out of existence, then the second, then the third.

"We did it," Johnson spoke in breathless disbelief. He swung around to face McShane, more confidence in his voice. "We did it. We beat 'em."

McShane's mouth opened, but he couldn't reply to his co-pilot. After all the unsuccessful battles they'd had against the Jotnar, his brain found it hard to accept they had actually defeated the stone bastards.

Cheers from the other pilots over the radio hammered home the reality. They had won a fight against the Jotnar without help from Tuzvihar.

"Quiet! Everyone quiet!" ordered Ironhide One Three.

The chatter ceased as the commander of the defensive line continued, "All helicopters clear the area. Take up orbit ten kilometers from the gateway. We are preparing air strikes to finish off the Jotnar."

McShane looked down. Half-a-dozen stone giants lay on the ground, only two with arms that worked at all. Easy targets for jet fighters.

He swung the Viper away from the battlefield, followed by the other choppers. They circled the forest, McShane watching plane after plane dive on the wounded Jotnar. F/A-18s, F-16s, F-22s, Typhoons, Tornados, F-35s, even a couple of old F-4 Phantoms from the Hellenic

Air Force. Multiple black dots fell from each aircraft. McShane gazed at the thick plumes of smoke and dust the explosions threw into the air. He'd seen Jotnar survive direct hits from one or two bombs. Could their rock hides fend off a dozen or so?

The bombing runs ceased, the pilots unable to target the Jotnar with the black and brown clouds lingering over them.

"I don't care how tough those SOBs are," said Nunez, "no way could they have survived all that. No way."

McShane didn't respond. He silently prayed Nunez was right.

A single aircraft appeared over the smoke and dust, circling the area. Probably a drone doing BDA – Bomb Damage Assessment.

Several minutes passed. No one spoke on the radio. McShane tensed, on edge, waiting for someone to report the Jotnar were all dead . . . or that a second wave of them had charged out of the gateway.

"This is Ironhide One Three."

McShane jerked at the sudden voice in his helmet.

"We have confirmation. All remaining Jotnar are dead. Repeat, all remaining Jotnar are dead."

The news sent a blast of emotion through McShane. He forgot all discipline drilled into him since his first day in the Corps, threw up a fist, and let out a shout of joy.

***

Dinner that night at the FOB mess tent turned into a party. Boisterous conversations rang out from every table, pilots swapping stories of the battle.

"You see how those things were flailing in the water?" exclaimed one U.S. Apache pilot the next table over from McShane. The man swung his arms wildly in the air while pretending to gasp. Other pilots howled with laughter.

"The buggers better bring water wings next time they come over," hollered a British pilot from the table across from him.

"That's if they come back." Koosman grinned wide. "You see that one Jotunn? Big dumb son-of-a-bitch was looking around at his buddies all like, 'Damn, these little humans blew off their legs. They really are badasses.'"

Pilots hooted and banged on their tables, McShane included.

"Yeah!" Eastwick got up on his chair and shouted, "Chopper pilots rule, and jet jockeys . . . can go fuck themselves!"

The whole room exploded with cheers. Some pilots banged their cups or silverware. McShane pointed to Eastwick and yelled, "Oo-rah!"

Someone brought in an MP3 player and cranked it up. A variety of music blared through the tent. Rock, hip-hop, dubstep, metal, including some band singing about an 18-day battle between Belgian and German forces in World War II that McShane thought kicked ass.

Gotta find out the name of this band and listen to more of their stuff.

One of the German Tiger pilots, a lieutenant named Vogel, put on - of all things - a country song.

"What the heck do Germans know about country music?" asked Cain.

"My family went on vacation to Arizona when I was young," said Vogel. "We visited Tombstone, Bisbee, Prescott. I loved all the western themes, and the music."

He stepped over to where Hunter sat. "Would you care to dance?"

Hunter raised an eyebrow. "I never learned to dance to country music."

"Then allow me to teach you." He flashed a smile.

She returned it. "Teach away."

"Yeah, Clubber!" cheered Eastwick.

"Go, Clubber." McShane gave her a thumbs up while the rest of Hammer Flight whooped it up. Even Johnson nodded and clapped.

Vogel and Hunter danced in the middle of the tent to the cheers of the other pilots. As they began their second dance, the Norwegian mess personnel came around with trays with powdered rolls and cups.

"For the conquering heroes," declared the senior sergeant in charge of the mess. The pilots took the whipped cream and jam-filled pastries, called *fastelavnsbolle,* and the cups. McShane looked into his cup, filled with a gold liquid.

"Hansa." The senior sergeant grinned and nodded to the drink. "Good beer. Need something stronger than coffee for proper celebration."

Still grinning, the sergeant continued on.

Johnson shuffled over to him, looking at his drink. "Are we supposed to have this? We are still on duty."

McShane stared at his own Hansa. The Corps has some of the strictest rules in the armed forces when it came to officers drinking on duty. Commanders could administer breathalyzer tests at any time, and a Marine could wind up in big trouble for a reading as low as .01.

And I already used up my free pass for disobeying orders.

He looked around the tent at the happy pilots, especially the members of Hammer Flight. How many aviators and grunts had been lost during their previous battles with the Jotnar? Hell, he and Johnson could have been one of those statistics had it not been for Tuzvihar saving their asses.

Today, finally, they had a victory of their own. They could kill the Jotnar if they hit them with enough high explosives. They had not lost a single person during the battle at the gateway. They won. They were alive.

Fuck the rules.

"Technically, this is a Norwegian base, not a Marine Corps one. And I don't see Colonel Esposito or Lieutenant Colonel Whitaker around. So I say fuck it, drink up."

"Yeah!" his Marines cheered, Eastwick adding, "Go, Mack!"

They downed their Hansa. So did everyone else. Even Johnson shrugged his shoulders and gulped down his beer.

"Hell yeah." Nunez slapped him on his back. "You're not such a tight-ass after all, Go Around."

Johnson grinned.

McShane laughed and finished off his beer, then took a bite of his *fastelavnsbolle*. Very tasty. Nice and sweet. Amazing what these Norwegian cooks could whip up in a field kitchen.

He took another bite when he overheard a British Apache pilot, one who looked young enough to still be in high school, say, "What if the Jotnar come back? Can we beat them again?"

A Polish Hind pilot gave him a dismissive wave and replied in a heavy accent, "Bah! They come back, we blow them up again. Giants not so tough." He shrugged. "Maybe they don't come back. You see how they run away. Maybe they scared of us."

McShane rolled the cup back and forth in his hand, mulling over what the pilots had said. Yes, they had scored a victory, proven the Jotnar were not invulnerable to their weapons. But would they really stay on their side of the gateway? They had to have taken lots of casualties in the war over there, and they apparently didn't give up and quit.

His lips pressed together in a flat line. He gazed around the tent. Pilots continued to talk loudly and down their Hansa. Hunter and Vogel kept dancing. Were they celebrating too much? No way this war with the Jotnar could end so easily. Would they be able to turn back a second attack? Should they start preparing for it?

Again, his gaze swept around the tent. The cheerful voices, the music, this whole joyous atmosphere. No. These men and women deserved it.

At least for tonight. Tomorrow, however . . .

THIRTY-ONE

The night passed without a Jotnar sighting. So did the morning.

Maybe they did decide to call it quits, McShane thought as he and Johnson headed to their Viper. He sighed softly and stared at the grass. No, that was wishful thinking. That was carryover from the celebration of last night. The Jotnar wouldn't give up that easily.

But what if . . .

He gave a slight shake of his head, trying to erase that thought from his mind and focus on the job at hand.

McShane and Johnson went through their pre-flight checklist and took off with Eastwick to begin the 1200 to 1400 patrol. Joining them were a pair of British Apaches and two Portuguese Alouette IIIs. They took up orbit three miles from the gateway. McShane gazed at the defensive line, reinforced by a few more tanks and armored vehicles. All was quiet.

He flew around and around, the routine racetrack pattern and inaction allowing his mind to wander. It wandered mostly to Ylva. Damn, he missed her. How much longer would they keep him at the FOB? Would they send him back to Gardermoen or another base in Norway? If weeks passed with no Jotnar sighting would they send him back to the States? What would happen if –

"Jotnar coming through!" someone shouted over the radio. "Jotnar coming   through!"

McShane's head snapped to the left. He spotted four stone giants running through the river. Then a fifth, a sixth, a seventh. All running.

"What the hell?" blurted Johnson. "Why didn't the *Jegerkommandos* warn us?"

McShane grimaced. "I have a bad feeling they're not gonna warn us about anything again."

He heard Johnson swallow over the ICS as he banked the helicopter toward the invading Jotnar. More poured through the gateway, all running, throwing up waves of water. McShane tensed when he noticed all the monsters gripping pine trees.

Only a few tank guns and missiles fired. McShane figured the defenders were still scrambling to ready their weapons, taken completely by surprise.

He aimed the Viper's nose at the closest Jotunn, watching as it and its buddies stomped out of the river, never breaking stride. A far cry from how they lumbered out of the gateway yesterday. But with NATO forces guarding their path to this world . . .

My God. They do have intelligence. Maybe not genius level, but they knew enough to adapt their tactics. To not emerge from the gateway without a care. Instead, charging through, taking them by surprise, making it harder to target their knees.

He counted twenty Jotnar, the forward elements closing in fast on the defensive line.

"Targets of opportunity," ordered McShane. "Fire at will. Fire at will."

"I have lock," said Johnson. "Selecting Hellfires One and Five. Ready –"

Two Jotnar threw their trees at the approaching helicopters.

"Evasive action!" McShane threw the Viper into a hard left. He counted to two and leveled out, checking around him. None of the six choppers got hit.

Two more trees hurtled toward them. The helicopters jinked and banked. Another tree flew at them. Another.

"Dammit!" Johnson cursed. "I can't lock 'em."

"Well I'm not gonna stand still and get a pine tree up my ass."

Another big wooden spear tore across the sky, well away from his Viper.

But right into one of the Alouettes. The tail spun away from the bulbous fuselage, which spiraled out of the sky. McShane clenched his teeth when it smashed into the ground and vanished in a fireball.

The Jotnar neared the defensive line. A cold, invisible hand clutched McShane's stomach. Between flying trees and running monsters, they had no chance to use their Hellfires.

Missiles flew up from armored vehicles and infantrymen. Some missed, some burst against the Jotnar. None hit their knees.

Enormous feet stomped armored vehicles. Several soldiers leaped out of their foxholes and ran, most leaving behind their missile launchers. Jotnar crushed them with their feet or trees.

"Forget missiles," said McShane. "Use rockets. Take some pressure off the groundpounders."

Dozens of yellow flashes zipped toward the ground. Explosions tore up the grass or jumped from the Jotnar's thick bodies. A few flung their trees at them. McShane dodged one. Eastwick and the other pilots also avoided the projectiles.

The barrage did nothing to slow the Jotnar. Three tanks went spinning across the ground from kicks. Two Jotnar snatched armored vehicles and threw them at the helicopters. One struck an Apache. Fuel and ammo detonated, turning the chopper into a mass of orange and black.

A Jotunn drove its fist into a tank, turning it into twisted metal. More stone monsters filed through the gateway, all running, all gripping trees. Sweat broke out on McShane's forehead. There had to be sixty of them, maybe seventy.

And they kept coming.

"Ironhide One Three to all personnel." The voice from the CP sounded near panic. "Fall back. Everyone fall back to second defensive line."

The surviving tanks, armored vehicles, and troops fled into the forest. The Jotnar chased after them.

"Johnson. Fire rockets."

Flames spat from the pods on the wing stubs. The other helicopters unleashed their own rocket barrages. Tongues of fire and smoke sprang off the giants.

"Nothing," Eastwick spat. "They're totally ignoring us."

Three more trees flew at the choppers. McShane banked hard right to avoid one.

"Not completely." He switched frequencies to the FOB. "November One Five, Hammer Four. First defensive line overrun. Repeat, first defensive line overrun. More Jotnar coming through the gateway. Estimated enemy strength in excess of eighty."

A couple of seconds passed before he got a response. "Copy, Four. Pull back from area. Air strike inbound."

"Copy, One Five."

He and Eastwick headed back east, along with the surviving Apache and Alouette III. McShane checked his mirrors, watching the Jotnar storm through the forest. Anger burned in his gut. He gritted his teeth to keep from raging. They just got their asses handed to them. Taken completely by surprise. Had they become overconfident after their victory yesterday? Should they have done more to prepare for the next Jotnar attack instead of partying because they lucked out and killed a handful of the bastards?

"Fast movers coming in," radioed the British Apache pilot.

McShane glanced behind him. Two Harriers from the Spanish carrier *Juan Carlos I* dove on the Jotnar army. A string of bombs fell from each of them. A roiling mass of fire rose among the monsters.

Next came two Norwegian F-16s, followed by two Swedish Gripens. More bombs exploded among the stone giants. It barely slowed their advance. McShane's shoulders sagged. Easy to drop multiple bombs on a single, limbless Jotunn that couldn't move. Hard to concentrate several bombs on individual Jotnar moving en mass.

The creatures swung eastward, knocking down trees or ripping them from the ground to give them new weapons. Two more jets roared toward them. F-22s. Bombs fell from their internal bays and wing-mounted hardpoints. A line of fireballs rippled through the enemy ranks. Several emerged from the fiery maelstrom with cracks and holes and scorch marks. One giant had its right arm hanging limply at its side, barely attached to the elbow.

But they still kept coming.

McShane stared ahead to the line of armor and infantry that made up the second defensive line. Beyond that was the third defensive line that stretched to the outskirts of Nome. If the Jotnar broke through both of them, that little town would be wiped off the map.

Maybe all of Norway will be wiped off the map.

He exhaled loudly. Not if he had anything to say about it.

The four choppers reached the second defensive and hovered over it, noses pointed at the tree line.

"Everyone standby missiles and rockets," radioed McShane. "Soon as the Jotnar break through the trees, fire everything we've got at their knees."

Eastwick, the Brit, and the Portuguese pilot all responded, "Copy."

McShane steadied his breathing, watching dozens and dozens of Jotnar crash through the forest. He estimated they were a mile from the tree line. He barely registered the thumping rotors, all his focus on the approaching monsters.

He jerked when explosions burst from several of the Jotnar. Clouds of thick gray smoke rose from the forest in front of the monsters. He hadn't seen any of the tanks or APCs below open fire. Had to be artillery from a few miles away.

The Jotnar just charged through the smoke. What rounds hit them barely scratched their hides. McShane tensed. Any second.

The first few monsters crashed out of the forest, trees tumbling over in their wake.

"Fire!" he hollered.

Missiles blasted off the rails of the helicopters. Rockets flashed through the air. Below, smoke spat from tank guns and contrails from anti-tank missiles raced over the ground. Explosions erupted from the Jotnar's stone hides. Other rounds blew apart trees. Three of the giants stumbled and fell, their legs severed at the knees.

McShane had no time to celebrate. More Jotnar streamed out of the forest. Trees soared over the battlefield. McShane jerked the Viper left to avoid one. Eastwick dipped his helicopter, letting another tree fly over him.

One tree smashed through the cockpit of the Alouette III. A spray of glass and metal shot off in all directions. The wreckage dropped to earth and burst into flames.

Two jets shot into view. F-35s. Several bombs fell away from the first one. Blasts of fire, dirt, and rock flew up around the monsters. One toppled onto its side, its right leg missing.

The second F-35 lined up for its attack run. Four Jotnar hurled their trees at the arrow-shaped fighter. Three missed. One clipped the left tail. The jet corkscrewed into the ground. A trail of fire rolled across the field.

More rockets zipped away from McShane's Viper. The tanks and missile crews on the ground kept up their barrage. Hazy smoke settled between the attackers and defenders. Another Jotunn went down, its left leg gone. The others ran past it.

McShane's jaw clenched as they surged over the NATO line. One giant picked up a tank and drove through the top of another. Another Jotunn swept out its tree, knocking infantrymen across the field. A Boxer armored vehicle shot a Jotunn in the knee point-blank with an anti-tank missile. The giant staggered, glared down at the eight-wheeled vehicle, and kicked it away.

Rockets flew from McShane's Viper, a few exploding against the leg and waist of the Jotunn. It turned toward them and flung its tree, missing the helicopter.

"That's it," said Johnson. "All rockets expended."

"I'm out, too," radioed the British Apache pilot.

"We only have a few more shots left," said Koosman.

McShane reported their weapons status to the FOB.

"Return to base to rearm and refuel," replied the air controller.

He glowered at the battlefield below. Jotnar stomped through the defensive line. Another tank went flying through the air. A Boxer got crushed by a huge foot. McShane did not want to run out on the groundpounders, but with the exception of his useless gatling gun, the Viper was unarmed.

He swung the chopper toward Nome, followed by Eastwick and the Brit. More helicopters appeared in the distance. The rest of the squadron from the FOB, including Cain and Hunter.

"Save us some for when we get back in the fight," Eastwick tried to joke, though his tone was flatter than usual.

"I think there's plenty to go around, unfortunately," replied Cain.

"Good luck," McShane radioed as he passed the helicopters. Other jets and choppers had to be heading here. Would it be enough to stop the Jotnar?

He grimaced, thinking about the city he and Ylva found on World Bravo, imagining the same thing happening to Nome, and Oslo, and every other city in Norway. Maybe all of Scandinavia.

McShane kept up with the battle on the radio. He wished he hadn't. The second defensive line had crumbled. The helicopters had put down three Jotnar, but at the cost of two Tigers and an Apache. The rest of the giants kept coming. Like a *banzai* charge the Japanese did during World War II. Though those attacks usually ended with the soldiers falling to a hail of bullets. With the Jotnar, it wouldn't be that simple.

The three helicopters set down at the FOB. The rotors barely stopped spinning when the groundcrews swarmed the aircraft, connecting fuel hoses, attaching Hellfires, and shoving rockets into the pods. McShane pressed a fist into his leg, anxious to get back to the fight, fearing the Jotnar would hit the last line of defense before his Viper was ready for takeoff.

C'mon, c'mon. He urged the groundcrew, though fought the urge to yell it at them. Their asses were on the line, too. He doubted they could move any faster.

One of the Marines shoved another rocket into the starboard side pod, then looked up, eyes bulging. Two more members of the groundcrew also stopped their work, gawking at something.

"What the fuck?" McShane banged on the canopy. "Hey! Get back to work!"

One of the Marines looked at him, then pointed behind the Viper. McShane craned his neck around. His eyes went wide.

Tuzvihar rose from the river.

THIRTY-TWO

"Yes!" McShane punched the air.

"Holy shit!" Eastwick blurted over the radio. "The big guy's back. Fuckin' A!"

"Check it out," said Johnson. "He looks good as new."

McShane nodded, his gaze still locked on the dragon. Talons pressed on the river bank, Tuzvihar pushed himself out of the water. The wings were no longer mangled. McShane saw no other marks from the battle in Drammen. Had the Asgardians' bioengineering technology included the ability to self-heal?

The dragon hauled himself onto dry land, curtains of water cascading off his dark red body. His mouth opened, unleashing a trumpeting roar. Nearly all the groundcrew personnel covered their ears.

McShane got on the radio. "Stripes. Clubber. Good news. We've got big help coming your way."

"Is it the kind of help that flies and breathes fire?" asked Cain.

"Damn right it is."

"Just what we need," said Hunter. "The Jotnar are about four miles from Nome. There has to be over a hundred-and-fifty of them."

McShane gritted his teeth. As powerful as Tuzvihar was, could the beast hold his own against so many Jotnar?

But he won't be on his own. We're backing him up.

He swung his hand in a circle, urging the groundcrew to finish their work. In less than a minute, the last rockets were loaded, the hose disconnected, and the rotors began spinning. Eastwick and the British Apache took off seconds later.

So did Tuzvihar. The huge wings flapped, kicking up dust clouds throughout the FOB. Several men and women had hats go flying off their heads. A few fell on their asses.

They flew over fields and forests, then over Nome proper. McShane took several glances at Tuzvihar, flying alongside the three choppers. The beast's mere presence bolstered his confidence.

Black dots appeared on the horizon. More helicopters and jets. Armored vehicles and missile-armed field cars sped through the streets, heading for the fields outside Nome to bolster the defensive line. Puffs of smoke belched from self-propelled artillery and field guns positioned in open areas around the town.

Dozens upon dozens of Jotnar tore through the forest. Many raised trees over their heads. Cain, Hunter, and the other helicopters hovered a mile from the tree line, ready to hit the Jotnar's knees when they emerged in the clear.

Adrenaline raced through McShane. He felt it to the core of his being. They would either stop the Jotnar here or die trying.

He closed his eyes, thought of Ylva, thought of his family.

"Arm all weapons," he ordered. "Fire the moment you have a clear shot."

"Hellfires armed. Rockets armed." Johnson blew out a breath. "We're ready."

Trees collapsed as the Jotnar pounded forward. Artillery rounds burst on and around them. The monsters just ran through the explosions . . .

And surged out of the tree line.

"Fire!" shouted McShane.

A wave of missiles streaked through the air. Tuzvihar shot ahead of the choppers. A blast of sunset-red flame gushed from his mouth. It burned through the torso of one Jotunn, and the one behind it. Both monsters fell.

Missiles exploded in the ground or on Jotnar. Four of them tumbled to the ground, each missing a leg. Another volley of missiles soared away from the choppers as Tuzvihar drew back his wings and plunged into the Jotnar ranks.

McShane watched the monster's tail lash out. The spiked club smashed through the head of one Jotunn. The dragon claws slashed another giant's throat. Two more hammered its back with trees. Tuzvihar whipped his long neck around, lowered his head, and snapped it up. The curved horns drove through the throat of a Jotunn. The dragon strained his head as he pushed up, up . . .

And ripped off the Jotunn's head.

Its comrade punched Tuzvihar in the gut once, twice. Two Apaches battered the Jotunn's back with rockets. It turned slightly.

That was all Tuzvihar needed. His right foreleg swiped at the other monster's neck. It stumbled back. Two missiles from the ground forces struck the gaping wound in its throat. McShane could not see any obvious damage.

A second slash from Tuzvihar severed the Jotunn's head.

Three more Jotnar stomped toward the dragon. He turned toward them and loosed another fire blast, sweeping his head left to right. The flames burned through their massive chests, slicing off their heads and shoulders.

More Jotnar converged on Tuzvihar. Two threw trees at him. He deflected one with his tail and caught the other in his mouth. He bit down, and both halves dropped in front of him. The stone giants closed in on the dragon.

Johnson let fly two Hellfires. Both missiles exploded against a Jotunn's right knee. It sagged to the side. Three more missiles blew off its leg.

More missiles and rockets ripped into the Jotnar. Several stumbled, chunks of their kneecaps missing. The dragon swung out his tail. The spikes smashed through the legs of three Jotnar.

McShane moved the Viper left and fired off a volley of rockets. A few burst against a Jotunn's knee. It turned toward him.

Eastwick's chopper fired another rocket volley. The monster's kneecap shattered in a storm of smoke and rock. It fell on its back.

Several Jotnar looked away from Tuzvihar to the NATO force. McShane grinned. Just as he hoped. They forced the giants to split their attention between a familiar enemy and the alliance troops.

Trees flew through the air. McShane banked right to avoid one. Other helicopters jerked away from the improvised spears. One struck a Tiger in the rotors, sending it tumbling to the ground. Another tree slammed into the side of an Apache, knocking it from the sky.

Tuzvihar slashed one Jotunn across the face. A breath of flame took out six Jotnar. Another barreled into the dragon with its shoulder. Three others battered him with fists and trees. Several more giants broke off and charged the defensive line.

"Ironhide Three Three to all helicopters," radioed the command post. "Take some pressure off the dragon. If they kill it, we might lose this battle."

"Copy, Three Three." McShane looked out the canopy. "You heard the man, Hammer Flight. Let's help out our buddy."

"Semper Fi," Eastwick blared.

Cain and Hunter repeated the Marine Corps motto and drew closer to the melee.

"Hellfire Four locked," said Johnson. "Fire."

The missile impacted several feet from one of the Jotnar.

"Dammit. Going with rockets."

Flames snapped from the pods. Fireballs sprouted up and down the Jotunn's leg and waist. Two Hellfires exploded against another giant's leg. Two missiles from a Hind hit the back leg of a third Jotunn. It turned to the chopper. More missiles and rockets bombarded its legs. It threw out its arms and collapsed.

A tree sheared off the cockpit of a Tiger.

The dragon raked a Jotunn's chest with its claws. The spiked club raked the eyes of another Jotunn. It spun away, covering the fissure where its eyes had been. Two Apaches moved in and blew off its legs with Hellfires.

A giant punched Tuzvihar in the back, slamming him into the ground. The Jotunn raised its foot.

Two missiles from Hunter's Viper exploded against its leg. It toppled on its side.

Another blast of superheated plasma ripped through the Jotnar. Seven fell. Other giants stomped into the defensive line. They crushed three tanks and a couple of infantry fighting vehicles. Two M1s fired at a Jotunn. Shards of stone flew off its left knee. Anti-tank missiles exploded against the injured leg until the Jotunn toppled over.

Jets dove into the fray, unloading bombs and missiles. Clouds of flame and smoke rose across the battlefield. Trees arced into the air. An F-16's wing shattered, sending the jet spinning into the ground. Another tree took down an old MiG-21 from the Romanian Air Force.

Tuzvihar flapped his large wings and sprang into a trio of Jotnar. The tail whipped out, the spiked club cutting through the knees of one giant. Claws lashed out, decapitating the remaining two Jotnar. Two others advanced on the dragon.

JDAMS fell from a pair of F/A-18s. The sleek, guided bombs exploded on the legs of the two monsters. They collapsed into the mass of gray-brown smoke.

Another stream of dragon fire burned through half-a-dozen Jotnar. Several giants stomped on tanks, armored vehicles, and soldiers. One Jotunn snatched a Polish T-72 tank and hurled it at Tuzvihar. It slammed into the beast's head.

"Hammer Four," McShane radioed, "Several Jotnar have broken through the defensive line."

"Hammer Four, all helicopters, Ironhide Three Three," the CP responded. "Keep supporting the dragon. We'll handle any Jotnar that break through."

"Copy, Three Three."

A Jotunn clubbed Tuzvihar in the head with a tree. Another kicked him in the side. Cain launched a Hellfire, but missed. A Hind blasted one giant in the leg with rockets. Two Apaches then hit it in the knee with missiles.

The other Jotunn slammed the tree down on Tuzvihar's neck. It lifted the tree for another blow.

McShane thumbed the fire button. The rocket pods flashed. The tree exploded into flaming debris. The Jotunn stood still.

An A-10 roared in and hit the monster's leg with a Maverick missile. It then strafed it with its 30mm cannon.

Tuzvihar rose on his hind legs and slashed the Jotunn's throat. Two more slashes and its head fell off. The flying beast swung around and saw several Jotnar romping past the defensive line, headed toward Nome. He opened his maw, ready for another fire blast.

A Jotunn leaped across the field and tackled him. Both monsters tumbled across the grass. They bowled over two Jotnar. Two others turned and tromped toward them.

"Big guy's in trouble," said McShane. "Let's give him --"

A tree whipped across the air and battered the rotors of an Apache. The chopper spiraled into the field below and exploded.

A barrage of pines launched toward them. McShane dipped the Viper to avoid one. Another tree barely missed Hunter's helicopter. One pine crashed into the side of a Huey. The front end of a Tiger burst apart as a tree knifed through it.

"Dammit." McShane dodged another improvised missile, glimpsing Tuzvihar. Two Jotnar kicked it. The dragon swung his neck, the horns tearing through the leg of a giant. It staggered back.

The third Jotunn grabbed Tuzvihar's head and drove it into the ground. It wrapped a massive hand around the other creature's neck and squeezed.

Dread clutched McShane's stomach. "Someone get to Tuzvihar. Now."

Cain and Hunter started toward the dragon, but banked away when two trees flew their way. An Apache tried to circle around to aid the monster, only to have a pine crash through its cockpit.

Teeth bared, McShane grunted and shoved the stick forward. He ducked beneath another flying tree.

"Johnson. Weapons status."

"We've got about half our rockets left, but just two Hellfires."

He nodded. "Then make every shot count."

"I will."

McShane drew closer to Tuzvihar and the Jotnar beating him. The dragon thrashed as the one Jotunn continued to choke him. McShane swung the chopper to the left.

"Johnson. Put both Hellfires on that Jotunn's arm."

McShane glanced to his right. His entire body went rigid.

A Jotunn reared back its right arm, tree in hand, aiming right for his Viper.

"Locked up," said Johnson.

Fear kept McShane from replying. His brain screamed at him to bank. But any evasive action would break the laser lock for the Hellfires.

Tuzvihar could be dead before they reacquired. If the dragon died, they'd probably lose the battle.

He held the chopper steady, his throat constricting.

The Jotunn's arm started forward.

Rockets hammered the stone giant. The top half of the tree blew apart.

McShane checked his rear and smiled as Cain's helicopter banked away from his attack run.

"Thank you, Stripes," he radioed.

"Fire!" Johnson hollered a split-second later.

The two missiles rocketed away. The Jotunn leaned forward, pushing down with its weight, threatening to crush Tuzvihar's throat. The dragon's legs spasmed. How much longer . . .

The first Hellfire missed.

"Shit!" Johnson raged . . . just as the second missile plowed into the Jotunn's elbow. The monster jerked. It released its hold on Tuzvihar's throat. The Jotunn swung around, staring at McShane's Viper. The other two also stared his way.

Fireballs rippled below the waists of two of the Jotnar. Two newly arrived Norwegian Hueys lobbed rockets at the giants. A pair of Italian Mangusta attack choppers followed, launching Hellfires. One Jotunn had its left leg blown off.

Tuzvihar crawled away, standing on trembling legs and shaking his crocodilian head. Concern rolled through McShane. How long would the dragon need to recover?

The Jotunn that had choked Tuzvihar stalked toward him. McShane fired a volley of rockets. A few struck the giant's legs, making it pause.

Two winged, bullet-shaped JSOW glide bombs dropped by an F/A-18 exploded against the Jotunn's gut. A huge cloud of smoke and dust enveloped the monster. McShane knew the Jotunn wasn't dead, but the impact probably stunned it. Hopefully long enough for . . .

Tuzvihar straightened, raising his head. He swung around as the Jotunn lumbered out of the cloud, a chunk of its stomach dug out by the bombs.

The dragon lunged forward, forelegs extended. His claws tore through the Jotunn's wound. Tuzvihar's claws burst out the monster's sides. The torso fell away from the legs.

Wings flapping, he took off after the Jotnar that had broken through the defensive line. McShane launched a few rockets at the knees of a Jotunn, then caught sight of a jet of flame gushing from the dragon's maw. It cut through all but one of the rock monsters. The survivor turned to face him.

An F-35 dove on it and dropped a JSOW. The bomb blasted off its right leg, sending the Jotunn falling face first. Tuzvihar finished the job with a few slashes of his claws, decapitating it.

Several Jotnar ran for the tree line. McShane sucked down a breath and straightened. Were they retreating?

No. The monsters ripped out trees from the edge of the forest, reloading for another standoff attack.

Problem was, they blocked the path of other Jotnar trying to emerge from the forest. The advance stalled.

McShane grinned. Yes, the Jotnar had some intelligence. Not a lot, thankfully, just some.

The jets took advantage. Tornados, Typhoons, F-16s, F-35s, and A-10s rained bombs on the tightly packed monsters. Fire and smoke washed over the trees and the monsters among them.

"Make a hole," radioed Eastwick. "Looks like ol' Tuzvihar's ready to light it up again."

The dragon hovered in place, eyes locked on the dozens of Jotnar in and around the forest. Helicopters moved out of the way. His line of fire clear, Tuzvihar let loose.

The jet of flame burned through the Jotnar ranks. The dragon moved his head left to right and back again, cutting a swath of death among the giants.

"My God," McShane stammered. He couldn't even count how many Jotnar had been taken out with that one blast.

The remaining giants froze, gaping at what remained of their comrades.

Until an F-16 dropped a couple of JDAMs on them. The explosion got the monsters moving again.

"All units, all units, Ironhide Three Three," radioed the CP. "Heavy bombers approaching. Time on target, five minutes. Repeat, five minutes. All ground forces, fall back to Nome immediately. All air units, continue attacks until ordered to disengage."

McShane nodded. Just what they'd been waiting for. To have the Jotnar in one place so they could unload a massive storm of high explosives on them.

He spotted troops scrambling aboard tanks, APCs, and field cars. The vehicles then sped toward Nome. The Jotnar burst through the tree line. McShane swore they set their sights on the fleeing ground forces. Rockets and missiles roared away from the helicopters. Contrails stretched across the battlefield, then struck the advancing Jotnar. Many paused, but continued on. A handful fell over.

Tuzvihar launched himself at the stone horde. He skimmed over them, tail whipping back and forth. Shards of stone exploded from the heads of a few Jotnar. A small number swung their large, makeshift clubs, striking Tuzvihar. The dragon staggered, but kept flying. More jets screamed toward the monsters. Bombs and missiles erupted among them. Very few struck their legs. The Jotnar continued their charge.

"All air units," radioed the CP, "disengage and clear the area. TOT two minutes. Repeat, two minutes."

McShane scanned the advancing Jotnar. Tuzvihar dove on them, blasting several with his fire breath. He raked his claws across the heads of a few more. One Jotunn nailed it in the gut with a tree. A swing of the spiked club on his tail tore through the giant's right eye.

"Ironhide Three Three, Hammer Four. Dragon is still in target area."

"Copy, Hammer Four, but we have the Jotnar concentrated in one area. This is our best chance to finish them all at once."

"We are under orders to not attack the dragon."

The command post didn't reply for a couple of seconds. "Roger, Four. Do what you can to lure it out of the target area. If you can't, get the hell out of there."

"Copy, Three Three."

McShane swung the helicopter around when Cain contacted him. "We'll give you a hand, Mack."

"Negative. All you guys haul ass out of here. That's an order."

He could hear Cain sigh through his headphones. "Roger that, Mack. Good luck."

McShane watched the rest of Hammer Flight fly east, then faced forward. Johnson looked up at him, lips pressed tight.

"Worried, Go Around?"

"Yeah. But Tuzvihar saved our asses. I guess we owe him."

McShane nodded at him. "Good man."

Tuzvihar took out a Jotunn at the knees with his tail, then impaled another through the neck with his horns, ripping off its head. With a few flaps of the wings, he backed off. Probably gearing up for another blast of fire.

McShane buzzed alongside the dragon. Flares spat from the dispensers on the side of the Viper. Tuzvihar's head snapped in his direction. McShane hovered in front of him.

Okay, genius. What now? The dragon sure as hell didn't have a radio. Could it even communicate with a human? Maybe the Asgardians gave it that ability. Even if they had, he doubted Tuzvihar understood English.

Time was running out. He needed to do something.

McShane jerked the Viper right once, twice, three times, the tail pointing to the south. *Go that way. Now.*

Tuzvihar's ink black eyes just stared at him. McShane swore the thing looked dumbfounded.

"Get the fuck outta here, dumbass!" He swung the tail south again. The dragon remained in place.

"Mack!" Johnson pointed skyward.

In the distance, McShane spotted a plane with enormous wings and eight engines. He recognized it instantly. The old, iconic B-52 Stratofortress. One of the symbols of the Cold War. Instead of the nuclear bombs it carried back then, this one packed 70,000 pounds of conventional ordnance.

All of it about to drop right on his head.

"TOT one minute," reported the CP. "Repeat, one minute."

"Dammit, Mack," radioed Cain. "Get out of there."

McShane ignored him. He swung the chopper around and flew about a hundred feet away. Tuzvihar just watched him.

He circled around and again and flew farther south. *C'mon. Figure it out.*

McShane kept going.

The dragon whirled around and followed.

McShane had no time to celebrate. He gunned the engine and screamed over the forests and fields. A check of his mirrors showed Tuzvihar kept pace with him.

"TOT ten seconds," announced the CP. "Five . . . Four . . . Three . . . Two . . . One."

McShane didn't look behind him. He sped over the green terrain, trying to put as much distance between him and the falling bombs as possible.

"Damn, look at that," Eastwick stammered.

McShane checked his mirrors. The air stuck in his throat. A string of massive, roiling orange plumes stretched across the forest.

The Viper shook. McShane clenched his teeth against the blast wave. His jaw loosened as the tremor subsided, the chopper still airborne.

A second B-52 appeared. A long line of bombs fell from its underbelly. More explosions rocked the countryside, like a mass of mini volcanoes erupting at once.

Another plane followed, sleeker than the B-52s. A B-1 Lancer, capable of carrying 125,000 pounds of ordnance. A downpour of black dots descended from the bomber. Columns of fire and smoke turned the Jotnar's path into a raging hellscape.

McShane blinked repeatedly, trying to absorb the sight before him. He'd seen footage of attacks by heavy bombers in World War II and Vietnam War documentaries. But seeing it on a TV or computer screen barely did justice to the conflagration he'd just witnessed.

He eased back on the speed and turned the Viper around, hovering in place. Tuzvihar settled on the ground nearby. Both stared at the gigantic cloud of smoke and dust in the distance.

It took a while for it to dissipate. When it did, McShane and the other chopper pilots moved in for bomb damage assessment. Tuzvihar joined them, probably to finish off any surviving Jotnar. Would there even be any?

"Damn," Johnson said in barely a whisper.

Large chunks of the forest were gone, replaced by uneven row after uneven row of smoldering craters. Pieces of Jotnar lay everywhere, jagged and blackened. To McShane's amazement, a few of the giants had survived the carpet bombing. All, however, were dismembered, those with arms weakly trying to crawl away. Tuzvihar finished them off with slashes to the neck.

"I guess the people on World Bravo programmed him to really hate Jotnar," said Hunter.

The choppers swept over the charred, battered landscape, unable to find any more barely living Jotnar. McShane sagged in his seat, exhaling.

Tuzvihar pulled next to his Viper, the large, black eye on the left side of his head staring into his cockpit.

"Hey, Mack," said Eastwick. "Looks like you got a new best friend."

McShane chuckled, staring back at Tuzvihar.

"Thank you." He gave the dragon a salute.

He swore Tuzvihar nodded to him before flying off in the direction of the gateway.

THIRTY-THREE

A steady thumping drilled through McShane's sleep. His eyes fluttered open, becoming conscious of the bed he lay in. He thought the noise was part of some now faded dream and closed his eyes.

Another round of thumping echoed through the little cottage.

Ylva stirred next to him, letting out a soft moan. McShane pushed himself to his elbow, grunting. That's when he realized someone was knocking on the door.

Da hell? He glanced at the digital clock on the nightstand. 7:17 in the morning. No way the maid staff would be doing their rounds at this hour. Even if they did, he had a "Do Not Disturb" sign on the door.

A third series of knocks came from the door.

"What the hell?" He threw off the covers and rolled out of bed.

"What's going on?" Ylva asked sleepily.

"Some dumbass is knocking on the door." McShane threw on some gym shorts and a t-shirt with a grinning skeleton in fatigues that read "USMC -- Uncle Sam's Misguided Children." He looked at Ylva in the bed, thought about their fierce night of sex, the feel of her body against his. He figured they'd pick up where they'd left off when they woke.

Now . . .

He stomped into the living room. "I swear I'm gonna go R. Lee Ermey *Full Metal Jacket* on this ass-hat."

McShane grabbed the knob and swung the door open. "What's go -
-"

He gaped at the person before him. A trim Japanese woman a couple of inches shorter than him in a dress suit, her hair in a tight bun. A computer case was slung over her shoulder.

"Mom?"

Lieutenant General Kokoro McShane (neé Hayashi), Director of the Defense Intelligence Agency, lifted her chin, staring him in the eyes. Her narrow face stiffened, then relaxed. She stepped forward and wrapped him in a tight hug.

"You had me so worried," she said. "I'm so glad you're all right."

She held him for a few more seconds before letting go. McShane noticed moisture in his mother's eyes. She blinked a few times, her face forming a rigid, professional mask before entering the cottage.

"What are you doing here?" McShane shut the door.

"A mother can't see her son? Especially after he fought a war against a race of stone giants?"

"Point taken. Still, you had to drive to one of the most out of the way spots in Norway to do it?"

"Don't worry. I won't take up too much of your time. You certainly earned this three-day pass."

"Sounds like this visit isn't just for personal reasons," said McShane.

"I have meetings scheduled with various NATO intelligence officials," Mom explained.

"Starting in Norway. What a coincidence."

"Rank, and being a mother, has its privileges." The barest hint of a smile came and went on his mother's lips.

"Um, hello." Ylva stepped out of the bedroom, wearing sweatpants and a *Fullmetal Alchemist* t-shirt.

Mom turned to her. McShane winced as his mother's head dipped down, then up. Sizing up Ylva, like she had every girlfriend he'd ever had. He wondered what fault she'd find in Ylva. Probably her anime t-shirt. Mom certainly hadn't thought highly of Ella, his cosplayer girlfriend from college. Considered her immature for dressing up as cartoon characters.

"Ylva, this is my mom. Mom, this is --"

"Ylva Tande, Professor of History and Mythology at the University of Tromsø." Mom walked over to her, again doing the full body scan, her gaze lingering on the gray armored figure and yellow-haired boy on the t-shirt. Ylva winced and looked away.

"I believe a thank you is in order." Mom stuck out her hand. "Were it not for your contributions, we might never have found World Bravo. Good work, Professor."

Ylva's eyes widened with a mix of shock and delight. "Thank you, Mrs. McShane." She shook her hand. "Or, um, is it General?"

"Either is fine." Mom moved to the couch. "I'll make this brief so you can get back to . . ." she looked first to McShane, then Ylva, "well, get back to what I apparently interrupted."

Now McShane winced, his gaze falling to the floor.

Mom sat down, waving for him and Ylva to join her. She slid the case off her shoulder, removed the laptop, and set it on the table.

"Turn away," she told them.

"I'm sorry?" Ylva's face crinkled.

"I need to type in my password. My eyes only."

McShane looked to Ylva. "I told you Mom's serious when it comes to security."

"I'm one of the few people in Washington who is. Now turn away, both of you."

He and Ylva faced away from Mom. After a few taps on the keyboard, she said, "You can turn back around now."

They did. McShane glanced at the screen, saying, "If you wanna go to Netflix or Amazon Prime, just so you know, the WiFi here sucks." He grinned at his lame joke.

Mom did not. She just raised an eyebrow and huffed, her usual response whenever he or Dad made a wiseass comment.

She clicked on a file. "Two days after the Battle of Nome, we conducted an aerial reconnaissance mission on World Bravo. Because the gateway interferes with radio and satellite transmissions, we couldn't use a UAV." She used the acronym for Unmanned Aerial Vehicle. "Instead, we used an Apache helicopter, stripped of weapons and with external fuel tanks to extend its range. This is what it found."

Mom brought up a few clips showing not just the ruined city he and Ylva flew over, but two others in similar states.

"Looks like there was some sort of large-scale war over there," said McShane.

Mom nodded. "That's the general consensus."

"Have you found any survivors?" Ylva leaned closer to the laptop.

"No. Not human ones anyway."

McShane grimaced. He knew what his mother meant.

The next image showed Jotnar moving through a forest. McShane counted twenty-two. Four more images from the Apache turned up more of the monsters in groups ranging in size from six to forty.

McShane leaned back on the couch. "So there are still more Jotnar out there."

"You didn't really think the ones you fought were the only ones," said Mom.

"I was hoping." He frowned. "But deep down, I didn't think so."

"The most concerning part is we have no idea how many Jotnar are left on World Bravo."

"Hopefully not too many," replied McShane. "Hopefully the side that made the dragons took out a lot of them before they got wasted."

"I would have thought they could have defeated them, knowing the Jotnar's weak spots." Ylva folded her arms across her knees. "Their weapons had to be much more advanced than ours."

Mom looked at her. "They most likely had weapons more advanced than we can imagine. But if you have thousands, tens of thousands, of Jotnar charging en masse, they could overwhelm any army, no matter how advanced. The British learned that lesson the hard way at

Isandlwana during the Zulu War. They had rifles, field guns, even a rocket battery, while the Zulus mostly had spears and cow-hide shields. Even with such an impressive arsenal, the British numbered around eighteen hundred, while the Zulus had twenty-thousand men. Sometimes, quantity has a quality all its own, as the Russian military is fond of saying."

She moved the cursor to another clip. "And Jotnar may not be the only creatures to worry about."

This footage had the Apache flying over a body of water, maybe World Bravo's version of the Skagerrak Strait.

"My God," Ylva blurted, nearly lunging toward the laptop screen.

McShane's eyes locked on the large, snake-like object cutting a path through the water.

"That thing looks enormous," he said.

"Our analysts estimate its size at anywhere between eighty to a hundred feet," Mom told him.

Ylva pointed at the screen. "This could be where the legends of the Midgard Serpent originated. It was said to be so large it could wrap itself around the entire world."

"I guess whoever saw this thing was exaggerating," said McShane.

"Oh yes. But I doubt something that large could have swum through the narrow rivers and fjords leading up to the gateway. So either someone from our world went to Asgard . . ." Ylva glanced at Mom. "Sorry, World Bravo. They went there, saw it, and told everyone when they returned, or . . ." She straightened, staring straight ahead.

"Or Nome isn't the only place that has a gateway," Mom finished the sentence for her. "There might be others throughout Scandinavia. Perhaps the whole world."

Ylva took a slow breath. "That could be the explanation to many monster sightings and mysterious disappearances throughout history. These creatures could have accidentally crossed over into our world, and people, ships, and planes could have gone through a gateway and never found their way home."

"If that's the case, we could be facing threats on multiple fronts," McShane pointed out. "From who knows how many different monsters."

"At least we have Tuzvihar," said Ylva. "And if he survived that war, there could be other dragons out there who can help us."

"If there are, the Apache didn't find any on its reconnaissance flight." Mom pressed her hands against her knees. "Of course, we've only just begun to explore World Bravo, and are trying to come up with a doctrine to deal with any threats from there. Which brings me to why I'm here, because you two will play important roles in that."

McShane and Ylva exchanged glances as Mom continued. "You, my son, in spite of your gross insubordination at Drammen . . ."

His cheek twitched. Suddenly he felt like a seven-year-old who came home from school with a report card full of F's.

Mom went on, "You are considered by many in NATO as one of the most experienced pilots when it comes to fighting the Jotnar. As such, you will be reassigned to the Joint Non-Human Lifeform Threat Planning Staff subordinate to Allied Joint Force Command Brunssum."

McShane snorted. "I'm gonna get stuck behind a friggin' desk? Sounds like a punishment to me."

"It's a good assignment for your promotion track. And you will not be stuck behind a desk. You will help develop tactics and training to deal with future Jotnar attacks. And if they do attack again," she paused, pressing her lips together, "you will likely be back in the cockpit of a Viper. Additionally, the planning staff will be based at Gardermoen. You'll still be in Norway, which I'm sure will please you." She glanced at Ylva. "Both of you."

Both McShane and Ylva eyed one another and smiled.

"And you, Professor Tande." Mom turned to her. "Given your expertise and all of your insights during Operation Beast Slayer, you are being offered a position in a newly formed working group, also based at Gardermoen, to help with the study of World Bravo and to see what other mythological creatures we might encounter in the future. This work will also include expeditions to World Bravo. Again, if you are interested."

Ylva bounced on the couch, her mouth agape. "Yes, I am interested. Thank you so much for this opportunity, Mrs. McShane."

"No need to thank me. You earned it on your merits."

"If Ylva is going to hike through Asgard, she is going to have a big security detail with her, right?"

"There will be more than a security detail, Makato," said Mom. "NATO is drawing up plans for permanent bases on World Bravo. The hope is a year from now, we have at least two divisions of armor and infantry on the other side, along with a sizeable air wing."

Her face tightened in a determined look. "We don't intend to wait for the Jotnar to come through the gateway. The next time we fight them, we will do it on their world."

The End

About the Author: Sci-Fi, sports, action/adventure, cryptozoology, history. John J. Rust loves writing about all of them. A native of New Jersey, John graduated from Mercer County Community College and the College of Mt. St. Vincent with degrees in communications. He worked for New Jersey 101.5 FM before moving to Arizona, where he serves as the sports director for KYCA radio. When not broadcasting high school or college sports, John is at his computer writing about whatever genre strikes his fancy. He has authored 17 books, including *Sea Raptor, Demon Flyer, Dark Wings,* and *Weird and Interesting Stuff from World War II.* Beyond broadcasting and writing, John likes to exercise, collect t-shirts and ballcaps, and bang his head at heavy metal concerts. His favorite bands . . . too numerous to name.

Praise for John Rust's Books

"I really enjoyed this book. His character development and multi-layered plot held my interest. There were some superb action sequences that spanned multiple chapters and kept the action flowing, and I genuinely cared about the characters in jeopardy." – *Steve Yeager, author of "Raptor Apocalypse," on "Sea Raptor."*

"A must read for action/horror fans." – *Amazon review for "Reptilian."*

"This was Rust's best FUBI novel yet." *Amazon review for "Demon Flyer."*